ISABEL OUT OF THE RAIN

ISABEL OUT OF THE RAIN

A NOVEL

CATHERINE GAMMON

MERCURY HOUSE, INCORPORATED
San Francisco

Published in the United States by
Mercury House
San Francisco, California

Distributed to the trade by
Consortium Book Sales & Distribution, Inc.
St. Paul, Minnesota

Printed on acid-free paper
Manufactured in the United States of America

Library of Congress Cataloging-in-Publication Data

Gammon, Catherine.
  Isabel out of the rain : a novel / Catherine Gammon.
    p. cm.
  ISBN 0–916515–96–6 : $18.95. — ISBN 0–916515–97–4 (pbk.) : $10.95
  I. Title
PS3557.A46I8   1991
813'.54 — dc20
                                                        90–49383
                                                           CIP

for Heather

Acknowledgments

For the Vietnam chapters of *Isabel out of the Rain* I consulted many sources, chief among them: Philip Caputo, *A Rumor of War;* Frances FitzGerald, "The Tragedy of Saigon," in *The Atlantic Monthly,* December 1966; Michael Herr, *Dispatches;* Myra McPherson, *Long Time Passing;* J. Smith, "Death in the Ia Drang Valley," in *Saturday Evening Post,* January 28, 1967; and James F. Veninga and Harry A. Wilmer, eds., *Vietnam in Remission.*

Other works that contributed to the writing of this book include Philip Berryman, *Inside Central America;* Jonathan L. Fried, Marvin E. Gettleman, Deborah T. Levenson, and Nancy Peckenham, eds., *Guatemala in Rebellion: Unfinished History;* Marthy Jones, *It's in the Cards;* Victor Perera and Robert D. Bruce, *The Last Lords of Palenque;* and Dennis Tedlock, trans., *Popol Vuh: The Mayan Book of the Dawn of Life.*

The lines from Gaston Bachelard's *The Psychoanalysis of Fire* that appear in the "Trespass" section are adapted from the translation by Alan C. M. Ross (Beacon Press, 1964).

Finally, I would like to take this opportunity to express my gratitude to those organizations that have supported my work over the years: the Fine Arts Work Center in Provincetown, the Corporation of Yaddo, the New York Foundation for the Arts and its predecessor, CAPS, and in 1979 the National Endowment for the Arts.

Trespass

Trespass

A woman picks up a younger man—in a bar. A passion. He lives with her—after three weeks she is dead. There is no third party. No witness. Only the man and the death. This is the story. Stop here. There is no solution.

Intervention—she wishes to intervene. In her personal history. In the life surrounding her. In the future. She would like to go back to that time when she was a child in Los Angeles riding with her father in the car at night and he pulled over to the curb and got out and in the darkness pissed against a tree. She would like to stop there and say little girl, don't be afraid, your father's drunk and it's not your fault. She would like to go back and warn the child, herself, you're not crazy, your father's lying, don't blame him, don't forget what you know, don't let your mother pretend—don't lose track of your life for their sakes. She would like to go back and stand up to those people, the mother, the father, and speak the truth, and force them to speak it. She would like to go back and find the truth. But she is a ghost in that past, as for you—as I write, as you read (because I have told you)—she is a ghost already.

Hers will have been a cold story. It was a hot night but the woman was cold. Cold inside her skin. She felt the shivering start and lost her power of concentration. She had been reading and put the book facedown on the nightstand. In the bar she saw the man — dark-haired, lean, and beautiful. He was looking at her. He was watching the door and didn't move his eyes from her as she walked in. He didn't smile. He was something out of a movie. A silent movie. Where everything was in the seeing, in the look. She watched him and didn't smile. She ordered bourbon and forgot him, then saw him in the mirror. He stood next to her. They leaned together against the bar. She felt his breath against her shoulder — briefly, passing, he turned around, leaned back into his elbows and looked for her face. She gave it to him: this is my face.

On reading Derrida: She picked him up in a bookstore. She brought him home. Three weeks later she was dead. She also brought home Lao Tzu, Thomas Merton (the wisdom of the desert), Kierkegaard (either/or, volume one), and the Bhagavad Gita. But it was Derrida that killed her (dissemination) because it was Derrida she began to read and left abandoned on her night table when she got up and got dressed and went down to the corner for a drink.

She did not like his face in the mirror. He sensed this. In the mirror his face was false. She averted her eyes from his mirror face. He was careful from then on not to meet her face in mirrors.

Bourbon had been her father's drink. She rode beside him in the car, just the two of them. He reached his hand into his pocket, pulled out a pint, drank from the bottle, left hand still on the wheel. She would see this image clearly, in her memory, never knew if it was once or many times she saw it, knew it didn't matter, the thing itself was constant and repeated, whether seen by her or not. He drank far more than her mother knew, more than her mother either could or would imagine. With her drinker's heart she knew this, then and now.

Intervene. *1. To enter or occur extraneously. 2. To come, appear, or lie between two things. 3. To occur or come between two periods or points of time. 4. To come in or between so as to hinder or modify. 5. To interfere, usually through force or threat of force, in the affairs of another nation. 6.* Law. *To enter into a suit as a third party for the protection of an alleged interest. [Latin* intervenire, *to come between:* inter-, *between* ± venire, *to come (see* **gwa-** *in Appendix of Indo-European Roots).]*

They made love and slept and ate and drank and made love and slept and drank. They did as little as possible of what had to be done: they excluded everything. She called in sick and un-plugged the phone. She brought the mail up and didn't open it. No one knew where to find him. He had nothing and no one to leave.

She would like to return to the past to which she can't return. She would like to find answers to questions to which she can find no answers. She would like to say to her mother: I was a child. I didn't know the word *pissed*. *Pissed* is a word that protects me, now, from the darkness and the fear when Daddy stopped the car and left me and leaned against a tree. I followed him. (Did I?) He yelled at me. (Did he?) How long did I sit alone in the car before I got out? (Was he too sick to yell at me? Was he sick, or only pissing?) Why do I remember this? So much and so little? I remember the darkness and the night — the tree — fear. I remember, maybe, that Daddy was crying.

She woke up one morning and saw the man had become a loathsome bug. His face, which had been so beautiful, was suddenly cunning and sly. He wore his mirror face beside her and she recoiled. She lit a cigarette. He spoke to her. She didn't understand the words. He asked her a question. She began to answer it. He asked another question. She drew back. Every question he asked pulled her further away from the original question, and pulled her further away from herself and from him. He became ugly. She got up from the bed screaming. She grabbed the nearest thing to hand and threw it back across the room at him. It was the book she had been reading the night they met. He followed her into the bathroom. In the mirror he was beautiful. He pounded his hand against her image — his image. The mirror shattered. His hand bled, dripping down into the sink. She stood frozen, looking: the white sink cold and gleaming — tiny mirrors glittering and in the bigger shards her face — his bright dark blood. They both stood arrested — as if suddenly sober: time suspended, battle done — white, red, silver. She pulled a towel down and wrapped his hand.

In the bar they had talked about political violence: Star Wars, apartheid, Central America, intervention. In bed they shut the world out. They saw the sun and shadows move across the floor. When they got restless, she connected the phone and called out for cigarettes, liquor, and food. There is no third party. They were alone.

In Los Angeles in some neighborhoods the trees are planted in a narrow strip of grass that runs along the curb, between the street and the sidewalk, one tree per lot. It was an old neighborhood, they were old lots. It was a big tree, relatively speaking. Not young and skinny like the tree outside their own house. Not thicker than a person like trees she knows now in the East. But relatively speaking, a big tree. As big around as her father's leg, maybe, his thigh, maybe a little bigger. Yes, she got out of the car. She sees him clearly, leaning in the night against the tree. More than this she has never remembered. Only the mood of shame and fear and the knowledge that she saw what she was not supposed to see. There is no one to speak for her. She wants to intervene on her own behalf. She wants to say wait, this is not an isolated incident, this is important — wants to shake the man, the sick drunk man against the tree, lean and beautiful, dark-haired and fair-skinned in the moonlight. But she is inventing the moonlight. She is looking at her lover's dark eyes, his tousled hair — brown, almost black, like her father's. She is living in the smell of old bourbon, Camel cigarettes, and sweat — her father's smells — and sex, the dirty sheets. Don't forget, she wants to cry — don't let this little girl forget — and wants to pull him away from the tree and slap him and push him down to the ground, to his knees, to force him to cry — to cry so that he'll remember, so she will remember, so she'll know what really happened, what she saw, what she felt, and before that, in the car, when he stopped the car, and before he started it again, and later, when they got home, when they faced her mother, and when they hid — wants to pull her father around and pound his chest, make fists and beat his chest, naked, hairless like her lover's, and cry you lied to her, all her life you lied, don't you know what you did? — she'll think she's crazy because you're her father and you lied — it's not what you did — she doesn't know what you did — it's that you lied — look at her — she's seen you lying and you're her father and when you lie there is no truth — but it's her lover's chest she's pounding and while she weeps he holds her wrists, waiting for the screaming and weeping to pass, waiting to let loose his grip and pull her head to his shoulder to soothe her and stroke her head, her hair, when she will weep more quietly against his skin.

Gwa-. *Also* **gwem-**. *To go, come.* 1. *Germanic* *kuman *in: a. Old English* cuman, *to come:* COME; *b. Germanic* *kuma-, *he who comes, a guest, in compound* *wil-kuma-, *a desirable guest (*wil-, *desirable; see* **wel-***), in Old English* wilcuma, *a welcome guest, and* wilcume, *the greeting of welcome:* WELCOME; *c. compound* *bi-kuman, *to arrive, come to be (*bi-, *intensive prefix;* BE-***), in old English* becuman, *to become:* BECOME.

The word *pissed* is an intervention. Language is an intervention. In her mouth all speech intervenes. In her mind words come between — hinder and modify, interfere, usually by force or threat of force, enter into suit, allege interest, attempt protection. They come, they appear, they lie between — they lie. Extraneous, they enter. Like this lover, this stranger in her body.

She woke up. She felt a body in the bed behind her, breathing against her neck. She shivered and pulled away, curling into herself. Her skin crawled. Lavender light came in from the street in slivers that outlined the desk, the lamp, the bookshelf, the door. Desk. Lamp. Bookshelf. Door. She couldn't identify them. She didn't know the room. It was too dark. The lavender edges of things gave back no information. She pulled the sticky sheet tighter around her shoulder and shivered in her skin. She felt her heartbeat, fast, fluttery, doing double time, depthless. Her skin was cold and clammy. The lavender outlines began to move in the room, sinuous and swirling, became cartoon shapes, illegible words written in air, welcome, whispering, grasses twitching, wild eyes watching from the other side of the night. Her mind was clear. She knew she was awake. She knew these visions were in her mind, projected into the room. She wanted to see what would come next. But they scared her. She closed her eyes and saw nothing. She opened her eyes and saw the wild lights. She closed her eyes and rolled away to the stranger's body. If she looked at him she would see a stranger's face and hallucinate love. She lay there, stiff, cold, curled up against him. She felt her heart beat in her chest, fast and shallow. She took deep, slow breaths. She kept her eyes closed. She waited. She expected to die. The night went on.

He had become a loathsome bug. His hand bled. They were out of booze. She tried to make coffee but she was trembling — the blood, the breaking glass, the screaming — the shock of seeing his face so ugly. And maybe too much bourbon, she thought. She didn't know what day it was, how long he'd been here, she wasn't sure she knew his name. But the sight of his blood had made her tender. She leaned over him in the bright reading light next to the bed and painstakingly with shaking hands and a tweezer pulled out slivers of glass. They called the liquor store for vodka to wash his wounds and to celebrate the fact that it wasn't Sunday.

According to Bachelard (the psychoanalysis of fire) alcohol is a creator of language. It enriches the vocabulary and frees the syntax. The alcoholic unconscious is a profound reality. Alcohol does not simply stimulate mental potentialities, it creates them. Alcohol incorporates itself with that which is striving to express itself. What Bachelard does not say — or if he says it, she failed to notice, or if she noticed, the caution eluded her — is that for some people this alcoholic incorporation is irreversible (incorporate: to unite with or blend indistinguishably into something already in existence; to give substance or material form to; embody), the exchange vampiric, Faustian; that for such people, to enact this bargain (given, not chosen) is to die or to live in hell.

In her nightmare her father is in the bed with her, the breath on her neck is her father's breath, the leg against her leg her father's leg, the heat and wetness in her body for her father's pleasure, the searching fingers her father's fingers, the erection moving against her skin, against her bottom, the back of her thighs, her inner thighs in search of welcome, her father's. In her nightmare she wakes up screaming, but in reality her lover is coming into her and when she starts to scream he pushes her head into the pillow until their lovemaking is done. In her nightmare her father was in the bed wrapped in sheets and she stroked him, half-erect. In her nightmare he was an old man, the man he was just before he died. She was asking for information, stroking and waiting, cajoling, until a rush of potency scared her and she withdrew her hand. "Did you ever make me do this?" she asked, and he told her once, that night he got her loaded. "Did you get me loaded?" she asked, and already in her nightmare she saw the bottle on a chair in the other bedroom where her mother sat in bed, the way she did every morning, reading prayers. In her nightmare a third person was in the bed with her and her father—a shadowy person, almost no one. In her nightmare her father pressed himself against her from behind and she felt his probing fingers. In reality at the age of four she was suddenly afraid of the dark. In reality whatever happened her father will remember nothing. This is the moment in which she would like to intervene. But to intervene is to wake herself, and in reality she screamed. She remembered nothing of reality, only the nightmare, and pressed against the pillow by the violent hand of a stranger, unable to breathe and heaving under the effort and sweat of his young body, she tasted her own juices, and vodka, and blood against her cheek.

Wel-. *To wish, will. 1. Germanic* ★wel- *in Old English* wel, *well ("according to one's wish"):* WELL. *2. Germanic* ★welon- *in Old English* wela, weola, *well-being, riches:* WEAL (WEALTH). *3. Germanic* ★wiljon- *in Old English* willa, *desire, will power:* WILL. *4. Germanic* ★wil(l)jan *in Old English* wyllan, *to desire:* WILL, NILL. *5. Germanic compound* ★wil-kuma- *(see* **gwa-***). 6. 0-grade form* wol- *in Germanic* ★wal- *in Frankish* ★wala, *well:* GALA, GALLANT, GALLOP, WALLOP. *7. Basic form* ★wel- *in Latin* velle *(present stem* vol-*), to wish, will:* VOLITION, VOLUNTARY; BENEVOLENT, MALEVOLENT. *8. Suffixed form* ★wel-up *in Latin* voluptas, *pleasure.*

Freud is no help. Freud said the little girls desired the unthinkable and repressed the desire. Recent scholars say the fathers did the unthinkable and Freud repressed the facts. The debate continues. She will find no answer: there is no solution in theory, her mother knows nothing, and her father is dead. Her triangle can be unraveled only by opening it up in time. But she is out of time. The delivery boy from the liquor store rang the bell for 5-E as he had done almost every day for three weeks. The first morning they were laughing and wrapped in sheets. The man said they were having a honeymoon, they expected to see a lot of him, and gave him a ten-dollar tip. At first they ordered bourbon, then switched to vodka. Sometimes he brought them one bottle, sometimes two. At first they paid with cash, later with checks. The boss said he knew the woman a couple of years, her checks had always been good. At first the delivery boy liked going to them—they were happy and sexy to look at and generous with the money. They gave him an extra five dollars to stop at the corner and bring them a carton each of Marlboros and Camels. They always buzzed him up right away and let him inside when they opened the door. They were nice with him—in fact, they excited him. But rapidly he decided they were pigs. The air in the apartment was stale and stank of something skunklike and deadly. Their faces became ashen and their eyes dark-hollowed. They were like junkies, he told the boss. The tips dried up. The woman reeked of ammonia, as if it came oozing out her skin. Once on the other side of their door he heard screaming that suddenly stopped. The man came to meet him alone, wearing jeans and a khaki shirt, unbuttoned. His skin was scratched and bleeding. The check he gave him was crumpled and almost torn. It was the woman's check. Her handwriting was illegible. The man slipped him an extra dollar to carry down a bag of empties. "Don't come back," he said. "No matter what we tell you, promise you—don't come back." But he had come back. When they called and gave the boss an order, he had no choice but to go. Every day then he dreaded them. Until the morning when he stood on the stoop and rang and got no answer. He was carrying two quarts of cheap vodka and a carton each of Camels and Marlboros. He rang and rang. He went back to the store and told the boss. "I spent twenty-four bucks on cigarettes for those people," he said. "That's your problem," the boss said. "They're killing each other," the boy said, and the boss said that wasn't his business, as long as the checks were good. The boy walked out. He came back to the building and rang for the super. They went up together. The super pounded. There was no answer. He yelled, he said, "We're coming in." They waited. Slowly, the super unlocked the door. The boy gagged on the threshold. The skunk smell was overpowering, and all the human fluid smells, and fear. The boy crossed himself in the presence of what he knew was death. Neither he nor the super went in.

Replete and fearful—feeling exists but she is willing to know it only in the mind. She thinks she wants illumination, reality, the absence of deceit, but she is too absent from herself, too well protected. She is too old, she thinks, to wait for miracles. But pleasure is terror: If I take a knife to him, she wonders, will he give me back the truth?

She would like to intervene. Here perhaps: She had been reading for several hours when she began to get an inkling of the method and laughed out loud. She realized she would be too stimulated to sleep. She put the book down on the nightstand. Or here: He wore an overcoat in houndstooth plaid, black and ivory. Invented like the moonlight. Or not. He gave her a drink from his bottle. She asked for more. He gave it to her: Don't tell your mother. Later he was crying.

In a mirror, across the room, the man: huddled, so small and naked as almost to be invisible—he, who had been so beautiful. In the mirror, a bloody sheet, and everywhere the traces of its passage. In the mirror, his hands bloody, his chest, his skin cut and torn. In the mirror, in his lap, in his bloody hands, a telephone—suddenly familiar. He remembers where he is. They were sitting in separate corners, each with a bottle. The blood surprises him.

Here and now: She wishes to speak. Too much is missing. Nothing is right yet. Her story is not complete. There is more to say: I am a little girl who lives in a jail. Outside a neighbor is yelling at a dog to shut up. Every day she yells at the dog to shut up. I hate it when she yells at the dog to shut up. I also hate the dog. Most of the time I ignore the yelling neighbor and the dog. I let my jailer hate the yelling neighbor and the dog. Most of the time I ignore everything. I live in a dark jail. I came into this jail when I was a little girl and I'm still a little girl. I am alone in the house. Most of the time I like being alone in the house. In the house alone I act out fairy tales — mostly Cinderella — my favorite part is when she buries her head in her arms and cries on the bench. The coffee table is just the size of the bench in my picture book and I act it all out up to the part where she weeps because her wicked stepsisters have ripped up her dress and she can't go to the ball — up to the part where she weeps crying on the bench — right before the fairy godmother comes. I am the little girl crying, waiting for the fairy godmother to come and send her off to the ball and the handsome prince and the triumph over the wicked stepsisters and the happiness ever after. That's how old I really am, in my heart. And there's more to say. There will always be more to say.

For a while they watch television, soap operas, anything. She soaks in the bathtub, sleeping. He pulls her up by the hair. She holds on to his shoulders, her grip is slippery, she falls. Water splashes. They have bruises. In the tub they examine each other's bruises. Next they study the scars. His hand bleeds. Together they take time to dream. They can leave this city. They can go anywhere. They don't have to live like this. They are free. The sun is coming up. The little bit of sky out her window is almost blue. She lights a Marlboro and watches the smoke blown to nothing by the fan. The ash falls, she scatters it away.

Isabel

OUT OF THE RAIN

1

His heart aches when he looks at this child. It is nothing sexual. But who would believe him? He is forty years old. She is seventeen. She is beautiful. He has two wives behind him, a daughter somewhere in France. His feeling for this girl is not paternal. She lives with him. She has no family. She is alone. She makes his heart ache — all of him, he twists inside his skin. Whenever he looks at her. When he looks at her slowly. Or when she takes him by surprise. When he sees her. This child. She has been with him three years. He found her in the rain. She told him her name was Isabel. Black curls clung dripping to her cheeks. He still calls her Isabel even though he knows it's not her name. Her eyes are blue — not pale or gray, but dark, like ocean water in deep summer — and slightly crooked: a stranger can't tell if she's looking at or past him. At first, he thought she hadn't seen him. He was staring, arrested by her beautiful face — as if it were the face of someone he knew, or once had known and impossibly forgotten. Then suddenly he felt her eyes and understood that she was watching him, had seen him first, that her stare alone had drawn him to her face. Yes, she said. What? he asked. She shrugged. I'm hungry, she said. He didn't understand her. He wants to take her away from this city where for a year or more (two, three — her story changes) she lived on the street, begging when she had to, selling her body when she could. He would like to give her a childhood. But she laughs at him. She had a childhood. She lived in a thousand places, she can tell a thousand stories. Not a childhood then, he says. A future. But she laughs. There isn't one, she says. A paradise, he says. What kind of paradise? she asks. And together they dream a while of a world less cruel and more enduring, more magical than the one they know. This is love he thinks. But what kind? She came to him like a lost kitten. He took her in out of the rain. She's a collector. Where there used to be bare white walls, now he has feathered earrings, dusty bottles filled with sprays of dead flowers, a fan of scattered playing cards picked up off the street — one by one, each read like an omen then slipped into her pocket to be added to the others, pushpinned together, a hand about to be played amid objects and materials she's carried home from trash piles (bits of metal, leather scraps, packing paper in rippled sheets) and stapled up to make a kind of sculpture, haphazard, accidental, changing with the shadows that fall away from the ceiling lights or the windows or rise up from the lamp she's brought down to the floor, where with book and hair hot under the light bulb and legs swinging in the air she slaps her rubber flip-flops against her callused feet.

Lately these calluses disturb her. She fills his biggest pan with steaming water and a powdered soap made from borax, iodide, and bran. Every morning she sits at the big kitchen table — the only table — soaking her feet and drinking coffee, the radio on as if she's listening to the news. But she isn't listening: stooped over, determined, one foot pulled up to her thigh and resting on a towel, giving it all her concentration and working as if driven, she rubs a broken pumice stone back and forth against her thickened skin. Her motive for this ritual isn't vanity, it's fear. "My mother had calluses," she told him the first time he watched her. "She could be a nun in that order like Mother Teresa for the calluses she had." She has seen them in the subways, their white robes edged in blue, their wooden beads and crucifixes, their worn leather sandals, their cracked, callused feet. "I dreamed about her. I dreamed she was one of those women." Her calluses are all that's left of her existence on the street.

Before she came to him Russell lived in a world in which everything was distant. Looking at her, he knows how he has changed. He sees with her eyes, he lives in the rhythms of her speech. Alone he was a shallow, self-centered man. He doesn't recognize what he was before. He looks at the books on his shelves as at the books of a stranger, someone he sees in windows and mirrors when they catch him by surprise: a lonely, handsome man who has always believed his life to be one of profound intention.

Isabel flexes her toes, slap-slap go her flip-flops, his heart breaks. "Isabel," he says, and she turns her head. Her long dark lashes cast articulated shadows down her cheeks. He doesn't understand how they got here — not her, not himself, not anything. She looked at him in just this way, almost two years ago, just before she said, "I haven't been telling you the truth."

"What?" he asks.

"I didn't say anything." She watches him curiously, patiently, like a cat called for no reason — quizzical, superior, self-contained. "What's the matter with you?"

"Is something the matter with me?"

"You're strange tonight."

"Dreaming."

"No," she says.

"It's the rain."

She shakes her head.

He tells her: "I'm afraid."

The tip of her tongue licks her upper lip, a darting, unconscious movement that indicates she is thinking — hesitating, to ask or not to ask, the obvious question: Of what?

She doesn't ask it. Maybe she knows. Maybe she has asked herself and in her heart heard the answer he is waiting to give: Without you. "Read," he says. "It's nothing." She smiles, quick and grateful, and disappears into her book.

She's right. He's not himself. He sits here looking for the reason and expects to find it in her — as if she's the one who's strange. He is looking for the thing that changes, the thing that makes a change, like the ringing of a bell — in a mystery the crime, in a romance the meeting of the lovers, the problem that drives the action through a play. This morning after she scraped her feet she poured the water into the sink and turned around saying, "I read there's a white gorilla in the Barcelona zoo." She wants to see it. He wants to take her away. For her sixteenth birthday he took her to Jamaica. In Jamaica, they danced. They drank champagne. Then she said, "I have to tell you the truth." She was born in California in 1967; he was in California in 1967. Sterilizing dishes in the kitchen of Herrick Hospital. Getting his head together, he used to say. He'd been in Berkeley since New Year's Eve when he got back from Southeast Asia. He wasn't in the military. He had a job with a voluntary service organization and on his own did photographs and interviews for anyone who'd pay. Maybe some intelligence — he was green, he didn't always know. He went over there believing he could do something about it. By witnessing the misery, make up for it somehow. Change people's thinking. Turn things around. Just by showing up. There were others like him — relief workers, teachers, churchpeople, nurses, doctors — civilians, volunteers — angry young idealists from America, camp followers twentieth-century style. (Only yesterday he got a phone call from a woman he'd known then — she was leaving for Manila to watch the revolution, did he want to come?) He was a civilian, he wasn't supposed to kill people. Sometimes he carried a gun. Before Isabel came he had pretended these things didn't happen. Sooner or later he has always pretended everything didn't happen. Someday he'll be pretending Isabel didn't happen. She was born the day before Thanksgiving, in Herrick Hospital, where he was working in the kitchen (without coincidence, he tells himself, there is no story), watching the steam and remembering the rain. Today he mostly remembers the rain. Only the rain was human, he thinks, and the people we were killing. (He says "we," but he knows who he means.) He was young. (We were all young.) He doesn't look back.

On her seventeenth birthday Isabel told him she had been in touch with her mother. "She's drinking too much," she said. He was afraid. "You won't leave?" he said. "Not yet," she said. Not yet.

She had come to him out of rain, like an angel in a movie sent to save him from despair. But movie angels were funny old men (and once Cary Grant) — never a beautiful girl, barefoot and shivering and offering herself for a slice of bread, a bowl of soup. Only minutes before, he had been sitting in a restaurant looking blankly at the menu, unable to conjure from the words on paper the possibility of food. He'd turned away to watch a stream of raindrops run down the window when suddenly, in the reflected stem of the solitary rosebud rising from the vase on his table, he had seen how small and narrow, how cramped he'd let his life become. He stood up. He left money for his abandoned waiter and went out into the street. Now it is the summer of 1985, Isabel has brought him back among the living, and tonight he is afraid. Outside it is raining. The balsa slatted shades billow into the room. Water accumulates on the deep, gray sills and runs down the white brick walls to the floor. Time is passing. He hears it in the morning when Isabel works at her calluses, when she says *white gorilla in the Barcelona zoo*, when she slaps her flip-flops, in this moment when she jumps up to answer the ringing phone. She's getting ready for something. She's leaving him. It's a tropical summer. The city is in a drought; upstate the reservoirs are going dry, and here it rains. Every few days the streets turn to rivers and a minute outside soaks you through to the skin. When it starts like this you think it will never stop. You're standing in water, surrounded by water, breathing water — you'll never get dry. Drought is impossible, but it continues. All over New York people wear white, pastels, Hawaiian shirts. As if it were Miami. Drought or no drought. The weather follows fashion.

He should get up and close the windows. But he wants to hear the water beating down into the street. Sometimes it lasts only minutes, stops, starts. Last night he dreamed of snow. He was in a snow-buried valley, with Isabel. He heard the pounding rain. In his dream it was snow, and it was silent. Tomorrow the air will be drier, Mediterranean, the sky blue, the clouds white, the trees and buildings out these windows sparkling clean. She wants to go to Barcelona. She gets letters from abroad. He doesn't know who writes them. She doesn't tell him. She is careful with the envelopes—doesn't leave them lying around, never throws them away, at least not here. She doesn't read the letters in front of him. She takes them to her room. On her desk she has a box where she keeps her private things—the box from the first pair of shoes he bought her. Once he opened it—once only, a few months after she arrived. He had come home early, knowing she'd be out. Being at home without her excited him; his excitement filled him with shame. He had felt this with Lucinda—on Saturday mornings when she went to the farmers' market and waiting at home without her he searched desperately through the trash. Now, he went into the bedroom—Isabel's room—and lifting the lid off the shoebox, saw peach stones, an avocado pit, pomegranate seeds, and two thin blue envelopes edged with airmail stripes. He couldn't read the postmarks, couldn't read the return addresses or the stamps. She had put the peach stones and avocado pit and pomegranate seeds each exactly into place: if he moved them, even one, no matter how carefully, she would know that he had been here. She had set it up deliberately. "You're doing it again," Lucinda had accused him. But Isabel was new: that she had taken these precautions made him cry. A tear fell onto the thin blue paper: his confession. She would understand that he had gone this far and no farther. She wouldn't say anything. He knew she wouldn't. Or hoped. Or hoped the opposite—that she would challenge him—beg him to tell her why, get angry, make a scene, throw her letters in his face, tear them up, read them aloud—what? He put the lid back on the box and left the room. As he closed the door, he sobbed. Before Isabel came he hadn't cried in years. Now tears were an almost daily occurrence. He sat at the kitchen table and poured himself a drink. He looked at his hands. They were shaking. He was afraid. He had resisted knowing his reasons for leaving work early: to be here without her, to look into her room, to find her secrets—just one secret, any secret. But his failure left his reasons impossible to deny.

    That night she was especially kind. She told him a funny story about her early life with her mother. It was a gift. As if to say— you can't have that, poor man, but here, take this. He realized only much later that the story she told him that night might not have been true.

Isabel turns to him now from the phone. "He says his name is Angelino."

"Angelino?"

"He says you'll know him when you see him. He wants to come over."

"Should I talk to him?"

"He wants to surprise you."

When he came in tonight, she was on the floor, up close to the television, watching the local news, a police drawing: lean face, shaggy hair, sunken eyes. "Who is that?" he'd asked her. "Who does that look like?" She had answered, "It does, doesn't it?" but the sketch had already left the screen, and in his mind now Angelino wears the face of the wanted man.

She is standing in the shadows, still talking. Giving directions maybe, speaking softly, twisting the phone cord around her finger, tossing her head. She laughs, nervously maybe, and he hears Billy Santana, during a poker game on the floor of a concrete, street-level room in Saigon, saying, "This is how death arrives — you say sure, I'll talk to him, and you open up the door." Outside, war-crazy people shouted at each other, sometimes at no one, music was playing — American rock and roll — distant explosions, animals, children, seconds of silence, someone pounding to get in, and the rain, just like tonight. Russell tells himself this story. Like Isabel's stories, it can start anywhere. In Saigon he knew a French girl. She was his lover and his translator. She was pregnant when he left her. Later she wrote to tell him she had taken their daughter to France. He was searching for an active way of loving. He has learned this from Isabel — that all his life he has been searching for an active way of love. Since she came to him, every day he has prayed. In the beginning he didn't know it was prayer, and even once he knew, didn't know what he prayed to. He still doesn't. But his ignorance has changed. Like everything else. This, his short life of prayer, started the first morning; it started with tears. She was sleeping on the mattress he kept for visitors and temperamental lovers. He walked out of the bedroom into the kitchen and there she was, asleep at the far end of the loft. He listened to her deep, even breathing—safe and trusting. The tears came suddenly to his eyes. *Dear God,* he said—but not he—heard said inside his body: *Dear God, where did she come from?* Words spoken into his body. They shook him, and he went back into his room and punched his fists into the pillow, crying *God*—a stranger, nothing, not even a word, a cry of pain, not faith, not belief, empty, a sound without content, not even hope—*God God God,* over and over. But his sobs grew quieter and his breathing slowed. The tears washed out of his eyes like water overflowing the rim of a glass. They were no longer his tears. He was confused. He didn't know why he was crying. It started with the snores of a sleeping child on a mattress that retained more of his history than he did. He was grateful. He didn't know for what. For being alive. For the sleeping girl. For the mattress filled with history. For the girl. For the inexplicable tears—for relief. It never occurred to him that she would stay. She stayed for days, weeks, and still it never came to him that she was staying. What he thought about, when he thought at all, back then at the beginning, was the sensation of emptiness suddenly filled: it was gratitude. He called it gratitude. It was love. It was immobilizing. Whenever he felt it, he cried. It began with emptiness and ended in tears. It began with Isabel.

Now, she is standing in front of him, wearing faded blue jeans with a rip in one knee and a baggy peach-colored shirt with long tails and rolled-up sleeves. She shifts her weight from one foot to the other and back again. She wants to tell him about the man on the phone. She is chewing on a fingernail, the little finger of her right hand bent and pushed between her lips to meet the teeth. Her eyes look baffled. "He says you'll want to see him," she says. "He says he's coming over." So now they are waiting for Angelino, and Russell doesn't know who he is.

He gets up to close the windows. Already the rain is gentler, and he leaves the windows open and lets it blow against his face. The street is lit orange. Teenagers gather on the far corner. Brooklyn teenagers. He's had this loft five years. He wanted room. Air. Space and light. He'd been living in a hole on East

Fifth Street with seven narrow windows, barred and facing air shafts and other narrow windows like his own. He left everything behind. He had a new bed delivered and spent a week just walking in this vast empty room full of air and light—every morning, every evening, back and forth along the windows, stopping to look down at the street. It was November. Ronald Reagan had just been elected president. Russell began to regret having left his books behind. He went back to East Fifth Street. His books were piled up on the sidewalk, next to the garbage cans—his books, his old mattress, old clothes, the contents of his desk drawers—already well picked over. Tax records, letters, spiral notebooks containing sporadic memories, thoughts, instructions to himself, occasional dreams. Loose yellow pages, drafts of articles—unfinished work, years of unfinished work. Photographs. Notes from interviews. But no tapes—no tape recorder, radio, iron, clock. It was Sunday afternoon. He was standing there taking inventory, mentally saving what he could, even the mattress, when a pretty blonde walked past him, up the stairs, digging for keys. He'd never seen her. He asked if she was new in the building. She ignored him. "I just moved out," he said. "Last week. I left these things. If I could stash it all, till I can find a way to get it across the river—"

She took pity on him. He didn't know why. Women always took pity on him. They supplied their own reasons. Maybe it was the vision of the labor he faced. He was holding a book in his hand, *Being and Nothingness:* maybe she liked Sartre—maybe she liked Brooklyn, maybe she liked him. "I just hauled all this down," she said, "and now you want it up again?" But she was laughing. Her name was Margot. She gave in. "You do the work," she said. He thanked her. Within hours they were lovers, and off and on for the next two years. He almost doesn't remember what she looked like. A few days ago he noticed in the *Times* that she'd got married. She came from that kind of family. He recognized the name before the face. She had never met Isabel. But she talked to her once on the phone.

"Who was that girl?" she asked him.

"Isabel," he said. "My niece."

"You're an only child."

"My half niece. My half brother's — "

"Mother's or father's?"

"Mother's." In this, he was telling the truth.

"You never said you had a half brother."

"He's kind of a jailbird," he said, lying again, as far as he knew, making his brother up as he went along, not thinking, just answering, as fast as he could, to justify Isabel.

"And there's no mother."

"Not lately."

"Which is why you haven't called in two weeks."

"Has it been two weeks?"

She hung up. He hardly noticed. What he noticed was Isabel: sprawled on the old mattress, reading under the light. He didn't know how long she'd been here. He didn't know how long she meant to stay. She probably didn't know either. She was alone in the world, except for him. At least for now. As far as he knew. That was how she wanted it. The first day she'd slept and eaten and soaked in the tub and washed all his dirty dishes and even started to scrub the bathroom until he told her she didn't have to play Cinderella. She smiled. She asked could she stay another night. "As long as you like," he said automatically. He had already forgotten his tears. He was leaving for Margot's, for dinner and a movie. He told Isabel to help herself to food. "Don't wait up," he said, and in the morning came back with the Sunday paper and cream cheese and bagels. In the days that followed, she ate and slept and took baths and read his books. She wasn't interested in television but she listened to music so he bought some new tapes. It pleased him to watch her enjoy what he gave her. Like fattening a hungry stray on milk and sardines. When he came home one night and found her gone, he was surprised — then surprised at his surprise. He poured himself a drink and looked around to see what was missing. He felt dejected and ashamed. He poured another drink. The door buzzer jolted him out of his chair. Her voice came over the intercom: "It's me." She walked in with a bag full of treasures from the street. "And look at these," she said. A bouquet of dead flowers. The next day he had a set of keys made for her. After Margot hung up on him, he decided to give Isabel the bedroom. He ordered lumber and plasterboard and spent Thanksgiving Day partitioning a room for himself at the far end of the loft. Isabel cooked and they had dinner by candlelight, listening to Bob Dylan and Haydn and Patsy Cline.

That night he had been happy.

Now, on the corner, a boy and a girl are wrestling. Two old women sit on the sidewalk in folding chairs. One of the land-lords walks his lover's dog. The rain has stopped. Across the street, the Mae Son Waste Paper, Inc., is deserted. The RV painted *Leisure Time* parked outside Belinda's Lounge is quiet. From beyond the low buildings a plane appears, rising into the big Brooklyn sky. The first night he slept here he dreamed an air war—a phalanx of red-starred, khaki-colored missiles bearing down on these low green, red, and yellow buildings until the faster, prettier good-guy missiles rose up all erect and red-white-and-blue, rushing in like cavalry from over the horizon to drive the enemy away—as clean and artificial as any battle in a *Star Wars* movie. He told this dream to Margot the day he met her. He told her it pissed him off that his subconscious bought those images, that scenario—offense and defense, the Russians drab and evil, the all-American high-tech heroes bright and innocent as toothpaste. She didn't laugh. She asked him what he thought the dream really signified. He can remember this conversation: sitting at his old kitchen table, drinking her iced wine, the blond hair wisping around her face, falling down from the clasp she used to pin it up at the back of her neck—but it's as if the man there with her is someone else. Most of his memories are like this now; whatever he remembers didn't happen to him.

Outside, the air is dense. *Blade Runner* light—wet and orange. If he stands here long enough, the rain will start again. In the street two fat boys throw a football. At the corner the teenagers turn a radio on: loud, Bruce Springsteen, "Born in the USA." A siren swells, from nowhere, shutting out the music. Russell's heartbeat accelerates. As if the siren is for him. He is closer tonight to the man he was before Isabel came than he has been at any time in these three years. He turns away from the window and looks at her. She was beautiful from the first, when she was homeless and scrawny, lonely and scared. Yes, her face is beautiful — but it is not her face that has had such power over him, not her beauty, not anything she says, not what she does: just the fact of her, Isabel. If he speaks to her, she will answer. If he leaves without speaking, she will ask herself what's wrong. It is too simple to say his feeling for her is not sexual. He would like to get rid of her dead flowers. They remind him of the time when she will already be gone.

2

He had been sitting in a restaurant on the East Side not far from Bloomingdale's, staring at the menu and failing to come to terms. With what, he didn't know. He disliked his job, but it was adequate; he'd been there long enough that the money was good; it required nothing of his soul. He read words all day — nonwords: *gray matters, classic styling, exotic fantasies of flourish and form, S-M-L-XL, order by phone toll free, 7 days a week, 8 a.m. to 12 midnight,* etc. — and suddenly in that moment the words on the menu lost their power to mean. Outside it was raining. He had thought about going to a movie — eating something, drinking some wine, then going to a movie. By himself. To be alone without being alone. To be among people without having to talk. He disliked his own distress — it was universal, he thought, taken for granted, so commonly suffered that it was rude — thoughtless, indiscreet — to bring up in conversation, as if to speak of it would be to claim some infantile uniqueness, like a child whining about what others had grown old enough to endure.

When he looked at things objectively Russell knew his life was not in any way exceptional. Yet in his heart he believed it was — had always believed it — had always sensed the workings of fate in the patterns that formed themselves around him, accepting equally good fortune and bad, secure in the conviction that whatever befell him was written by some larger intelligence and destined toward a future in which his true depths, his reach, his scope — his free self — would be revealed. Had he examined this belief he would have denied it; most of the time, he managed to keep it at a distance: blurred, the invisible ground of action, the black light of dreams. Nevertheless, occasionally awareness broke to the surface to ripple the stillness of his routine: sometimes at night, alone in a shadow with a drink in his hand and a vision just outside the range of speech; more often in coincidence, where he encountered inevitability, communion with greater powers, verification from another world; and in that moment in the restaurant, when turning away from the menu to look out the window at the rain, he had seen his failed life in the stem of a rosebud, reflected onto the darkness, barely visible in the glass. The contradiction terrified him. He ran.

Outside he stopped: arrested by the presence of the girl beyond the light. She seemed to be looking past him, and he stood still and stared. He felt as if he already knew her, had known her long ago. Her eyes were beautiful, and her skin. She was watching expectantly, he thought, waiting for someone. Then her eyes seemed to shift focus, and he understood she was waiting for him.

"Yes," she said.

"What?" he asked, alarmed, as if he might have spoken or she had read his thoughts.

"I'm hungry," she said.

He didn't understand.

"I'm hungry," she said again. She shrugged and stepped into the light.

She had short black hair, maybe not its true color, curls dripping down her cheeks. Kohl lined her eyes. Her lips looked bruised, as if they had been painted and the paint rubbed away. A moment before she had been beautiful. Now all the pieces broke apart. He saw that her eyes were crooked. He saw that her skin was pale, almost bloodless. She carried a big red beaded cotton bag over her shoulder. Her black hemless skirt came to an end, fraying, three inches above her bony knees. Her feet were bare. She shivered. She said, "I'll do anything you like."

"Jesus," he said. He flushed. For an instant he had desired her — as she spoke, as he understood her words.

"Listen," he said. "What do you need?"

She laughed. A sad little laugh, a child's laugh. She was a child.

"What's your name?" he asked.

"Isabel," she said.

"Who're you doing this for?" he asked.

"For?" She laughed again. "There's nobody," she said.

"Nobody?" he said.

She shook her head.

"Don't you have any shoes?"

"In my bag," she said. "The rain," she said.

"You'll get sick out here like this."

"I can do anything," she said. "Anything you want. You tell me what you like. I can do it."

"No," he said. He had known girls like this in Saigon. In Saigon he had not always said no. He asked himself what the difference was. He hated himself for the answer. He was helpless, standing outside the restaurant, looking at this girl.

"Come on," he said. He took her arm and pulled her along.

"Where to?" she asked.

"I don't know," he said.

Her arm was scrawny in his grip, so tiny inside her thin black sweater that it was painful to hold. He let her go. He opened his umbrella and tried to shelter her under it. He listened to the rain come down.

She stopped suddenly, bent to the sidewalk and stood up again. "Two of diamonds," she said. In her hand she held a soggy playing card.

"Does that mean something?" he asked.

She shrugged. "Might," she said. "I'm hungry," she said.

"There's a coffee shop," he said. "Keep walking."

He shook out the umbrella and pushed her through the door. She stood just inside and fumbled in her bag. In the bright light she looked more pale, more sickly, than she had on the street. She pulled out a pair of ragged black Chinese slippers and put them on, and he followed her in and sat with her in a booth next to the window, thinking there had never been a moment so forlorn: the bedraggled girl in the overbright foreground, beyond her the street corner, the bobbing, dark umbrellas, the cabs racing by. But immediately he felt that there had been such a moment—he had seen this moment before—and with the rush of déjà vu came the certainty that in the next instant the girl would jump up and vanish back into the night. Involuntarily, as if to stop her, he asked, "Who *are* you?"

"What?" She seemed alarmed. "Isabel," she said. "I told you."

She drained a cup of coffee, full of sugar and cream. She asked if he had a cigarette. He told her not for years. She shrugged, she said she didn't really smoke anyway. She had put the playing card facedown to dry on the white plastic table top. A battered cocker spaniel held a leash between its teeth, looking up pathetically, pleading for a walk. She had ordered a bagel and cream cheese.

"That's all?" he asked.

"It's what I'm used to," she said.

He wanted to buy her something more. A bowl of soup, maybe.

"Not here," she said. "It'll be Campbell's or something, in a place like this. Soup has to be homemade."

"How long since you had homemade soup?"

She shrugged.

"Or homemade anything?"

She shook her head instead of answering. "So where do you live?" she asked.

"Brooklyn," he told her.

"Brooklyn," she said. "Yeah?"

She asked for another coffee. Her bagel came. He watched her eat—with big bites and in a hurry, paying no attention to him, as if she hadn't eaten all day, or longer.

"So what're you doing on the street?" he asked when she had finished.

"Living," she said. "What do you think?"

"Why?" he asked.

"Why do you want to know?"

He didn't answer.

"Not for the fun of it," she said. "If that's what you think."

"No," he said.

"What do you think?"

"I don't know." She looked at him steadily. He understood that she was challenging him to guess. "You're a runaway. Probably from close by. Right here maybe."

She waited for more.

"You want to go home."

She turned her face toward the window, not before he had seen tears in her eyes.

"Sorry," he said. He signaled the waiter and ordered more coffee and another bagel. "What's with the card?" he asked.

"I always pick up cards," she said.

"Omens?"

"Maybe," she said. "Sometimes."

"So what does it mean?"

She turned it over. He noticed her hands — square-shaped and bony, awkward fingers with heavy knuckles, a tarnished silver ring with a scratched paste pearl, nails painted red and peeling — old hands, not the hands of a child.

"Diamonds," she said. "Money, security, business — maybe service, giving, helping. The two is . . . well, two: you and me maybe" — she smiled at him uncertainly, then gave him a pouty, coquettish look that was odd and disquieting on her little face. "Partnership," she said, "or an exchange, or just this conversation. Also ups and downs, strength and weakness, health and illness — wealth and poverty, warmth and cold . . ."

"Beauty and the Beast?"

Her face went blank, almost angry. "Happiness and melancholy," she said, "friendship and loneliness," and then she stopped, picking up half her new bagel and spreading grape jelly on it. She didn't seem to notice that the bagel had just come or that she'd already eaten the first one, but she ate more slowly now, and Russell tried to imagine for a moment that she was an ordinary girl, a schoolgirl, the child of a friend, say, a niece, his own daughter. But he could not imagine it. Most of the children he saw — on the streets, in the subways, the few he knew to speak to — even the young ones were old enough to be afraid of this world they were living in, but not old enough to be afraid very often, not so old they made their fear a way of life. It was in

Cheyenne that he had seen this before, this refusal to be a child.
It was Cheyenne she reminded him of—wasn't it? She even
looked a little like Cheyenne. He studied her face and asked
himself if this could be true. He didn't much like to be reminded
of his brother. He had appeared after their mother died, back in
May, down in the street, yelling up at the windows, looking like a
cowboy, covered with dust, backpack slung over his shoulder—
an open quart of tequila in his hand. He was drunk, and when he
came up, they drank together. He told Russell about their mother
dying, how it had gone on and on. He told him how he had
refused to call him, how he had lied to her about calling, how he
had tried to keep Russell's father away. He sat there whispering
I'm the angel of death—you don't know when I'll strike. He giggled a
lot. He was crazy. Doing a James Dean act. Quoting lines from
Rebel Without a Cause. Then he brought out the coke and got
angrier, got scary. He hung around for days, drinking and snort-
ing and spilling his guts out. In the end he said, "I'll kill you,"
over and over, until suddenly his voice was dead. It was morning.
He was sitting naked on the mattress in the loft, head buried,
hugging his knees. He couldn't move. Russell had left him like
that, and when he came back Cheyenne was gone—no note, no
message, nothing missing—just gone.

The girl was talking. He had missed the beginning. If there
was a beginning. "I ran into this man my mother used to love,"
she said. "He took my picture. I looked straight at him. I dared
him to take my picture. I was across the tracks from him. He
wasn't carrying a camera. I didn't run from him. I held my hands
up to my face. I mimed. As if in my hands I held a camera. He
was on the opposite platform. I clicked the shutter, aimed at him.
I took the invisible camera down from my face. I smiled. I waved.
I pointed at my wrist as if I had a watch on. I held up five fingers.
Five o'clock my fingers said. I waited for him to understand. I
didn't come back at five that afternoon. I thought if he thought I
meant that, it was possible he would bring my mother. I wanted
him to suffer one defeat. I came back at five the next morning. I
was cautious. But I didn't have to be. He had understood me.
Across the platform—he was there. I posed for him. I didn't

move. I didn't smile. I stood with the vacant look of someone
waiting for a train. On the platform with me were two or three
other people. A fat black woman carrying a plastic Duane Reade
shopping bag, just come from cleaning an office building, office
buildings maybe. A young guy nodding out on a bench, drunk or
drugged. A few pillars away a boy, my age maybe, maybe older,
wearing a shiny baseball jacket and a woolen cap. We would all be
in the picture. I stood and looked at my mother's former lover.
He had a camera but at first he didn't lift it. It hung limp at his
side. I waited. I waited for a train. A train came. Everyone got on
except the drunk. Two more old women came from their night
cleaning, one white, one black. Both were fat. They talked
together, tired and quiet. An old man came, shuffling, wearing
ragged shoes, newspapers wrapped around his ankles. Then a
young man, wearing work clothes. In the photograph he will
look derelict and dirty. But it isn't ground-in dirt that covers his
hands and face, not dirt that's worn into his pores and stains his
overalls. It's chocolate. I can smell the chocolate as he passes,
close to me on the platform. I smile when I smell the chocolate.
He smiles at me. He leans against a pillar to wait for his train. I
stare at my mother's lover. I challenge him to raise his camera.
Without moving, without expression. At last he does. I can see
his hands shaking. Across four empty tracks I see his hands
shake."

She stopped suddenly. Russell didn't know what to say. This
story had something to do with him — that's what he was thinking. The whole thing — the girl, the bare feet, the ragged Chinese
slippers, her crooked eyes, her hunger — it all had something to
do with him.

He wanted her to know he had been listening. "You let him
take your picture?" he asked. He didn't know what he was
thinking. Chocolate. Roses. He was confused. He ordered more
coffee. "Why did you let him take your picture?"

"I thought he would show it to my mother. I thought — it
would help her."

"She'd know you're alive?"

"That."

"And?"

She shrugged.

"So your mother is here?" he asked. "In New York?"

"Can we go now?" she said.

"Go?" he repeated.

"Don't you want me to come to Brooklyn?"

"Why?"

"Well, we can't do it in the ladies' room."

He flushed. "Isabel," he said. It was the first time he had used her name. He would remember this moment for years; then, it had passed right through him — or rather, he had hurried out of it, away. "How long have you been alone?" he asked.

She shrugged. She turned her head to look out the window at the people walking in the rain. "A year," she said. "Going on. Not that long, really. I had a boyfriend for a while."

"You ran away for him?"

"There were reasons. He just helped me. Look," she said, turning back to him, "are you taking me home or not? 'Cause I have some money I have to earn."

"I'll give you some money. Just sit here a while. Relax. Eat."

"You're asking too many questions."

"What's wrong with questions?"

She picked up the other half bagel and began to eat it, staring at him. "You want to help me or something? Is that it?"

"I don't know," he said.

"I'm not asking for help," she said. "I'm making a sale. If you don't want to buy, I can leave."

None of these words seemed to come from her mouth. It was like listening to Cheyenne. Through thicknesses of glass. Dubbed speech. Bad lip sync. Wrong voice for the body. Wrong words for the voice.

"How old are you?" he asked.

"That's not your business."

"You're a child," he said.

She laughed. "Illegal. Is that what you mean? I'm illegal? Look at my breasts," she said. "They're tiny and hard." He could just

see the shape of them under her sweater. "I'm illegal, all right."
She laughed. "Afraid? Are you afraid?"

"Yes," he said. "I'm afraid."

She looked at him. Gently, he thought. Suddenly gentle. She
was beautiful again. "I'm sorry," she said. Tears were in her eyes.
He reached for her hand and held it.

"Isabel," he said. Her name was painful in his mouth. His
throat closed around it and for an instant he fought for breath.
He felt nauseous and was glad he hadn't eaten. He felt tears in his
stomach. His legs were light, liquid. Her hand was hot in his
hand. A night came back to him from Saigon: Billy Santana
across a filthy oilcloth-covered table in their favorite little ragtag
bar, ice-cold fingers gripping his wrist — "Paranoia is the hunger
of power," he said. They'd been sitting there for hours. Santana
was talking, getting ready to disappear, but neither of them had
known that then. "I'm not who's paranoid, Jacks," he said, "don't
you get it? It isn't me or you or us or Dominique or anybody you
can talk to in the face. It's them." Then: "Paranoia is the hunger
of power," and in that night the words had been as physical as
Santana's fingers on his wrist. Russell remembered his mother,
the innocent victim going crazy, protected by her righteousness;
instead of loving her, Russell had loved his father: "The guilty
party needs our love," he had written on a scrap of paper. "From
his guilt comes a deeper innocence." He was fourteen years old
then, not any older than this girl maybe, and like Billy Santana's
years later, his words had seemed as tangible as flesh.

"I'm sorry," he said suddenly. He let go of Isabel's hand. He
didn't know how long he'd held it. From the expression on her
face he thought it must have been a long time. She looked
frightened now, not for herself — for him. His heart was beating
fast. He felt himself sweat. "I don't understand myself," he said.
"I'm sorry," he said again. "I want you to be an ordinary child,"
he said. "I can't — it hurts me to think of you — a child — like this.
It hurts me," he said.

"It's got nothing to do with you," she said.

But nothing had hurt him so intensely in a long time. Maybe
ever, he wanted to think, although he knew it couldn't be true.

"It's nothing to do with you," she said again. "What would I be," she asked, "if I weren't what I am?"

"An ordinary girl."

"I've lived too many places to be an ordinary girl. I've been too free."

"An extraordinary girl, then. Anything. Pretend."

"Pretend what?"

"Anything. Three wishes."

"You don't think like that when you live the way I do."

"Try," he said.

"No," she said.

He stirred his spoon in cold coffee. He watched her. "You're thinking about it though."

She shook her head.

"Where would you be right now, tonight? What would you be doing?"

"If I hadn't left?"

"Okay."

She shrugged and looked out the window. "I don't know. Anywhere. My mother was always moving. We could've been in, I don't know, Barcelona by now."

"Why Barcelona?"

"Sometimes she wanted to go there."

"You're in Barcelona with your mother then. What are you doing?"

"I don't know. I've never been to Barcelona."

"So you didn't go out tonight. It's raining. You're at home. With your mother in Barcelona."

"You really want me to play this game, don't you?"

"I really do."

She looked back at him. "I'm alone with my mother in a little room. Two little rooms, one with a kitchen and a table, it's a big table — the table is always big. It has books all over it, and cups and plates, a bottle of wine maybe, some fruit, some cheese, paper and pens, newspapers, magazines, an ashtray somewhere, filled, packs of cigarettes, empty packs, matches. After the table, the rest doesn't matter. But we're in the other room tonight, sitting up on the bed — the bigger bed, it's her bed. We're talking. She's drinking — what? — wine maybe, in Barcelona. And she's a little bit sad, but she's laughing while she drinks and she's telling me about it, whatever it is, and I'm remembering things from before, to make her laugh and forget whatever it is she's sad about. For a while it works and then after a while it doesn't and she hugs me and tells me maybe she'll go out for a while, to meet some friends maybe, or just to walk a while, and after a while she goes. And then I'm alone in the room."

She looks back out the window at the rain. "So you see it doesn't matter where we are," she says. "I'm alone in a room. Reading a book. A book I could read anywhere."

"What book?"

"I don't know. Something I haven't read. *The Brothers Karamazov* maybe. Or *Crime and Punishment*. I loved *The Idiot*. Did you ever read *The Idiot?*"

Yes, he said, he'd read *The Idiot,* and he understood as he said it that he was meant to help this girl: that he had bolted from the restaurant, had experienced terror at the image of his life in the window, had gone blank looking at the menu, because this girl was standing outside in the rain. She needed him — she had been sent to him. And he needed her. It was all one. An equation. A providential algebra. Understanding this exploded in his body like rising bubbles shattering the surface of a pond.

3

Since Isabel came to him, sometimes he thinks about God. Sometimes he talks to God. He doesn't know who God is. Or what. Or if. Just someone to address, to speak to — found in the addressing, in the speaking. Or something. Which might not listen. Or listening might fail to hear. Or hearing might not need to listen. Or knowing all, needs nothing, not even Russell Jackson's intention to address it. Our animal groans, he thinks he remembers from somewhere in the Bible. Our inarticulate wretchedness. The less articulate the better. The closer to the truth. Since Isabel came to him, he cries for his mother (she whose virtue he never forgave, whose guilt he never acknowledged) and for her son, the other one, second-born and fatherless: Cheyenne, dark-eyed child of perpetual accusation. Russell was sixteen when Cheyenne was born. His own father was newly married to a woman so young she might have been Russell's sister, his mother abandoned in what he then thought was middle age. Divorced and spinsterly, she lived quietly and alone with him until suddenly she was pregnant — sitting at the kitchen table telling him she was pregnant. She was drinking coffee and the morning sun illuminated the steam that rose from her cup. She sat there looking at him through it, telling him no abortion, and he was surprised she even spoke the word. No adoption either, she said — a child that would be hers alone, a child who wouldn't betray her in the name of its father. He ignored the accusation and asked: But who? — convinced it was his own father's, that somehow she had tricked him, won him back for a

40

night to steal for herself this calculated revenge. She wouldn't
answer. No abortion, she said. No murder. She was going to
church again. To a Spanish church, in Oakland. No adoption
either. She is not a divorced woman, she said. She is an adul-
teress, and this child is the child of her adultery, this child will be
her cross. She christened the baby William, but when Russell
came back from Vietnam he told the kid his true name was
Cheyenne. Cheyenne, he said, was a wild man, a rebel and a hero,
and he filled his brother's head with stories of Billy Santana. He
came around a lot and let the kid love him and then without
warning he disappeared. That was in the days when everyone was
always disappearing. He never went back. Cheyenne kept the
name. When he showed up years later, what Russell saw was their
mother — not quite forty, blue eyes crazed behind a veil of silver
steam. Sometimes he sees her now, he thinks, when he looks at
Isabel.

"My mother grew up in Los Angeles," Isabel told him. In a
neighborhood that was bean fields until World War II. Airplane
country. Her mother was a talented woman. She wrote and
painted and wanted to make movies. She wanted many things.
Not things, Isabel said. Abilities. Knowledge. Achievements.
Lovers. Salvation, Isabel said. Exhilaration. Change. Sometimes
she worked for it all. And sometimes she didn't. When things fell
apart she ran. Always she drank too much. She lost what she had
and made new starts and never quite recouped her losses. Two
steps backward, one step forward — two back, three forward, two
back, one forward — staggering. "She could never catch up with
herself," Isabel said. "Her feet had these calluses. From the
sidewalks in L.A. She played barefoot all her childhood, on the
sidewalks and on the grass. She went barefoot wherever she
could. Her feet were tough. She wanted to be tough. She
toughened herself. But inside she fell apart. She cracked. No one
saw it but me. And sometimes a lover. Once or twice a friend.
She never trusted people after they saw that. Only me. She
trusted me. I didn't want to leave her."

He didn't ask why she'd left then. He'd heard too many
explanations already. Isabel's stories changed. He didn't want to

know anymore. He thought he didn't have to. He had also left his mother. His reasons weren't the same. But that didn't matter. He didn't like Isabel to talk about her mother. It made him anxious. Every morning when she scraped her feet he began to feel afraid.

"I dreamed about her," she said. "She was standing in a kitchen next to a plate-glass wall. Water beat against it. It was a room on a body of water, immersed in water. The tide rose halfway up the glass. Outside it was night. The water was black, like ink. My mother had called me. She'd said *Look, our first hippopotamus,* and we watched its back bobbing up and down just under the surface of the water. Then it rose up close to the glass: a pink yawning mouth, a dark tongue, a couple of peglike teeth, and suddenly it was in the kitchen, shaking itself out like a dog. It stood there next to the refrigerator, smaller than it had been in the water — safe, domesticated, waiting to be fed. My mother was wearing a robe like those sisters, like Mother Teresa, white with blue-striped edges. Her feet were thick with calluses. I dropped to the floor and looked at her feet. I held on to her ankles but she was moving away to feed the animal. Her robe came off in my hands, and then she was wearing silk, heavy with spangles and sequins — black, silver, blue. Her feet still had those calluses. She walked on glass and didn't bleed."

Russell doesn't know how they got here. Isabel is reading. He is standing at the window, waiting for the rain. Just now someone telephoned who said his name was Angelino. (Billy Santana maybe. Or maybe Cheyenne. Like Billy Santana, Cheyenne could be anywhere.) It is 1985. Isabel has been with him three years. He was happy when she told him Isabel wasn't her name. He didn't want to hear the real one. He thinks of himself as nameless. He doesn't like his names.

The rain begins. His mouth tastes like salt, as if he had been crying. He watches her read. She works days in a Burger King and saves her money and helps with the rent. She educates herself. She says she's making plans. She's taking math in night school, Spanish, sometimes an acting class. She wants to go to college, she says — maybe, and maybe not. She's getting ready. She is reading her way through the books on his shelves — first the

Dostoevsky, then the Kafka, the Tolstoy, the Beckett, the Freud — for fun Thomas Pynchon and the Latin Americans, on the subway the plays, diligently two nights a week the history, and soon, she says, the philosophy — Sartre, Marx, the Greeks. She's saving the poetry for last, she says. But this isn't true. She takes it to bed with her and reads it in secret, an act of prayer.

He doesn't know who he was when he bought these books and read them and filled the shelves — books by Joyce, Nabokov, Faulkner, Kundera, Fuentes, García Márquez, books on movies and semiotics and third world revolutions, books on American history from seventeenth-century Massachusetts to Vietnam. He doesn't remember himself. Since Isabel came what he remembers are the things that didn't happen — Dominique, refusing to be tragic, walking away from him in the rain; Cheyenne, unable to kill him; Billy Santana disappearing, a bottle of tequila in one hand, the other flashing the peace sign that once stood for victory; Lucinda packing for Guatemala, expressing no regrets — his first wife almost doesn't have a name. Sometimes now he sees her, playing volleyball in Tilden Park, under the eucalyptus trees. He married her to leave his mother and left her for the war. He wasn't in the military. Sometimes he carried a gun. When he came back he tried to live with her. But already it was too late.

"I was in love once," Isabel told him. "I was six years old. Or maybe five. This boyfriend of my mother's. I was five, I think, and everyone thought I was some kind of grown-up. I liked playing with grown-ups. I liked when they got high or drunk and acted more like me. We laughed more then. This man was more like me. He had long black hair. It curled down his back. He read me stories. He believed in fairy tales. Princes and princesses, unicorns and dragons, happily ever after. My mother read stories with me, too. But it wasn't the same. She was never a child with me. Except sometimes when she was drunk. But this man was the prince in all the stories. He believed in magic. After a while my mother didn't like him. She woke up one day, she said. Just woke right up. She didn't want him around anymore. He embarrassed her. It happened all the time. Suddenly like that. What saved her one day embarrassed her the next. Not what — who.

The whats never changed. Only the faces. And the geography. Wherever we went and whoever we went with or found there, it was always the same. She had a rebellious spirit. It attracted people to her and pushed them away. We all loved her. Even the men who left her loved her. Some way. I loved her too. And I loved some of the men. But this man was the one I fell in love with. Maybe not for any reason. Maybe just because I was five years old. One time I rode on his back while they were making love. It was afternoon I think. I remember the daylight and the sunbeams going blue and silver in his hair. I got up from my nap and heard them in the bedroom and there they were under the sheet and I just climbed up on his back and rode him like a horsie, laughing while I held his shoulders and watched my mother's face.

"Maybe that's why I loved him," she said. "What do you think?"

But Russell couldn't think. He recalled the daughter he'd never seen and felt afraid. He wanted to kill that man, and that woman, her mother, and Dominique too, who would have been just like her, who would have lain there fucking while his daughter clung to the back of a stranger, a man not her father, watching her mother's ecstatic face. He hated them all, men, women, mothers, children, Isabel, himself. He was stunned by the depth of hatred he suddenly felt in his body. It tied him in knots. A rebellious spirit, he thought. But no — those words Isabel had used about her mother. This was not a rebellious spirit. This was malevolence, it was rage. It was — paralysis, the end of things, the end of everything.

"Stop," he said.

"It wasn't bad," she said. "It was no big deal, we were all laughing. It didn't scar me."

But he couldn't answer. His hands were clenched into fists. He wanted to open his hands and wrap them around her neck. He wanted to squeeze until she stopped breathing.

"Grown-ups," she said. "You all think fucking is so important."

She made him want to change his life.

"Isabel," he says. He wants her attention. He wants her to talk. He wants her to take him out of this thinking. He wants her to tell him a story. But she answers, "Just a minute," and keeps on reading. "End of a chapter," she says. "Almost done." And he wants more: wants her to stay here with him, or better, to take him with her when she goes. He wants her to love him. He doesn't care how. He wants her to release him, to make change possible — no: necessary. She is his ticket — out. What he wants — well, what does he know? — he doesn't know what he wants, he wants her, without knowing what wanting her means. Not sex. It doesn't mean sex. Or maybe it does, but only incidentally. What then? He is terrified of her leaving. She has made him want change so absolute it's beyond his will to reach. He has done what he could. But nothing is enough. The gap between reality and imagination continues to widen, everything changes and remains the same, he is a stranger to himself, and still dissatisfied. In her presence, sometimes, he has found peace. But not tonight.

"Isabel," he says, and his throat constricts around her name.

She looks up at him, alarmed.

"Sorry," he says. "Read."

"I am," she says.

If I were her father — , he thinks, and stops. In Jamaica they were dancing. It was her sixteenth birthday. At dinner they drank champagne. She was beautiful. They danced and he forgot himself, his life became someone else's and all the world a party — black and pink and orange, yellow and more black, shiny black mirrors, black glass walls, black marble floors, and pink, blue, orange, lavender flashing off steamy bodies, clothes whipping like flags in a shifting wind, and the sweat and smoke and perfume and flowers and booze filling the air with a sweet smell he remembered of men and women and desire alive in a tropical heat. He felt naked, insubstantial — a vapor, he had no skin. He never lost sight of Isabel, dancing toward him and away, stomping her feet and shaking her hips and shoulders, her hair a mass of black tangled curls, her eyes closed even while she approached him, as if her body were pulled toward his by gravity, her muscles dancing in a frenzy, her spirit hidden inside its trance. There was witchcraft in her dancing—she was an obeah woman, glowing and beautiful and suddenly wholly strange. His body came back to him in a shock of electricity. Or panic. He moved toward her. His clothes were not his clothes, they were her clothes around his body. His breath was her breath. His heartbeat, hers. He was terrified but he went on. He had no choice. He felt her skin surround his skin. There was no one else in the room. He filled the room, and everything outside his body was still his body, dense with the power to hold her and break her. She danced toward him, she danced away. He pursued her. She opened her eyes. He froze. She looked at him. The music stopped. She said, "I haven't been telling you the truth."

They stood on the terrace listening to the rain beat down on the once-wild leaves in the jungle garden that backed up the hillside behind the nightclub. They watched moths and beetles and fireflies die in the white-purple bug lights half-hidden in the hibiscus growing along the railings. The music kept coming. Isabel's arms were bare, rosy from days in the sun. He couldn't touch her.

"I didn't come to you by accident," she said.

He didn't want to hear it.

"I have to tell you the truth now," she said.

But he was afraid. "Let's go in," he said. "Let's dance again. Tell me later. At the hotel."

"No," she said. "Now."

The air was heavy with rain and frangipani. She leaned over the railing and picked a red hibiscus flower. His desire turned to nausea. She had bought a shell on the street—a tropical shell that grew in logarithmic whorls, its conical peak white and crusty, onetime home to a thousand seed-sized tenants, then pulling down, inward, creamy orange and pink, curling in on itself, labial, vaginal—shiny, slick, and smooth. He had rubbed the heel of his hand along the slick smooth underside, and he had looked at Isabel across the room drying her hair after her shower, and he had cried. Innocent then. He had been innocent still. This night had not yet happened to him.

"Please," he said. An accident, he wanted to say. This was an accident — never again. But this nausea was still his desire.

"That night in the rain," she said. She twirled the hibiscus flower between her fingers. "I was looking for you," she said. "For you in particular."

"Isabel," he said.

"It's not my name."

"I don't want to know your name."

"I won't tell you then."

"I don't want to know anything you haven't already told me."

"Yes," she said. "You do." Then she looked at him.

He listened to the rain. He heard the insects dying. "The music stopped," he said. Her eyes were too dark to be blue. Her dress was white and fell off her shoulder, the shoulder nearest him. She had tied a green silk scarf around her waist. When she danced the skirt and scarf furled around her legs and snapped out again. "All right," he said, but he turned away, toward the spotlit ferns and frangipani and bamboo. "Let's walk," he said. "From the other side we should see the water."

"No," she said. "You have to listen to me. Why won't you listen to me?"

She was helpless. As helpless as she had ever been. Obeah woman or not, he thought, and with that thought he got a grip on himself. She was a stranger here without him. She was a stranger anywhere. She needed him — not as he was tonight, but as he had been for her, for more than a year: safe, trustworthy — protector and provider of shelter, listener, brother, friend.

"I'm sorry," he said. "Tell me."

"When you came back from Vietnam," she said. She hesitated. She tore at the crinkly petals of the hibiscus flower. Pollen dusted her fingers yellow. He stopped her hands. They were cold. "My mother," she said. She looked at him and pulled away. She threw the broken flower out into the rain. "I was looking for you," she said. "I knew your name, I knew where you lived, I knew where you worked. I followed you from Bloomingdale's. I followed you to that restaurant. I waited for you in the street in the rain. It wasn't an accident," she said again. "I found you."

He didn't understand. "I know your mother?" he said.

"When you came back from Vietnam," she said.

"In Berkeley?" he said.

"Yes," she said. "You worked in the hospital where I was born."

"And I knew your mother?"

"You knew my mother before that. You met my mother in the winter, when you came back from Vietnam. You met my mother — I think it was in February, or maybe it was March. You met her in a music bar called the Babylon."

"The Babylon," he said.

"It was little and dark," she said.

"Crowded and loud."

"You remember."

"The place," he said. "Rhythm and blues."

"And sex and drugs and rock and roll."

"And I met your mother —"

" — in the Babylon. You took her home."

"I was living with my wife."

"You took her home and you made love to her. You stayed with her all weekend."

She waited for him to acknowledge this.

"It's possible," he said. He felt a chill at the back of his neck, up his spine. He was unable to ask the obvious question. She went on.

"She fell a little bit in love with you," she said. "But you never saw her again. Sometimes she looked for you in the crowd at the Babylon. Once she saw you, but you turned away. You don't remember. Maybe you don't remember my mother."

Her eyes were wild. Like the eyes of the cat in the book from his childhood about the little island where the cat goes on a sailboat for a picnic with its people. It is a little cat, a little black cat with white throat and paws, and the island is wild, and Isabel's eyes were like the cat's eyes when it catches a fish and holds it under its claws, eyes wild and knowing and proud. Isabel was lying.

"She knew who you were," she said. "She knew where you lived. She knew where you worked. She knew about your wife and your mother and your little brother. She knew everything about you. You told her a lot in one weekend. All you did was lie in bed and fuck her and talk. That's exactly how she said it—All he did was lie in bed and fuck me and talk. And then she said—But I fell a little in love with him, maybe more than a little, and when I knew I was pregnant, I wanted you."

He stared at her. She was lying. He wanted to hit her. As if hitting her would erase the lie. He wanted to hurt her, he wanted to see her bleed.

"She was a senior in philosophy," she said, "about to graduate, with honors. She didn't know what to do. She didn't want to tell her father." Isabel laughed. "She thought she might run away to Canada and pretend to be a war widow. Then the doctor told her how to get welfare and she decided to stay where she was.

"I was tiny when I was born," she said. "I was one of the last babies born in that hospital. They stopped having babies there after that. The house we lived in got bulldozed for a parking lot. We went back once to see it and it was gone. She didn't want you in my life."

Something snapped in his head, like the beetles dying on the lights. He chose to believe her. He didn't care if it wasn't true. All of a sudden he believed her.

"I didn't come looking for you for her sake," Isabel said. "But she had told me what she knew. When I had to leave her, I tracked you down."

"Let's walk," he said. "I can't stand this phony jungle here," and on the dark side of the terrace, looking down on the water and the lights strung on boats, he cried. She stood beside him in silence, separate. The rain drummed on the metal terrace roof.

"Why didn't you tell me?" he finally asked her. "Why didn't you tell me as soon as you found me?"

"I was afraid you wouldn't keep me."

"But I did keep you," he said.

"I didn't know you," she said. "How could I have known you?

Now I'm sixteen. If you don't want to keep me it doesn't matter. I'm not a runaway anymore. I can do what I like."

And so in Jamaica she had let him become her father. He got used to it. She was not any kind of obeah woman, it had been a trick of the night. She was a child. His child. Still, for a while, his newborn desire stayed with him, and everything he saw or felt or touched was sexual, everything but Isabel, until gradually the sexuality of everything died away. Alone at night he prayed and for the first time his prayers found words — old, solid, traditional, English words: *Our father . . . thy will be done . . . deliver us from evil . . .* They were not his words, but in silently speaking them he made the old words his, as best he could. Sometimes he thought he was crazy — to believe Isabel was his daughter, to pray to a dead god — but he didn't care, he loved this girl, and only his faltering attempts to pray (. . . *I shall not want . . . for thou art with me . . .*) made it possible to believe her. He didn't know what being her father meant. The first little human god, he thought. And a powerful god, too. Larger than life. And what was a father anyway without his claim to godhood? Not much. A hose the sperm ran through. (Don't even dream about her, Dominique had written. She isn't yours. She will never be yours.) In spite of himself, uneasily, as desire gave way, he began to make fatherhood's ordinary claims: Isabel's debt to him, his natural authority, his right of command. He was uncomfortable wearing this mantle. It was a hair shirt. He didn't like himself. In a father's power, he thought, there was this catch, this necessity — a prison impossible to escape from.

Then Isabel saw her mother and came back to him with the truth. A new truth. He should have been angry. Instead he was free. "You won't leave?" he asked. "Not yet," she said. He had hardly known how uneasy he had been as her father until she told him it wasn't true. True, he thinks. Nothing has ever been true. The truth was whatever she said it was, whatever she wanted it to be. And the truth today is she wants to go to Barcelona to see a white gorilla, she has her own money, she might go to college, she gets letters from abroad, she is almost eighteen, and she's the one who's free. She doesn't need him. The truth today is that he would almost rather be her father. As her father, at least, he could act. Wasn't action the definition of fatherhood? Wasn't a father the man who acted on his children? No matter what? Even in withdrawal, stasis, death, a father acted on his children. This power he will never have over Isabel. Instead he has his hunger, and his freedom. But this freedom no longer means what it once did. Even here, where nothing has changed, she has changed him. Because he knows now that he is his own jailer, that he is separated from her by desire and by everything he wants to be. And by this relentless thinking, which he is powerless to stop. He is no different from the particolored man he saw this morning on the subway, an albino man with a big brown splotch across his face, like a pinto horse — a tall man, skinny, with square shoulders and turned-out toes, his hair black, his wrists white: talking out loud to himself, angrily, in an unfamiliar language, a language maybe all his own.

4

Every new truth became another story. From the beginning he had known she was not his daughter, he had known it was a game they were playing; and he had not known. Believing he was her father had inspired him to change his life. The lie — fantasy, delusion, self-deception, whatever he chose to call it once it was over — at the time had worked liked magic, a gift from heaven, news from God. He cut back his hours at Bloomingdale's and let Isabel help pay the rent. He quit drinking. He gave up television and poker. He stopped going to bars to find a one-night woman to take him home. He began to work with his old notes. Rereading them, he was struck by the innocence of his actions — going to Saigon, hanging out with Santana, letting Santana drive him deeper into the war; struck too by the naïveté of his anger, the helplessness of his compassion and rage; and struck suddenly by fear, a fear he had hardly acknowledged at the time: almost twenty years later, suddenly frightened for his own young life. He found himself grateful simply to have survived. He felt the same gratitude for Isabel. On her behalf. A gratitude she was still too innocent to know.

He built a darkroom in the loft. He photographed the streets. He covered the walls on his side of the partition with photographs of Isabel. He taught her how to use the camera, the darkroom, and when they weren't at their jobs, they went out together to shoot: to the zoos, the botanical gardens, Central Park, the Cloisters, every neighborhood in the city, and out of the city, to the beaches and ballparks and racetracks; they rode the ferry and walked the bridges; and when they came back and worked in the darkroom, he saw in their drying prints how they inhabited different worlds: his darkly shadowed, etched, defined—hers softer, restricted but larger, viewed up close and filled with light. Her world had people in it—not an obsession with one person (repetitions of her at every angle, in every shadow of the day) and not an abstraction of people (his distant figures dwarfed by crowds and buildings or space), but a world of eyes, mouths, hands, feet—skin, he thought—various and touchable. These strangers could be touched, Isabel had touched them. The light that filled each image was her own. He was jealous, looking at them. He can't bear the thought of the darkness he will live in when she goes. He will retreat again, withdraw, dig in again somewhere and hide. Slowly, in her way, with her shape-shifting and stories, Isabel had led him into the light. He will be blind again without her. He wants to cross the room and rip the book out from under her face and throw it. "Don't leave me," he says. But she doesn't hear him. He is speaking to the open window. The rain is loud in the street, and he remembers a night he sat through under a leaky tin roof with Billy Santana—hunched up under rubber ponchos, sitting high off the ground on wooden crates in a makeshift black-market warehouse in the Cholon district of Saigon, keeping dry while Santana told stories from before he left the war. They were the only stories Santana ever told. As if he'd had no life before he arrived in Vietnam, no family, no history, no place that he came from or meant to go back to. The person he had been before was missing, a deserter, absent without leave. He had papers in various names, and he shuffled his papers according to his need. Pretending to be a photographer, he slung empty cameras around his neck and became invisible—wearing army green (faded except where insignia had been) and mildewed combat boots for anyone to see. He tied a red bandanna Apache-style around his forehead and let his black hair curl out from under it, growing long. He was taken to be a rookie journalist who'd lost it somewhere in the jungle. Maybe in '65, they said. Maybe in the Ia Drang. Stories floated around. Sometimes Russell caught one.

They were close enough to the truth as Santana told it. They were his own stories, modified and recycled, the currency that covered him. He was left alone. After the Ia Drang (he said that night under the ponchos) he'd found his name in *Stars & Stripes*. Listed among the missing in action. If he laid low long enough, sooner or later he'd be dead.

The truth, Isabel said, is she ran away for adventure. She wanted to live the life her mother lived, or wanted to live, or would have lived without her. She had chosen the life she found, she said. She had asked for it. She got off the bus at Port Authority and walked out onto the street. She was naive, she said. But she learned fast. By the time Russell found her it was different—she was weak by then and always hungry, her brain wasn't right, she said—nothing was right. She was running, she said—on the run. But at first things hadn't been like that. She wasn't so scrawny when she got here, she was rosy-cheeked and ready for anything anyone asked her to do. She was curious. That's all it was. She wanted to learn what was out here. She wanted to know. For herself. In her body. With her own eyes. With her skin.

The truth, she said. She had been to see her mother.

They were looking for her when she came to him. Men, she said. Men she had worked for. She was hiding with him. She lived with him in hiding, in disguise. They still wanted her. She had seen something, she said. She had seen a child die. He was not her father. She had invented his fatherhood out of stories he had told her. She had recognized desire in him that night in Jamaica. And desire in herself. But she did not want his desire. She didn't want anyone's. The street had ruined her maybe, she said. Or maybe it was her mother. And maybe she wasn't ruined. But only for now.

The truth, she said.

But her truths were stories. Like Billy Santana's. They started somewhere in reality and ended in lies. They served the same purpose—they protected her. From what? He doesn't know. Sometimes they had no apparent purpose—stories for the sake of being stories. They might have been real, or not. Their reality didn't matter. Only the illusion: the truth.

He doesn't like this line of thinking. It makes him restless. He asks too many questions, thinking like this—who she really is, what she really wants, why she's really here. Questions that have no meaning. From day to day—here she is. What more does he need?

But—everything, this thinking tells him. He can stop it only by holding steady on her eyes while she talks, by listening to her voice, not her words, by holding her hands, by feeling her presence in the room. Her look, her body, her smell, her voice: the truth.

"Isabel," he says again. The rain comes down. The shades billow. One by one he closes the windows. The room gets quieter.

"I was in love once," she told him. "He found me on the street. We had six weeks together, then he got scared and ran. He came back and left. He came and left. I was in love with him. He was in love with me. Every time he left me I got thinner. He was like a drug. Without him I was in withdrawal. Then you found me. I don't know where he is."

"Isabel," he says. "Who was that on the phone?"

He can hear in his voice that he believes she knows. She can hear it.

"What?" she says.

"Don't lie," he says. A lie is not a story. Somewhere in a story the truth is concealed.

"Why would I lie?" she says. She closes her book and sits up. A story is coming.

A story then, all right, he thinks, tell me a story. "I want to know who that was," he says—no longer confident, no longer accusing. They will piece it together. He will ask questions, she will answer, they will construct another fiction. The truth will wait buried in it, sometime later to be dug out.

Later, he thinks. When she's gone. When her absence penetrates her stories and brings these fragments, isolated now, contradictory, out of their separate darkness into the larger picture her absence will reveal—the time of her absence, a negative of this time—what is dark now will be light, what is light, dark. And locked up in the light of her absence, he will be as blind as ever. He is waiting for her absence, hungry for it. Hungry for it and terrified. His fear has nothing to do with her. Is this possible?

"I should have talked to him myself," he says.

She crosses her legs, Indian style, and waits for him to go on, watching him, catlike, thinking.

"What did he sound like?" he asks.

She shrugs. Story time. "Ordinary," she says. She reaches her arms up over her head and stretches from the waist to the tips of her fingers, first one side, then the other, alternating, deep in concentration on the movement of her body.

"I don't know who it was," he says.

"Does it matter?" she asks.

She was in love once, she told him. She lived with an artist. She modeled for him and he fed her and let her sleep on the studio couch. He was good to her. A gentle man. "Like you," she said. She smiled. "He took good care of me." But he wanted her to go back to her mother. She told him the truth about herself and he wanted to send her back.

"So you stopped telling the truth?" Russell asked.

"I still tell the truth," she said. "Just not all at once."

"You didn't know him?" he asks her now. "He wasn't anyone you knew?"

She shakes her head. He can't see her face.

"Isabel?" he says.

She looks up. "He had a nice voice," she says. "I liked his voice."

He was mistaken. She will not tell him a story. She is going to do her exercises now, she says, and from the bedroom he hears her thump-thumping to the music of the Talking Heads. "What's the big deal?" she asked before she left the room. "It's nothing to get so excited about. It's just some friend who wants to surprise you." But she is not as calm as she wants him to think her. She is not indifferent to this caller. She does not blush so easily. This giddy breath does not come into her voice. Her heart does not beat so fast. She is not made afraid by phantoms. He can feel these things. He felt them while she sat reading and when she put her book aside to wait for him to let her leave the room — as if he could have stopped her. He feels them now through the bedroom door, in the rock-and-roll music, in the energy of her workout. This man arriving is not anyone for him. Not Cheyenne, not Billy Santana. This man is coming to take her away. When she's done exercising she'll come out of her room all sticky and glowing with sweat. When the stranger arrives maybe she'll be naked, fresh from her shower, wrapped in a towel. One of those men in one of those stories. She was in love once, she told him. With her mother's boyfriend. He was like a boy himself, bashful; he cultivated secrets. "I was one of his secrets," she said. "That's why I had to leave her." Maybe it was that man. Or the artist. Or the guy who was like a drug who found her on the street. Or someone else, none of these inventions, someone he's never heard of, someone she just met. In night school or at the Burger King. In scene class or on the subway or in the park. Someone in one of her photographs maybe. Anyone. It could be anyone. Maybe she never went to night school or to scene class or to the Burger King. Maybe she still works the street. Maybe they're coming to take her back to themselves, whoever they are. Maybe they've found her, the men she's hiding from. Maybe she needs help now and doesn't know how to ask. Maybe she's afraid for him. Maybe she wants to protect him from the truth. Maybe that's the reason she tells so many stories — to protect him, not herself. As she would have told stories to protect her mother. Or maybe it was her mother.

"Stop," he says. The rain is orange in the heavy orange light. "Stop."

He has picked her up at the Burger King. He has taken her paycheck to the bank. He has watched her do homework in math and Spanish. He has cooked dinner for friends she brought to the loft to work on scenes. He is not afraid of her mother.

Liar, he says. He is afraid of her mother. But Isabel isn't. And whoever this caller was has made her afraid — breathless, blushing, happy, and afraid.

Who then? Someone she was in love with once. In love, he thinks. This kid. He wants to kill her. He wants a drink. He has never known love to come in the form of this anger, this physical rage. He wants to break things. He wants to put his hand through the window into the orange rain. He stares at the reflection of his fist, at the glass that wants to be broken. He can't move. It wasn't her mother. It wasn't for him, not Billy Santana, not Cheyenne. Who then? Anyone. The person or people who write to her from abroad.

His mind goes silent. Yes.

From Barcelona. Where an albino gorilla lives caged in the zoo.

He had seen the first blue tissue envelope sticking out of her shirt pocket on a Saturday morning less than a month after she came. It was one of his shirts. She'd brought the mail up and handed him a pile of political ads and appeals for money and a postcard from Margot, on vacation in Bermuda. He saw the envelope in Isabel's pocket and wondered and didn't ask. She was strange to him still, and he didn't want to frighten her, or anger her — from the start she had told him he asked too many questions. A few weeks later, he came home early and got the mail himself. He was disappointed. There was nothing but a concert ad from Carnegie Hall. What had he hoped for? He knew the answer when he found himself in her room. The tear that fell there — or the seeds arranged in magic circles of protection — rendered the subject of her letters permanently taboo. He has almost let himself forget that they exist. She's been careful. He has too. Their whole first year together he never saw her mail. Then he cut back his hours at Bloomingdale's and brought up the mail himself. The letters came, on blue tissue or gray, addressed to Isabel Jackson, sometimes from London, sometimes from Paris, two from Berlin, one from Vienna, one from Rome, one from Tel Aviv. They still come, from cities all over Europe. He leaves them on the table for her, and she takes them without comment to her room. Always typewritten, the aerograms and envelopes give no clue about the sender: no European handwriting, not feminine or masculine, young or old. No name appears in the return address, which always changes. Not even the typewriters used are the same.

From behind (he jumps — he didn't feel her come into the room, didn't hear her, didn't see her reflection), she tells him: "It was Billy Santana."

He doesn't turn around. Billy Santana. Billy Santana in Saigon knew the world was about to end, in Berkeley he knew the revolution was just around the corner, in New York he knew how to hide and where to go for documents, anything illegal — he knew how to disappear. He knew more than he told, and vanished, and when he came back, he brought rumors from the war zone — his war, which didn't change and didn't end.

"It was Billy Santana," she says behind him. But her story comes too late: in the street now Russell sees Cheyenne — long-legged and skinny and running to beat the rain.

"Why did you lie?" he asks her.

Her curls cling dripping around her face onto her shoulders, darkening the pale blue cotton of her shirt. (Like tears, he thinks. He is too old to be this melancholy.) She has taken her shower, washed her hair, changed her clothes.

"Did I?" she asks.

He doesn't know.

The door buzzes. A repetition. There is an excitement in her step now. He wants to stop her, to say: Don't go down, it isn't necessary, stay — a few minutes more. But he can't hold her. She's across the room and out the door. He listens to her bare feet drumming down the stairs. Maybe she does expect Santana. She had liked him when they met in Jamaica. But downstairs now, she laughs — "Wait," she says, "hold the door" — and Russell feels in the pit of his stomach that sickness he had known toward the end with Lucinda, when he waited at home on Saturdays, searching through the trash.

He listens from the top of the stairs: the rain, a bootstep, a car passing, and Cheyenne calling, "What?" The voice sends a shiver up his spine; it agitates a nerve. Breathless, Isabel answers, "Three of diamonds." The door closes. In the deeper silence, they whisper. Russell calculates Cheyenne's age. Twenty-three, or twenty-four. Young enough to take her away. The whispering continues. He can't hear the words, he makes up words: "Don't hurt him," Isabel says. He can't bear it. He withdraws farther, inside, to the window. Cheyenne, he thinks. Cheyenne — like a prayer, repeating it while he opens the window and, looking down on the empty street, breathes in the rain.

5

There are patterns here, mysteries he doesn't understand. When Cheyenne and Isabel come in, he turns around, willing himself to meet his brother, to hold out his hand. He is stopped by what he sees: Isabel waiting at the door, Cheyenne coming forward, and in the interval between them, visible magic. Even at this distance he can see it: Cheyenne is the truth, all her stories have been lies. He wonders how long she will take to reveal this. (She wanted things, she said about her mother once. Knowledge. Exhilaration. Lovers. Change. I didn't want to leave her, she said. I wanted to be like her.) Cheyenne hesitates in the middle of the room. The rain comes down harder. Water blows in the open window.

"You're getting drenched," Cheyenne says. The voice hurts.

Russell turns away to close the window and can't turn back around. (They came one day to the loft, a bunch of girls, four or five of them. It was late summer. They glowed, all brown and golden, dressed in colors, pink and yellow and orange and green. He made them spaghetti. They practiced scenes. When they worked they were beautiful—intense and concentrated, with the seriousness of children. When they stopped, they laughed. They were so young. They put their heads together and whispered and giggled. They sat up self-consciously straight at the table and made grown-up talk with him. For the first time, in the presence of these girls, he felt how unbearably young Isabel was.) In the window he sees Cheyenne reflected, and beyond him Isabel, still at the door. If he holds back any longer they'll come close to him, touch him, lie to him (to themselves), a hand on his shoulder maybe, a hug, a Judas kiss. He turns around.

Isabel stands at the door, soaked to the skin.

"I brought tequila," Cheyenne says, holding out a soggy, quart-sized brown paper bag—several days' growth of beard on his chin, hands shaking. "I thought we could make peace," he says. He smiles, a child, full of hope. "Jacks?" he says, and hesitates, and Russell goes forward to meet him. In his arms (the Judas hug), Cheyenne reeks of booze and cigarettes, and something else—old sweat, and maybe fear. His body is hot and trembling, and even through his bulky army jacket there's nothing to him but fever and bones.

"You're sick," Russell says. "You don't look good."

"I'm not. I don't think I am. Not very good. I'm in trouble, I think."

Isabel, trembling herself, comes away from the door. "What kind of trouble?" she asks, and Cheyenne's face goes gray.

"Food," he says, "maybe. I just need some food." To Russell he says, "Could we go get some food? I haven't eaten in days. I don't think I've eaten."

"I'll make something," Isabel says.

"No!" Cheyenne cries—too loudly—then looks at them, one then the other. "I was thinking maybe something from Vinnie's," he says. "Lasagna maybe, maybe food isn't what I need. Maybe that drink." He hands Russell the bottle. Isabel is at the refrigerator, opening the door. "What's she doing?" he asks. "Don't cook," he says. "Tell her not to cook, Jacks. I don't want her cooking."

"You have to eat," she says.

"I was at Belmont," he says. "I had a hot dog, I think. Maybe I had a hot dog. I was at Belmont all day," he says to Russell. "It was a good place to hide."

"From what?" she asks.

"From what," he says. "Where did she come from, Jacks?"

"Isabel lives here," Russell says.

Cheyenne looks at her, and turns away. "I need that drink," he says. "You have ice? That's all I need, some ice and a glass. And a cigarette, too. You don't have cigarettes, do you? I ran out of money. Maybe she wants to be so helpful, she can go get me some cigarettes. What's her name?"

"Isabel," Russell says.

"She makes me nervous," Cheyenne says. He looks at her, she blushes. She can't take her eyes off him. He turns away, glances around at the walls, goes to the window and looks down at the street. He comes back. "I was at Belmont," he says. "I didn't have money. Well, a little money. Money enough to get there. Some change. A cheap bet. I hoped maybe I'd get lucky. I thought I deserved to get lucky. Or not. I don't know."

Russell holds out his drink. Cheyenne looks at it, his eyes bloodshot and tired. He needs both hands to take the glass. Tequila spills over the rim. He gulps it down.

"Go look at the horses," he says then. "It was the only thing I could think to do. Go out there and watch the horses and get my head clean. I had a few beers. I listened to guys giving tips. I listened to people. I was hearing voices, words I didn't want to remember. I had to clear out my eyes. My eyes were so full of— ugly visions. Ugly things, ugliness. My eyes and my ears. I—I don't know, I won something. Enough to get me through the day and to call Santana—"

"You called Santana?" Russell asks.

"I wasn't so scared then, when I started winning. It was a long shot. Seventeen to one. I thought maybe it wasn't so bad, when I was winning. I thought maybe God was on my side maybe. I couldn't—I don't know. I lost it again. She raised me Catholic. That was something you didn't have to endure." He stops to drink, finds his glass empty, looks for the bottle.

"Why did you call Santana?" Russell asks.

"Why?" Cheyenne laughs a little. "Why not?" He seems confused by the question, almost sad. "Isn't he who to call when you're in trouble?" he asks. "You don't think I'd call you?" He falls silent then, as if he expects an answer.

"Where did you come here from?" Isabel asks.

"Where?" He's distracted, holding out his glass to Russell. "Didn't I just tell you?"

"Before Belmont," she says.

"Before," he repeats. He watches Russell refill the glass. He drinks. "I don't know," he says. "Maybe it wasn't today. What happened to that card? Can you tell me about that card?" She holds out her hand. The soaked three of diamonds hangs limp between two fingers. He drinks, his face beginning to change: the smile going lopsided, the color coming back. He turns to Russell. "Where did you find her?" he asks.

"Ask me," she says.

He laughs. He looks from one to the other—full of himself suddenly, lit with amusement. "Well?" he asks. "Cat got everybody's tongue? Let's hear about the card then." To Russell he says, "She ran out into the rain to get it. Dug it up off the sidewalk. She do that often?" He laughs. He walks around the room, around the table, stopping, as he goes, to examine the cards and feathers and leather scraps and paper shapes and dead flowers pushpinned to the walls. "Decor's different," he says. "She's been here a while." He stops, drinks, looks at them. "What's the matter? Do I scare somebody? Downstairs you said you wanted a card that was happier," he says to Isabel. "So you read cards. So tell me what's so sad about this three of diamonds. Tell my fortune off it—I need to know." He circles the table; while Isabel answers, she follows him with her eyes.

"As a person," she says, "it's someone torn between fear and love. A person who hides and lives in secrets and makes decisions abruptly and tells no one any plans. A stubborn person—who learns from first experience and then stops learning. A person in terror," she says, "who has too much hunger for too much he believes he'll never know. A soul in prison. Jailed."

Cheyenne stops. "And you think that's me? Is that what you think? Why are you shaking?"

He's right. The steadier he gets, the more she shakes.

"Is that love or fear, that shaking?" he asks.

"Don't bully her," Russell says. "She's wet. Her clothes are all wet."

"It's all right," Isabel says. To Cheyenne she says, "There's more to the card." She waits. He salutes her with his glass. She

continues: "Money or law. A dispute — a custody battle or adoption, marriage or divorce. Exactly what it is depends on other
cards. Commitment, mental incompetence, a question of iden-
tity, a crime or a trial that involves these things — legal privilege
or legal insanity."

Cheyenne stops pacing to look at her. "You're spooky, kid. Did
anybody ever tell you?"

"What trouble are you in?"

He turns away from her. "I talked to a priest," he says, putting
his glass down on the table. "Trouble enough that I confessed to
a priest." He takes his jacket off.

"Your shirt!" she cries, and his hand flies up to his shoulder.

Blood stains his shirt, fresh but drying, as if a wound underneath had broken open, bled through the khaki, and closed
again.

Finding it dry, Cheyenne says, "It's nothing" — his other hand
still holding the jacket, an army jacket, full of pockets. Holding it
away from his body, he looks at it in confusion, as if it belonged
to a stranger, as if he'd just picked it up wondering where it came
from and why.

"What trouble are you in?" Isabel asks again.

"The priest told me to turn myself in," he says. He drops the
jacket over the back of a chair. He looks at them both. He laughs.
"Joke," he says. "Legal privilege? It's a joke." He drinks. "Refill,"
he says to Russell. "So what does the judge say?" he asks Isabel.
"Let's have the verdict."

"The three is the question. It doesn't give answers without
other cards."

"Legal insanity," he says. "Maybe that card means I'm insane."

"Chey," she says, pleading. She stops. She hears herself. She
turns to Russell and raises her chin and meets his eyes with her
crooked eyes. He has heard her too. Her face goes as blank as a
stranger's. "All right," she says. "I know him. I know him before.
I know him on the street."

"Yes," Russell says, less surprised than suddenly empty, hol-
lowed out by the physical certainty that Isabel (obeah woman,
shape shifter, eyes of a cat) is giving herself (has given herself, will

give herself) to Cheyenne. It blinds him to his brother, blinds him to everything. Paralyzed, he remembers Cheyenne, drunk, drugged, unable to move, wanting to kill him. Rage fills him, like a gust of wind, fills him, leaves him. "I know," he says. When she came to him, her skin was pale, her face bony, her eyes dull with an absence he sees now he misunderstood.

She waits for him, as if he will have more to say. There is no more. "I know," he says again. "What's another story?" But his voice breaks. He wants to protect her, he wants to hit her, he wants to take her face between his hands and look into her eyes until they both know what the truth is. "Suddenly you remember things," he says. Her eyes are so dark. (No one cares what you remember. No one is left to care.) He shrugs. He shakes his head.

She turns away from him. "What trouble?" she says to Cheyenne.

"If I'd known you were here I wouldn't have come."

"Let me look at your shoulder," she says.

"Stop pushing. Who are you to push me? Who are you to me?"

"Even Russell knows," she says.

"I've got my own reasons. It's not about you. It has nothing to do with you. I have nothing to do with you."

"You're lying," she says. "You know you're lying."

He laughs. "Kids," he says to Russell. "Women. Jesus, she's just like our mother. Believe what they want to. Where do we find them, bro? What is it, heat-seeking radar?"

"Russell didn't find me," Isabel says. "I found him."

"Devious little fortune-teller, aren't you? Our mother would have liked you though. She was into all this shit, cards, Ouija boards, crystal balls — decoding the world — too drunk to do it the ordinary way. She didn't trust anybody but readers. Not me. Not doctors. At the end not even the priests. Just those crazy old women. As crazy as she was. If it wasn't one thing it was another — God, the Devil, or Peter Pan." He laughs. "All of them in love with sons or the dear departed, saints and angels, brothers and fathers, wayward husbands, dead sweethearts — anybody gone. Abandoned old ladies." He stops and looks at Isabel, up and down. "Kind of young for that trade."

"I'm not his lover," she says.

"Did I ask?"

"It's true," she says. She turns to Russell. "Tell him," she says.

"We should look at that shoulder," he says.

Cheyenne laughs. "Always did like strays, didn't you?" He pulls a chair out from the table and, sitting, is suddenly smaller. His trembling shows. He studies Isabel. "Would you go for me for cigarettes?" he asks her. "Camels, Isabel?" To Russell he says, "I always heard about you bringing strays home — animals, kids — even Billy Santana. This one's a woman though," his eyes still on Isabel. "I'll have to stop calling her kid now," he says. "Used to call her kid all the time. She was crazy about me I guess. But I mean I don't think she was even fifteen. Is it true what she said? That she isn't your lover?"

"It's true," Isabel says.

Cheyenne goes pale. "Get her out of here. I can't talk anymore with her here."

"I'll go for the cigarettes," she says, but she doesn't move.

"Here," Russell says. He digs in his pocket and holds out a twenty. "Get him something to eat. Peroxide too. Gauze and adhesive tape."

She takes the money and hesitates in front of him. She reaches a hand to his chest. "I'm sorry," she says.

"Go," he says. He would like to say more. She is so close. Her hand is on his heart. "You're still wet," he says. "Wear shoes."

"I guess I need a mother," she says.

"I guess you do," he says.

"I fell asleep on the train," Cheyenne says when she's gone. "Coming back from Belmont. I dreamed I was on a beach with a little stray dog. It was orange-haired. It looked like a cat. There was another little dog like it. And a cat maybe too. A black cat. I don't remember. I was running on the beach with this little dog and then we ran up to her — our *mother* I mean — your mother and mine. We ran to her and flopped down. I was a child I guess. I must have been a child. She was sitting there in the sand," he says, "and I sat in her lap or next to her lap, my head in her lap. The little dog—or the cat, maybe it was a cat, it might have been a cat—ran down to the water. There were buildings nearby, it was like a beach with buildings on it, small buildings, two stories maybe, little buildings, the water was close, right there. And the cat ran down to the water and this black insect like a fly, a big fly, a horsefly maybe, came zipping up from the water and the cat chased it and I was afraid. In the dream I had the memory of seeing someone stung by that kind of flying bug—not really a fly maybe, maybe a wasp, it was black and long like a wasp—I don't know—but I had the memory of someone getting stung by it, by one like it, and dying, just like that"—snapping his fingers.

"I wanted to stop the cat," he says. "I was afraid the insect would kill the cat, I called out maybe, I don't know, but the cat kept chasing it, and the insect flew right at me. All this happened in a second or two. The insect stung my hand. I was trying to brush it away from my hand and it stung me. Right here," he says—he opens his left hand. In the soft flesh between the thumb and forefinger he has an ugly wound that isn't healing. "Right here," he says again. "Where the skin is torn. It won't heal," he says. "It won't form a scab. It's infected. I don't know. My hands are all cut up. Maybe that's what's wrong with me. My shoulder is nothing," he says. "I need another drink." He goes blank. He looks at Russell.

"I was trying to brush it away," he says. "The insect. Like this"—brushing his right hand with his left. "It stung me. Here. I went into convulsions. Right there in our mother's lap. I had a seizure. I was conscious inside it. I was paralyzed and conscious, shaking inside this fit. I was going to die. I was trying to communicate it to her. I was lying there in the sand in her lap in this paralysis and convulsion and I was trying to tell her and I couldn't make any sound or say anything or do anything and she didn't seem to see that anything was wrong." He shrugs. "That's all," he says. "We're the same, aren't we? Growing up with her? I want to hate you, big brother, I've always wanted to hate you. But somehow we're so much the same."

He waits, as if for an answer. When Russell doesn't give him one, he laughs. "I may be the family symptom," he says, "but you think you're so tightly wrapped? I need that drink." He tries to stand up. "Maybe food," he says. "Maybe something to eat now — anything."

Russell serves him — bread, an orange, cheese, the bottle. Cheyenne pours himself a drink. He half peels the orange and picks at the cheese.

"She used to trail around after me," he says. "That girl, I mean. Followed me. Always waiting for me. She waited for me. I took her in too," he says. "Like you," he says. "I took her in. I found her on the doorstep one day. Down at Santana's on East Third Street. She took care of me, you know? I was getting clean. She took care of me. She used to cook for me. She used to go out and get my cigarettes." His breath catches. He drinks. "Women," he says. "Kiss them once or twice and they think they own your soul." He refills his glass. "I'm all scratched up," he says. "I met this woman — " He stops suddenly. "Aren't you drinking?"

"No," Russell says.

"I thought we were making peace here."

"Aren't we?"

"I thought I could count on you to drink with me at least."

"I quit," Russell says.

"What'd you go and do that for? Not for that girl? That girl doesn't care. She used to go out for my cigarettes and come back days later. She lies as easy as she breathes." He interrupts himself. "Like Santana, hunh?" he asks. "Quit just like Santana?"

"Not quite like Santana."

"Took your wife away, didn't he?"

"You talked to him today?"

"I've always wondered if that makes him my brother. You think that makes him my brother?"

"Did you talk to him?"

"Didn't he call you? Didn't he tell you I was coming?"

"He talked to Isabel," Russell says. "Unless it was you."

"Me," Cheyenne says. "If it'd been me I wouldn't be here. He didn't tell me she was here. He didn't say a word about her. Why is that, do you think? He's always got something hidden, you know? Something up his sleeve. Always figuring. Computing. Reasons for everything. He wants you to believe he just cares about you—you know, he just cares? But there's always more going on, some other agenda—secrets, something he wants. I've never figured it out. I never got it. I mean, did you? I mean he took your wife away. He's got your fucking wife and you just sit around here waiting for him to show."

"He is coming then?"

Cheyenne pours more tequila. "He's the only one I knew to call. I guess that counts for something."

"How did you know?"

"Know what?"

"How to get in touch with him."

"I've never not been in touch with him."

"In the highlands of Guatemala?"

"Then too. But today he was in L.A. He's been in L.A. He's been in L.A. for a while. Didn't know that, hunh? He didn't tell you? Maybe he thought he should stay out of your way? Old wounds maybe? Not because he's afraid or anything. Just not to hurt you. He doesn't want to hurt anybody. He's always telling you he doesn't want to hurt anybody. And every time he moves, somebody—God, I don't know—dies or something. Know what I mean? Did you ever notice that? How would you? I went down there in Guatemala to see him. He showed me around, you could say. I wanted a break, you know, from the rodeo. I was working the rodeo, did you know that either? I worked those ranches and then I went to the rodeo and then it just got old on me and I went down to Guatemala to find Santana. He showed me around, sort of a tour guide. He wanted me to stay in fact. On the ranch you know when I was working on the ranch I got in with this group, I got training, you know, war training, karate, knives, guns, that shit, we got real gung ho, we were going down there and kill commies or something, I don't know, I didn't take it so seriously maybe, but I did, too, because these were the guys I was hanging with, you know? And then I thought well I'd go look up Santana and he straightened me out. So I came back to the rodeo but it wasn't the same. I mean, did he ever do that to you? Change your life around and then leave you hanging? You get your life changed around and where are you? I mean you're nowhere. The rodeo was nowhere, I was nowhere. Then I started drifting again, I came back here. I even thought I'd look you up maybe. I did think about it. But I never got to it. I ran into this woman . . ."

His voice trails away. He looks at Russell suddenly, as if surprised, as if seeing him for the first time.

"He is coming then?" Russell asks. "He's coming here?"

"Who?" Cheyenne says.

"Santana," Russell says.

"Oh," Cheyenne says. "Sure. Santana. I guess he is." He looks around. He reaches for the bottle.

6

Billy Santana. Chameleonlike, sometimes flamboyant, always a sadness in him. He scares Russell sometimes, or his love for him does. They met because of Dominique. Or he met Dominique because of Santana. Which came first? They walked into his world one day and everything changed. Like Isabel. It transforms the present to know this: a repetition, rearranged, a different victim. A repetition. Santana couldn't sit still: "Don't look at photographs, keep moving, never let your sweat get bad" — his formula for staying alive. In the Ia Drang, he said, his sweat went bad. "You don't stay anywhere that gives you that bad sweat. That bad sweat is your death," he said. He was careful not to use army slang. Maybe he was careful, too, not to let his voice betray where he really came from. He spoke slowly, even drunk — drawling, not quite southern; speech from nowhere, an accent of the war. Maybe an expert could identify its origins — Russell couldn't. He took him at his word (a decision he made early), and about his prewar self Santana had nothing to say. He never carried film; he didn't keep photographs; anywhere he landed the news was bad. "Sweat control," he said, "is an inside job." He meditated like a Buddhist. He had a teacher. In Saigon he ate vegetarian but back in the world he said *when in Rome* and ate meat and whatever else. On television a monk burned himself alive outside the U.S. Embassy. "That man was my teacher," Santana said, and Russell asked, "How can you tell?" — the coincidence blew him away. "They're all my teacher," Santana answered. "Nothing is personal." They were sitting in Berkeley, stoned, eating hamburgers and french fries from McDonald's, drinking beer, and watching moving photographs on the evening news. "You don't believe half the shit you say, do you?" Russell asked then — and because of the dope maybe, felt he had noticed this suddenly, for the first time. "Man," Santana answered without laughing, "I don't believe any of the shit I say, Jacks," and it was hard to remember, in that moment, that he had known Santana in another world, that he had met him on a sunny morning the other side of the Pacific (down on his knees on a glossy tiled floor making newspaper kites with a handful of little slum kids), Santana appearing up into the light from beyond the terrace, the sun bright behind him and on his arm a French girl (chattering at the children, in French, in Vietnamese), the skirt of her dress flowered, sheer, its pale spring colors vanishing into the light, her legs so long and Western, so visible and clean — Santana and Dominique coming together into his life out of the sunshine as later Isabel would come in out of the rain — and it was hard to remember, even that night on Kains Street, so soon after, eating hamburgers and watching the war on his mother's TV, with Cheyenne squeezed in between them sucking a chocolate shake, that he and Billy Santana had ever been in Saigon or anywhere in Vietnam at all.

Billy Santana. Dominique was afraid of him: the way she held his arm that morning — tentative — the uncertainty in her smile. They were friends, maybe lovers — lovers or not, standing next to him she was charged, a live wire. Russell stood up to meet them.

"You entertain the children," she said.

"They're teaching me, in fact," he said.

They all shook hands. Santana was dressed in fatigues. They had just come back from three months in the country, they said. "The pacified country," Santana said. Dominique left them. They watched her climb the stairs. "So what do you think?" Santana asked, and Russell blushed, as if the question had been about the girl. "Is this what you came here for?" Santana asked. He held out a pack of cigarettes.

"English," Russell said. "I came to teach English."

Santana smiled, very quietly. They stood there smoking.

The house faced an open street lined with tamarind trees. Behind it, invisible, the slum spread out to the next canal — our slum, Russell called it in his thoughts, our personal slum in a city filled with slums hidden like this one on the backsides of prosperity, pulling away from the paved roads, the whitewashed buildings, the tamarind trees, each one a labyrinth of alleys and mudways that led only deeper into hunger and cholera and smallpox and plague and worms, nameless swamp fevers, greed, political terror, and more ways to die than he could ever have imagined, each little slum snaking out through the human backwash of squatters and refugees from the countryside and the chronic urban poor, until it ran up against a canal, hesitated, and, leaping it like flames leaping a fire trail, spread out again on the other side into another backside world. This was the true city, he thought. These nonstreets, this marshland flooded with people and rotting garbage and stagnant red mud, not Tu Do — Freedom — with its glut of bars and black-market PXs and prostitutes and drugs, not Tu Do Street, but these back alleys, where Viet Cong moved freely and Americans were warned not to enter. This was the diseased Saigon, the patient Saigon, the Saigon that remembered who had built this city, and why, and what it really was. This was the war as Russell knew it — its overcrowding, its wormy hunger-distended bellies, its air that never moved and stank of contagion and waste, human and animal, and of all the animals, and the anger and the fear and the heat. From out of these alleys every morning came his children. Only the weakest and the youngest came. Their older and stronger brothers and sisters and cousins went to work the American streets. The fiction was that in teaching these children English he prepared them for more education, for democracy and the larger economy — the public economy, the American economy. (Somehow in San Francisco this had seemed almost a desirable object. And English, after all, was the only skill he had to sell.) Four months later, he knew it wasn't true. Many of their parents had been taught French, and the only American economy his English prepared them for was the economy of Tu Do. In the afternoons he did have an advanced class of teenagers who would find work

in the national and local bureaucracies, and the best of them—
following the dollar—in the city's burgeoning American office
complexes. But those weren't the kids who counted most for
him. They weren't hungry. Whatever happened to Saigon, those
kids would escape it. Of course they're advanced in English, he
thought—they know where they're going. Only one of them
came from the slum, a drug dealer with big ambitions, and after
the first month Russell was buying opium from him almost
daily. As for the rest—these little kids—most of them would take
his phrases, his games, his colors and pictures and numbers and
American gestures and smiles, his smattering of learning and a
season of healthy lunches and join their comrades on Tu Do.
Some evening he'd be out walking and there they would be:
shining shoes, picking pockets, selling birds and monkeys,
pimping, whoring, dealing PX whiskey and pharmaceuticals,
grenades and ammunition, marijuana, opium, hash and smack
and speed. And why not? American money created the demand
for more American money. It was the most addictive drug in the
world.

No, he answered Santana. This wasn't what he came here for.
"I've seen you before," he said. "More than once. You haven't
been in the bush. You were right here in Saigon. Wearing
cameras. I heard you were a journalist."

Santana shrugged. "Sometimes I am."

When Dominique came down from the office (her legs again)
she smiled and gave Russell her hand.

They met that evening for a drink. The sky was a color that
would photograph orange. They sat outside on the street, and
dusk came quickly and quickly turned to night. There was a dry
breeze and for a rare half-hour the air was almost fresh, almost
cleared of its hell-smog of exhaust and decay.

"So why aren't you drafted?" Santana asked him.

Russell answered—he'd been a student, he had a wife.

Dominique smoked most of a pack of Marlboros and stared
into the street—listening, she told him later, for the undersound
of chimes. "In odd moments," she said, "suddenly one hears
them."

From his first weeks in Saigon, Russell had had an intermit-
tent fever — fever of unknown origin they called it. Commonly
found among men in the field. It would end when the rains
ended — maybe. But the rains ended and the fever stayed.

"Fever of unknown origin," he had said to Santana that night.
"This whole fucking war is a fever of unknown origin."

"You want to know something?" Santana said. "It's not." He
nodded toward Dominique, who seemed not to be listening.
"Ask her. She was a child here. So was her mother. This war is too
old for us. The world is too old for us."

"Us who? — do you mean exactly?" Russell asked and felt like
laughing from the way the tequila and the fever made his words
turn and from the way the quiet absence of the girl across the
table seemed to call him out of his skin.

But Santana was angry. "You came over here, babyface, you
wanted to do something? You wanted to do something about it?
You wanted to do somebody some fucking good? Was that the
idea? Until you saw what you were up against? So you and
everyone like you, what do you do? You feed, you clothe, you
inoculate, you treat, you Band-Aid, you shoe — do you shoe? —
you read, you write, you add and subtract, you sing — I bet you
sing, don't you? — Beatles songs, am I right? — they like that
here — everybody wants to hold your hand. Especially if your
wallet's in it. Well, dig it" — he emptied his glass — "I'll tell you
how you do some good here — you go home and tell people —
and I don't mean you tell them about the orphans in the streets
and the burned-out villages and dead civilians and GIs with ears
strung around their necks and that shit, what I mean is you tell
them how this started, where it came from and who these people
are, you sit down and study some history, Jacks, and you tell them
who these people are and what the fuck we're doing in their lives
you want to do something about it, you get the history straight
and maybe they can't con you anymore with their Camelots and
their princes and heroes and their honest little countries in
goddamn distress."

He stopped. His face changed. (He struggled to change his
face: Russell read the struggle as if Santana were an actor in a

close-up on the giant screen. It went on forever and all three of them were silent and in that moment, she told him later, Dominique heard the chimes.)

"Sorry," Santana said. "I'm talking to myself, okay? I'm trying to dump this load on myself, you know that don't you?"

Russell didn't know it, but he nodded anyway.

Santana stood up. "Excuse me," he said. "More drinks. All around."

"Jacks," Dominique said while he was gone — already they both called him Jacks — "come home with me tonight."

From her windows they watched the artillery and tracer fire falling over the marshland south of the city.

"Every night it is the same," she said. "A display of peacocks. Otherearthly color to attract and hypnotize. Not power — but the illusion of power — the fan dance behind which power or its absence is concealed."

Maybe a week later he went out with Santana alone.

In a little stucco bar, a right and a left into the slum — a princely establishment by neighborhood standards, its neon sign in the high window casting a pink aura over the room — they looked at each other across a tiny oilcloth-covered table. In the light of the neon and the candles stuck in halved American beer cans Santana's face was rosy and when he turned his head at a certain angle, the dilated pupils of his eyes, like a cat's, seemed to go an iridescent red and green.

"Can you read this?" he asked. He pointed to his fatigue shirt, above the heart — an older shirt than the one he had been wearing the first time they met, a shirt rubbed thin and faded and stained, many times mended, by hand. A relic, he said. A keepsake. He lifted the candle close to his chest to illuminate a block of words from the Bhagavad Gita, tightly stitched in fine yellow silk on a field of black, inked indelibly over what once had been his name: PERFORM EVERY ACTION SACRAMENTALLY, AND BE FREE FROM ALL ATTACHMENT TO RESULTS.

Russell told him that was a formula for chaos, and Santana laughed, saying, "Not to worry, it's almost never achieved."

It was some kind of truce, Russell thought. They hadn't mentioned Dominique. He wasn't sure that she mattered. He had spent most of the week with her, day and night. She wasn't with them but she might as well have been, he could feel her all over his skin. He didn't know what Santana knew. He didn't know if Santana cared. They kept a silence about her. They began a conversation — or continued a conversation that had already begun — a conversation that survives in Russell's memory as if it had been spoken all at once, that first night together maybe, while Dominique sat smoking, staring at the street, or here in the little slum bar whose only (probably stolen) electricity was used to light the window and the night, or up on Dominique's roof, drinking black-market scotch and watching the war, or even at the end, when he and Santana huddled together under rubber ponchos and tried using words to hold back the rain. In reality it was a conversation strung out from night to night, from bar to bar, throughout the dry season and when the rains came, a fragment here and a fragment there, a conversation that snaked its way through Saigon, a thread never quite dropped in the midst of public events and private, holding together crazy nights played for tragedy and comedy, melodrama and farce, nights otherwise lost, turned drunk and melancholy, vanished into formless hilarity, poker, Tu Do sex and hallucinogens, nights gone numb; but what remains at the core of Russell's memory, as if it had been the center and only fact in those long nights, is the conversation — one conversation — until Santana sent him up to the war and the conversation stopped.

"What do you want here?" Santana asked him. "You came here thinking what? — this war was evil? — you're one of these guys who already knew that before you came. Myself, I only learned it when I got here. I had to be here to find it out. But you — you're one of the already wise — the just — so why did you come here if not to get wiser and juster? This is our war, yours and mine I mean, the only one we get — you know that much, don't you? — ambitious little suck is what you are I think — tell me I'm wrong, Jacks." But he wasn't wrong. "And stuck here in Saigon with the kiddies. Not what you had in mind? Don't protest. I know your

heart is pure. But wouldn't you also like maybe to see some
action, in the highlands maybe, down the delta — maybe all the
way up in I Corps? I mean, kid, don't you want to know?"

But Russell told him he knew plenty, right here in Saigon, he
knew from the children what was happening in the countryside,
he knew from their hunger and from their frail little bird-bones
and from their blank, black eyes. He had seen enough death and
mutilation right here in Saigon, what grenades and land mines
did to a body — right here at the project, the old man on wheels
who survived with nothing but arms and a head and half a torso,
who slept under the porch when it rained and when the sun was
out made the children laugh in rapid-fire Vietnamese that Russell couldn't follow, who disappeared for days at a time and when
things were going well for him had opium to sell. The one-
legged orphans were among the lucky. Russell didn't have to go
up-country to see a goddamn thing. Every night he could watch
the bombing on the perimeter. Everything American was packed
in sandbags. He had witnessed public executions in the center of
the city, men bound to the stake and shot by firing squad while
crowds looked on in silence — Americans, yes, averting their eyes.
He had felt the anger under the surface in the mobs that
sometimes formed, waiting for an excuse to riot. He had been
caught in riots. What did he need to go to the war for? All the war
was right here in Saigon. And where did this "kid" stuff come
from anyway? "I'm two years older than you are, Santana, and
you fucking know it."

"How do you know?"

"Somebody told me."

"Maybe they lied."

But that wasn't the point. "No one knows plenty," Santana
said. "Not here or anywhere, there isn't any plenty — even if it's
illusion, there's always more to know." The idea, he said, is
doesn't he want some press credentials — Bao Chi? — a Bao Chi
card? A piece of magic plastic to hang from his fatigues, a reason
to wear fatigues — PX privileges? — doesn't he want to go explor-
ing is the point, doesn't he want to see the dawn come up in
seconds and every day new nameless shades of green, doesn't he

want to walk in the forest on the bottom of an ocean, surrounded by seaweed, underwater, and everywhere enemies—VC, tigers, booby traps? Doesn't he want to know his own body? The life in it and the death? *Out there?* Santana said. Out there where the war is clean, he said—not this filth here in Saigon, he said—doesn't he want to know what it *is?*

But *clean?* Russell asked. What did that mean? Nothing physical, for God's sake, so what then?

And Santana just laughed. "You got it, kid. You want it, you got it."

Anyone was crazy, Santana said, who thought he was staying by choice. He was staying till he could make his way out was all. Earning his passage.

What he signed up for, he said, the reasons he signed up— "You wouldn't believe what I signed up for," he said, "you wouldn't believe what I'm trained to do, the ways I know to kill a man, the ways I know to lie, and how to wait—you wouldn't believe any of it, babyface, and what am I good for now but to keep on doing it? I just do it for myself now, I take my own orders, I don't work for those liars anymore is what it is, only they don't necessarily know that is all, lots of people think I'm on their side, and more people think I'm dead, and maybe I am, in a certain sense, dead, but the me who's dead wasn't a real person anyway, never was here, who was here is who you see here, who's talking to you now, is me—this is the me who's here, and you got one too, Jacks, but maybe you won't find him ever—do you know what I mean?"

Sure, Russell would say, in a haze of dope smoke and tequila, of course he knew, and it always seemed, at the time, that he did. More than once he asked Santana how he got away with it, how he got out, how he disappeared, but until the night under the ponchos, his only answer had been "Magic, Jacks. You don't ask how." Then suddenly that night in the rain Santana started talking:

"There was a guy out there," he said, "you got the feeling he was looking at you the way a cat does, seeing things you can't see.

And then in the Ia Drang this guy was looking at me dead. They were all dead. Every guy I knew.

"Some mornings in the highlands," he said, "you can think it's the dawn of creation, you're Adam, and God's just over there in the trees. I heard the voice like catechism, *Do you denounce Satan?* The dawn comes up like *that*" — snapping his fingers — "like the light at the end of the world, and when you're in deep under forest canopy even the air you breathe is green — the sky — there is no sky, you're in the Emerald City, it's Oz. At night when the flares fall everything freezes — things go black and white, and light shines out behind them, and all you can see is the silver haloes, men moving in flashes, then moving again from some-place else, and layers of shadows, everywhere, shifting — you'd think nothing was real except the shooting reminds you, until you get so used to the shooting it isn't real either. And then one day it's different, your sweat goes bad, and everyone you know is dead.

"I hid under the bodies," he said. "I hid myself under the bodies. I was covered in mud and blood. I took some tags off a broken torso and buried my own in the bloody mud. Everything was clear to me. Do you understand? It was clear, it was night, lit by flares, or maybe it was the moon, or maybe just death, maybe it was all the death in there, the ghosts rising. I was clear in my mind. Every action was clear. I muddied my face and my name. I bandaged my head and muddied and bloodied it. I bandaged my leg. I made myself look like the walking wounded. I was the walking wounded but I didn't know it. A chunk of my arm was gone and I didn't even know it. I got rid of everything. No grenades, no pack, no rifle, no gun. I took a canteen and a machete to cut back the jungle. And I started walking. I needed water, to drink and to follow. I came to a stream. I filled the canteen and stayed close to the water. I stayed close to the water and away from the trails. I walked away from it. I didn't know what I was walking to. It didn't matter. I just left it behind. I was alive and I was a man and I was walking in the jungle with a machete and water within crawling distance and a canteen just in case. And that was all. It got very quiet. Quiet. And I walked. I walked in the night and I slept in the day. I don't know how long. Not long. A day or two maybe. For the first time I wasn't an alien in that country. I wasn't an enemy in a place where I didn't belong. Even my hunger was my friend. My arm began to hurt. I had a fever. I walked away from it. I just walked away.

"I was passed out by the stream when they found me. Women. I heard their voices. My face was in the water and I could have been dead and drowned. I heard their voices up above me and I thought they must be angels. Then I felt the sunlight on my neck and the ache in my arm where the meat was torn away and I heard the women leaving and I groaned at them, I turned my head and called—they stopped, they made gestures with their hands and somehow I understood them. They would come back. They would come back for me. When I woke up again I was in a shack and an old woman gave me bitter tea and a child stared at me without any expression and an old man came to speak English to me, not many words. I said Saigon to them. They nodded. They would take me to Saigon. Saigon? I said. They nodded. They fed me tea and soup and I slept and they fed me more soup and then some rice and more soup and one day fish and the old woman washed my clothes and I lay there naked under an American army blanket and the child stared at me and the rain came down like it is tonight and finally they gave me back my clothes and the old man nodded at me to say we were going and together we set out in the rain through the bamboo and the rice paddies and the elephant grass and the jungle and we joined the highway south of Pleiku and sometimes we stayed with it and sometimes we circled around it and we made our way on foot and in an ox cart and alone and with crowds of refugees and we even hitched a spell in a U.S. Army jeep and we passed through VC country and American country and ARVN country and we zigged and zagged and wherever we went we had a story and no one ever stopped us and then one night we were on the perimeter of Saigon and we crept in before the bombing started the same way the Viet Cong do and that old man, my friend and companion, sold me to this Chinese we're waiting for here in the rain in Cholon."

7

"God remembers," Santana said years later. "When you start talking to God, you remember too." That night in the rain he said, "You won't know what this war is until you touch your love for it—your love for it, Jacks, along with your loathing. You won't find it here in Saigon. This shelling's nothing but a tease. As if the VC sat out there waiting to get hit. You want to know the truth they do it because it's sexy—a thousand rounds a night so you and I and all the generals and journalists and construction engineers can get our rocks off on the war. Remember the inscription on my shirt?" It had been embroidered for him by a Chinese woman who spoke no English. "I wrote it out for her," he said. "She copied the letters. Shapes. They were nothing but shapes to her. I tried to tell her what they meant. So she would know. While she sewed. Maybe she did understand. I don't know how she could have. But she sewed it just the way the words meant. I used to watch her sewing. Laid out smoking opium watching this little Chinawoman stitching across the room. So I asked her to stitch a thing for me. It was raining then too. From time to time she'd bring it to me and show me and I'd nod and she'd go back to her corner and sew. She was like the guy I got the words from. He's dead now. He brought that book with him to the war, he read it all the time, dug in on the perimeter he read it if he could, once even in flare light I saw him trying to read it. He died walking point, right into a booby trap. Everything below the waist blown away. They triaged the hell out of him—plasma-bagged and morphined and med-evacked him back to base—and in the heat there waiting to die before they could fly him to Okinawa he told me to get his book for him and when I brought it he said: It's yours, I know it by heart."

What Santana was doing was dealing drugs for a Chinese gangster from Cholon. Mostly to journalists and low-level embassy types. A few balls of opium and a handful of Thai sticks bought Russell's MACV press card. Not that it would have been hard to come by — they seemed to give them out like Halloween candy, as if somebody figured any civilian crazy enough to want to get up there might just as well go. Santana arranged him a flight to Da Nang and got a black marine sergeant heading back from R&R to be his tour guide and sent him away to see the war. When Russell came back, Santana was gone.

He wrote then, but he wrote about Saigon. He wrote about the Buddhist crisis, the immolation of monks, demonstrations and riots, and underneath every word he felt the victory of the swamp and the slum — corruption, fever, decay. He got picked up by a couple of Sunday supplements. Santana's old customers let him use their phones. He went north again to see the war. He made notes. He stayed a while, long enough to feel the boredom, the dread — too long. He came back to Saigon. He was living with Dominique. She led him through the back alleys, all the way to the canal, and they did interviews in a depth that no one in the United States would ever want to read. They had Santana's cameras. Russell began to use them — thousands of close-ups — faces, diseases, amputations, bones. The photographs piled up and covered the walls and then the images got distant — masses of people, shanties, tin roofs, rats, geese. He wanted to fit everything into a single frame. He was in over his head. They were all in over their heads. The year was ending. Dominique was pregnant. Russell came home.

Home. On the flight back he felt the war and the people and the place blow away from him, staying behind. He willed it all to stay behind. If it wasn't written down, recorded on film, he lost it. The moments were lost — the life of the moments — moments of love and moments of terror: an instant when he held a gun and didn't shoot — an instant when he did — sounds (the screams of the napalm-burned, the creaking of bamboo) and images too big to hold that came back only slowly — himself trapped in a riot, the center of a minor eddy, hated and alone; a teenager jumping him, emerging from an alley with a knife in his hand (he saw it again, years later, in a subway car at midnight in New York) — a teenager, but who knew?; a morning when he stood in the cold gray rain listening for Santana's dawn of creation, mountains looming but invisible, occupied but silent, and heard no God (Santana the only man he ever knew who talked about God without embarrassment or apology) — heard nothing — not even nothing — just stood there in the rain.

He left these things behind. He was back in the world. Washing dishes in the kitchen of Herrick Hospital, living in his marriage and leaving it, hanging out with his baby brother, and smoking dope, drinking, running around. It was 1967. He watched the war on TV. Then Santana showed up on Telegraph Avenue — suddenly, out of nowhere, face to face. Santana had acid. They went to the hills and sat awake all night under eucalyptus trees and in the morning lay in the grass and watched the sunlight flash off the leaves. (For years it has been painful to remember this, another moment he has chosen to forget — lying there knowing his love for Santana. Before Isabel came he pretended these things hadn't happened. She brought memory with her, truth — Isabel, who lied to him, who has known Cheyenne all along.) Alone on the grass — Santana already standing, running, gone — Russell acknowledged Dominique for the first time since he'd left her. Dominique and now a daughter. He remembered her in the rain. It was the rain that they had shared, in the rain that they had held each other, hiding from the world outside, children lost in a nightmare, in a fairy tale. He had loved her then, alone in those hours in bed with the heat and her body and the steady drumbeat of the rain. Santana made him remember. He didn't want to remember: the oblique gray light, holding her wet skin, his eyes closing, his tears disappearing in sweat — she would never know, he wouldn't let her, but he held her even tighter and they fell deeper into each other and he lost himself in her, and the world in her, and her, until there was only the rain.

Back in Berkeley he couldn't make love to his wife. He didn't know her, didn't want to know her. She smelled sweet to him, like a baby. Her bones seemed big and lifeless, her flesh too much like his own. He told himself they had never meant to marry. He hoped she hadn't been faithful to him and convinced himself that she couldn't have been. He encouraged her to keep up with the friends she'd made in his absence and asked only not to have to meet them. He didn't want to leave her. He wanted her to leave him. Drifting apart, he called it. And he didn't care — until he lay burned-out in the grass that morning listening to Santana whoop and run through the trees and for the first time felt the woman he was losing: Susannah Smith, now Jackson, his first girl, first love — they had escaped from adolescence together, had helped each other to become a man, a woman, until he left her in search of some greater power of manhood, and in his absence she grew into this secret womanhood that he would never know. She had waited for him faithfully but in her solitude learned to hold herself within. Like treasure fallen to the bottom of the sea. He could sense it there, waiting to be brought up; but he couldn't raise it. He had no access, no magic, no map, no key. The sadness in her eyes sank deeper, away from him. In themselves her eyes were clear. She seemed to stop expecting him. He saw no reproach. They lived side by side as strangers. They didn't fight. They had nothing in common to fight about. They hardly talked. Now and then they had a meal together and watched the news or — rarely — a movie on TV. She went on with her busy teaching-assistant, graduate-student life. He had been home for months, and only in that moment alone on the grass did he notice what he had lost. He told himself it was the acid, being up all night, coming down — seeing Santana again, so unexpectedly — the letter he had brought from Dominique. (Cher Jacks, she wrote, and her voice came back to him in all its distance and abstraction, its grave formality, its absence and its need. Cher Jacks, I have come to France. I have a daughter. She is what I have left of you, and she is all mine. I fear this will sound to you like pain. It is not pain. I love her. She is what is left. Do you understand me? Don't think about her. She will never be yours.

What we had we had and out of it has come this little flower. More than this you will not need to know.) He fled moments like this one, moments when this ache, this love, opened up inside him. All his life he would flee these moments, until Isabel came.

He wanted a cigarette. Suddenly he was desperate for a cigarette. Coffee, he thought. A joint. Maybe a shot of tequila. He stood up and yelled for Santana. They had to get out of here, away from all this pretty shit.

During the night they had talked themselves back to the war. In the acid-intensified darkness he had almost seen tracer fire — green, orange — and magnesium arcing in lightning colors from brilliant white to ash to purple across the sky. He had almost heard the plosions, near and distant. His body twitched, responding to incoming. Santana began to talk. He conjured ghost towns, a starving chicken, a headless goose, flattened Coca-Cola cans, water dripping from layers of jungle and forest, green sun, monkeys, bats, birds, insects, snakes, and the sudden silence when every living thing stopped, when the jungle held its breath because — but you didn't know why, Santana said, because of you maybe, because everything knew you were coming. "You," he said. "Death was coming and death was you." But the silence went deeper than that, too electric, too much a mystery. "Listen to it," he said, and the California night filled up with mahogany trees. He conjured the heat and bloody cigarettes and the smell in the Ia Drang of a thousand bodies rotting, the smell of napalm and chemical fire and smoke, and the smells of relative safety — the rot of the living, shit burned off with diesel fuel, canned peaches, marijuana, after-shave — broken by mortar fire, melting rubber, body bags, the homebound dead. He conjured Saigon, the perimeter ("Even Saigon had a perimeter, Jacks"): helicopter lights beaming down on the marshes and trees, moving through outlying streets of outlying districts and along the barricaded roads leading into the city; more helicopters, rocket equipped, and DC3s like gunboats, tons of heavy metal waiting to rain fire on anything that moved, and intermittently an insect sound, the sizzle of parachute flares. He left the city then to conjure the cordillera, the mists. Through the night Russell saw everything, acid-lit, Santana's memories and his own projected onto shut eyelids, and whenever Santana went silent he heard the machetes, hacking.

He called out for him again. He didn't want to be here. Tilden Park was suddenly as spooky as the highlands of Vietnam. "Santana," he yelled again. He listened and heard nothing. He was going into a panic and he watched himself falling and told himself it was only his mind, but the panic didn't stop. He dropped to the ground and tore into the dusty grass, trying to dig his fingers into wet earth — he scratched through grass and dust and dug deeper, but the earth was dry. "Dry," he said out loud, and stopped moving. His heart was drumming as if his body would explode. "Santana," he yelled, but already Santana was beside him, and Russell laughed. Santana was like that. You never heard him coming. You never heard him coming and you never heard him go. Like an Indian, he would have said when he was a boy. He grinned. He thought of Cheyenne. "You've got to meet my baby brother," he said. "I'm dying for a cigarette, let's get out of here," and Santana produced a pipe and some weed and a stashed half-pack of Luckies and they started walking.

The war. Santana couldn't stop talking about the war. Everything about it bothered him, not just the war as it had been for him, but the war as it was here, now — the war as he read about it and watched it — the way it was covered, the way it was supported, the way it was opposed. "Napalm is nothing new in that country," he said. "The French used fucking napalm. Napalm's not the point," he said. "The Seventh Cavalry," he said. The Seventh Cavalry was in the Ia Drang Valley. "The Seventh Cavalry was Custer's unit," he said. Maybe that was the point. "Did you know that before you named your brother, Jacks?" He said, "In that country they believe in the mandate of heaven — they believe that without heaven's favor no man can rule. So who do you think has heaven's favor in that place? You tell me, Jacks — our Diems and Kys and Thieus? How many more before we admit defeat? But that's not the point either," he said, "is it? What do you think the point is, Jacks?"

The day was coming up hot, the dry sharp smell of eucalyptus surrounded them, and Santana wasn't waiting for an answer. Russell stopped walking to pick up a handful of dusty leaves and eucalyptus nuts to carry in his pocket and crush against his fingers and inhale. Then he ran to catch up with Santana, who had gone on talking.

"The napalm and the booby traps and the land mines are the will of man," he said, "but the mountains and the jungle are realities willed by God. It's God we're making war on," he said. "Prometheus taking revenge. We spent three days together, Jacks," he said. "That's what the point is. Just three days, and she put you in between us." Then he relit the pipe and drew on it and passed it and started off at a run, and whooping and hollering they raced each other down out of the hills. In a bar in Chelsea, years later, he said, "Now I'm going to tell you about Dominique."

She had just come back from three months in the countryside, her skin was golden, her eyes were blue. He saw her in the sun. They had known each other before. He had spent one night with her, a bad night for him, he had been afraid of her—he didn't know why—because of how much he wanted her maybe—he had been new in American Saigon then, had only for the first time left the safety of Cholon. He found her on the terrace of the Continental, picked her up, she might have been anyone. But she took him home, and suddenly he was terrified. He came as soon as he touched her, all over her beautiful belly, and then he cried. She took him to her breasts and stroked his hair and held him and all through the night he talked to her, told her what he still told no one, who he was, where he came from, what he had done—"More than I've ever told you, Jacks, more than I'll tell anyone again." They slept then for a few hours, and when he woke up she was gone. He didn't know she was leaving for the country, he didn't know anything about her. He hung around the bar where he had found her, thinking he would find her there again. She never showed. And then one day, months later, dressed all in white and shining, she was walking toward him in the sun. He wasn't afraid anymore. He wanted her. And she wanted him.

"It wasn't because you came along," Santana said to Russell. "You just made it easier." They stopped still in the street. Human traffic parted around them and closed, like water flowing around a rock. The air was heavy with exhaust and food smells and incense and sweat and garbage and heat. *Santana,* she said, and her breath rose cool at his face and with it came a perfume, gardenias; the moving crowd pushed her thighs against his thighs, and he would have fallen except for the crowd's pressure holding him up, all the strength flowing out of him when he put his hand at the back of her neck, at her hair; he meant to kiss her cheek but couldn't move. They spent three days together. They talked — they didn't talk. In a strange way, he couldn't remember. The days passed and at the end of them he knew everything about her. He kissed her neck where it met her left shoulder and he felt the shiver invade her whole body and he whispered — Now I know all your secrets — and it was true. She had red hair. He had not seen the red in her dark hair until that day on the street in the sun. The red in her hair — and at dawn in her room, when the room was red and her mouth was open for him and her eyes sank away and he died to her, dying, and love came up out of their bodies and the sun rose and her red hair got redder and he knew it was red for no one but him.

"She put you in between us," he said. He scared her. The nakedness of his love for her, his need. He was helpless and he showed her his helplessness and it implied responsibility and it scared her and she ran. Or something else — the way she surrendered to him, layer on layer — and the way he knew her surrender, and received it, and asked for more and for more. She scared herself with him, maybe that was it — she felt herself vanish. And all she knew about him: he had told her too much. Maybe she was a danger junkie — his danger attracted her, but up close it repelled. Her desire for him was addictive, compulsive, and fighting for her psychic life she blocked her desire with anything she could. "With you," Santana said to Russell. "As soon as we met you she knew she was free." There was a sadness in Santana, she ran from that too, and from the fear that he loved her, that he really would love her — ran from the fear of it: of being loved by one man with all that sadness, a large black-haired man with so much sadness and power to love her. Maybe it wasn't the sexuality she ran from at all, only the love, and the desire to save him. He came at her from behind, kissing her neck, the shudder went through her whole body and suddenly they made love again — he had been getting up, spent, stopping only to kiss the back of her neck, when the shudder went through her, and there they were. He had sprung some memory in her. She cried, whispering, in French, in Vietnamese. She lost her own reality in the presence of a large man, lost her own existence, her feelings, her knowledge. She had grand designs, big dreams, she wanted them private and held inside, she didn't trust them to the world, or to anyone ("Not to you," Santana said). She needed that crucible of privacy — or thought she needed it — a preserve where no one saw her, or knew her, or knew what she did, or what she dreamed or hoped for herself. He violated her, she let him violate her. He came into her with his helplessness and his need, and he took her away. He stole her secrets, knew everything from her body alone. He touched something — the fear of the size of a man, of feeling small, of being a child in his arms, the fear of being a child, of being vulnerable, unable to speak up for herself, erasable, deniable, her versions of things erased, denied. She couldn't accept her fear. She was creating herself in courage, bravado. "So she left me. Without explanation. Traded me in. It wasn't your fault."

He stood at her window smoking, naked in the darkness, and she came out of the shower and up behind him, pressing her cool wet body, electric, against his skin. He slid her around to the front of himself and pushed her against the glass, and in the night outside beyond her watched the war. Later she talked about her father — a good man, she said, but a soldier, stiff and domineering — it was a horror to see him break. It was this war that broke him. And her mother too. Her mother was born here. She died after a year in France. Of a broken heart, Dominique said — a broken husband, a shattered world, a refusal to live. I was nine years old and had my father to take care of. I could talk him into anything. I talked him into coming back to Saigon. He's alive here still, she said. He lives with an Annamese woman, they have three children. He took her in when we were girls, to look after me and play. We are the same age. My mother died from leaving this place, and he came back and started life over. He thanks me for it. Sometimes I want to kill him.

In the morning they went out for bread and coffee. When they came back the air-conditioning failed. She opened the windows and plugged in the fans. The shades billowed, the fans whirred. Time kept passing. He held her. He wanted to stop time. He wanted — but that was all. He wanted nothing. In that room with the fans and the heat and Dominique there was no more to want. Slowly the day went, the room and the air steamy and sweet.

She took him to meet her father. They sat in the shade of a courtyard and listened to the trickling fountain while the Annamese girl brought them drinks and didn't speak. The sun fell. The children weren't to be seen. The father refused to use English. Dominique translated. She clung to Santana. She wore a dress with no underwear. She pressed herself against him and whispered in his ear. Hold me, she said — I want him to see what happens when you touch my skin. He submitted. She was demonstrating something, he was a prop, part of a dumb show. He didn't care. They had come from her bed. In an hour they would go back to it. The old man drank and called for more drinks. Santana heard laughter, children calling to one another in Vietnamese, then hands clapping and silence, and on the breeze from the ceiling fans within, the tinkling of chimes. Buddhist chimes, Dominique said — prayers for peace. He surrendered to enchantment. Back in her bed she cried. She wanted him violently and scratched and chewed at his skin and he fought her until her kisses went tender and she fell on him and beat her fists at his chest. He closed his hands around her forearms. His stillness stopped her. They waited in the stillness. The stillness went on and on.

"Some sounds are too loud to hear," he said to Russell in Chelsea. "The war was like that." But Chelsea was years later. In Berkeley Santana still thought he knew what he knew. Toward the end there he studied Fanon and Debray. With romantic left-intellectuals, most of whom had never bloodied a nose in a childhood playground fight, he committed himself to theories of regeneration through violence. His activism arose out of his experience — not political experience, but personal — maybe metaphysical, even pathological. He had learned something about freedom, he said. He meant to keep living in it. Also during that time he tried giving up drugs and alcohol and discovered he couldn't get through it without checking himself into a hospital detox ward. A few years later, he went underground. Never known, he was never wanted. He had been living underground, after all, ever since he'd left the Ia Drang Valley. If he had been in the Ia Drang Valley — as time went on the past got murkier, the truth more deeply obscured. Possibilities rippled outward whenever Santana showed up, and Russell came to believe he might have been anything in those days — might be anything still.

"Vietnam," he had said in the dark in the Berkeley hills. "Magic is in the word. Heavy magic. Let us speak the word: Vietnam. In the naming of it, all this was written: the monks in flames, the young girls on bicycles, the ghosts out there on night patrols."

"Three days," he said in Chelsea. "I was walking with her and she stopped to buy a piece of fruit and fed it to a monkey for sale. She said she was making a wish. Half an hour later, we were talking to you."

One rainy afternoon in Berkeley, not long before Russell left for New York, a fortune-teller sat down to share their table at the Med. She offered them a reading — "Gratis," she said to Santana. "I like your eyes." She dealt the cards. "We live inside our stories," she said while she was dealing. She looked at the cards spread out in front of her and was quiet a long time. Russell got nervous. The café was crowded, loud. He wanted more coffee. The woman tapped a nail against a card. "The three of hearts," she said to Santana. "Disappointment in love. But here" — she indicated another — "you will get revenge." Santana laughed. In Chelsea, Russell remembered that laugh and for the first time thought he understood it — it had been a laugh not of denial, but of recognition, acknowledgment, maybe gratitude: Yes, it must have said, I will have revenge. "What's a wife, after all, between war buddies?" Santana asked that night in Chelsea, and for a few hours Russell believed him, even then.

8

It was 1975 and Santana had just come back from Guatemala. He said nothing about what he had done there but much about what he had seen. He was still thinking in Spanish. New York made him feel crazy. It was summer and the humid heat and the crowds on the sidewalks and at times the smell of diesel fuel and garbage brought him memories of Saigon. Russell and Lucinda had been married two years by then, but Santana had met her only once, in passing, shortly before the wedding, which he skipped. What he remembered of her was her head of long, tangled, curly sun-bleached hair. When she opened the door to him, he knew why he'd stayed away. In Guatemala he had lived among men and worked with his body; in his body he had a stillness that was new to him. He had noticed it only when he landed in the city: in the city he was a rock, unmoving, everything moving around him. Until Lucinda stood in the doorway and everything else stopped moving too. The stillness took her in. He watched it happen. There was nothing but the stillness. He followed her into the apartment. They waited for Russell, who was detained at work. They sat without speaking much. She offered him a drink. He declined. She went to the kitchen and began cutting vegetables for salad. Her knife sounded in an even rhythm against the board. They were enclosed in the stillness. He stood at the window and watched the sun and shadows change without moving along the street. Russell arrived. He asked about Guatemala. "Another time," Santana said. The silence became palpable. It made Russell nervous. "Tequila?" he asked. But Santana wasn't drinking. Lucinda took a glass of wine. "Come up on the roof?" Russell asked, and Santana followed. "What's going on?" Russell asked. "You're never like this."

"It's hard coming back," Santana said.

"It's always been hard."

"It's harder this time."

The building had six stories and the roof looked out on the backsides of other buildings, down into narrow dusty yards — on hanging laundry and ailanthus trees and patches of weedy grass in the dust and a piece of lawn furniture with a towel hanging over it and next to it a newspaper and an empty glass. The sun was low and the light came in hazy streaks of gold. The Empire State Building looked close enough to touch. Russell's nervousness was contagious. Those moments alone with him in the near-sunset made Santana fear for his new stillness more than anything yet in the city.

"I can't stay," he said.

"In New York?"

"Maybe that too. I meant now, tonight."

"We have a room ready — Lucinda didn't show you?"

"She showed me." Russell's desk in a corner, piled high with books and papers. Cardboard boxes full of photographs and notebooks that had never been unpacked. A bed, a lamp, an armchair, an empty closet. "Not writing anymore?"

"The war's over," Russell said. "I got this job."

"I saw the masthead."

"In Guatemala?"

"On the plane."

They sat on the ledge and smoked, watching the colors in the sky change.

"So where will you go?" Russell asked.

"Avenue C maybe."

"Give me a break," Russell said. After a while he said, "You're not looking for drugs again, are you? Because if you're looking for drugs we can get you anything you want right here."

"I'm not looking for drugs."

"What then?"

"I just have to go," Santana said.

He found a place on East Third Street between B and C. He didn't plan to be there long—till Christmas at the latest. He made himself known along the street. He was large, black-haired, and sun-baked, his Spanish was good, no one gave him any trouble. Twice he had lunch with Russell in midtown. Then he ran into Lucinda one morning on Canal Street and three days later on Church Street and on the steps of St. Patrick's Cathedral three days after that. In those encounters he learned that she was an artist, that she'd kept her loft for a studio, that she worked three nights a week as a waitress to cover the rent and buy canvas and paint, that she went to Mass sometimes (when no one was looking—"Don't tell Russell"), and that his eyes wouldn't leave her eyes. It was still summer. He had been in the city six weeks. He wanted to reach out and touch her. "Buy me an ice cream," she said. Her eyes wouldn't leave his either. He couldn't answer. "Three times in one week," she said, "all over the city—doesn't fate deserve at least an ice cream?" She was laughing—she wanted to laugh, but she was afraid. They were both afraid. Their words went on. He bought her an ice cream. They walked to Central Park. She talked all the way, pushing the fear off. He felt safe as long as she was talking. While she was talking their eyes didn't have to meet. But in the park she grew silent, and the only things real were the heat and the walking. Finally she spoke again. "Tell me about Guatemala," she said.

"Mostly it's poor," he said. "The government is vicious. We created the government. In 1954," he said. "We were very busy in 1954."

He stopped walking to face her.

"I can't," he said.

Her eyes held his. The breeze blew her hair. He put a hand at the back of her neck. The nightmare came. No exit. Time froze.

"I'll let you go, then," she said. (Was that what she said?) She gave him her hand. He held her hand. She held his longer. He turned, he left her. The park overwhelmed him: the heat, the traffic, the dust, the honking horns, the dogs, the bicycles, the roller skaters, the runners. He ran. He came out at the Museum of Natural History and on Amsterdam Avenue he went into a bar.

He ordered a Jack Daniel's. He wouldn't look at it, he wouldn't think about it. He picked it up and swallowed it down. "Another," he said. "This time with ice." His mouth tasted like poison. He drank the second more slowly and ordered a third before the second was gone. He hadn't had a drink in almost three years. Every time he'd stopped, stopping had been harder. From his first attempt, in 1969, he'd had to be detoxed. He couldn't do it on his own. Every time he started again he was worse than he'd been the time before. He didn't want these drinks, but he drank them anyway. Stop now, he told himself. But already the third drink was in front of him and waiting was only a game and he knew it was too late. He drank and ordered another and took it to the telephone to call Russell, who said sure, how about this place in Chelsea, but it would be a few hours, and Santana said fine, he'd take his time getting there, thinking the walk would do him good, he'd walk it off. He shouldn't have left her. They both knew. She knew, didn't she? He couldn't get her out of his head. She had lived in his head all week. For six weeks really but until he ran into her that day on Canal Street she had lived there quietly, at a distance. Then suddenly she was in front of him, coming out of Pearl Paint. Her smile was too ecstatic. The moment held too much joy. He couldn't get away from her face. He saw it when he closed his eyes. "Get to work," he told himself. But there she was again, on Church Street, and she laughed, and they sat in the shadows on the loading dock outside her building and smoked cigarettes without talking, dangling their legs against the concrete and trying not to look at each other, until he stubbed his cigarette out and said, "I'd better push off." His stillness was gone.

And now this.

It was clear to him, now that he was drinking, that it wasn't her, or the desire for her (if it was desire), that had set him off — it was only the fear. He shoved his half-drunk drink away and hit the sidewalk. He talked to himself. He gave coins to beggars. He said prayers in Spanish, *"Nuestro Señor. . ."* Nothing worked. All along Eighth Avenue he stopped for a beer because it was hot or a Jack because he was on a tear and it might as well be a good one because he didn't fucking want to be in love with his best friend's wife. He wanted to cry when he saw Russell's face. "I'm in love with your wife," he said, "is what it is, Jacks. But what's a wife between war buddies? I'm going to tell you about Dominique now." He interrupted himself. "I hate this," he said.

He ordered another drink and started again. "In Guatemala," he said, "sometimes in Guatemala I was awake for days. Without food sometimes. In darkness. In killing heat. For months I lived among Indians who spoke no Spanish but knew the use of modern weapons. Later I found three of them dead in a ditch — heads severed, penises stuffed in their mouths. I threw up the first time I saw that in Guatemala. It was as if I had forgotten. But I hadn't forgotten. Because in Vietnam I had never really seen. In Vietnam I was drunk, drugged — everything was some kind of vision. But in Guatemala I was clean. I felt what I saw, what I was part of — the death and the sadness and the violation, the fear and the rage. I threw up and I cried and I kept on and I put my rage to work for me. I worked and I walked and I lived in the terror. I stayed, and I stayed clean. And now, here in the city, on a sunny summer day in the park with Lucinda, the panic takes me — just like that." He snapped his fingers. He told him about Dominique.

"I hate this," he said again later. "You can't begin to know how I hate this. You think because I'm lucid I must be fine. But I'm not fine. And I'm not even drunk. I've been drinking all day, Jacks, and I drank myself sober. I've got to get out of here. If you take me home I'll be all right. I'll do it alone this time. Maybe alone is the only way I'll ever do it. I'll lie in my bed and I'll say my Spanish prayers."

When he woke up he was still drunk, drunker than the night before. For a moment he hardly remembered the night before, and was about to be grateful for not knowing, when everything came back. He saw where he was — in Russell's study, in the bed he had refused six weeks earlier. He sat up. He lit a cigarette. He saw the ashtray filled with butts. He didn't remember smoking. An empty vodka bottle lay on the floor with his shoes. He didn't remember drinking vodka. He didn't remember being here. He wondered if he'd seen Lucinda and suddenly saw her: a loose-tied dark kimono, tousled yellow hair, troubled eyes. He had kissed her. He had backed her into the wall and kissed her. She had pulled away. The robe fell open. "I'm not drunk," he said. "Tell her, Jacks, I'm not drunk."

He remembered all this and stayed in the bed. He heard their voices. His skin crawled. He had asked Jacks to help him. That much he remembered. He dug down into the bed and pulled the blankets up. He wanted to sleep. It was hot. He pushed the blankets away. Their voices seemed to get louder. Hammering sounds came up from the street. When he woke again he was shaking. He moved too fast and lost his balance. He held on to the walls and found the bathroom, the kitchen. He drank coffee, cold, more coffee. His skin felt raw. He needed a drink. One detox drink. A Guinness, he thought. Guinness is good for you. He would wait as long as he could. He took a bath. He soaked. He smelled of ammonia. His clothes reeked of booze. He watched Spanish soap operas. He took another bath. He ate: juice, cheese, a tomato, toast. He tried to shave. His hands shook. He had too much beard. He went out to buy a Guinness. He sat with it on the stoop. The sun got low in the sky and the light got hazy and he remembered the day he arrived here as if it had been a lifetime ago. Tears ran down his face and salt stung the cuts he'd given himself trying to shave. He watched the smoke rise off each cigarette. He drank the Guinness slowly. His cells were dry, his nerves. He felt them suck up alcohol with every measured swallow. It was soothing, he thought. And it was over. "It's over," he said. He said it again: "It's over. I surrender. You win, Señor. It's over."

Lucinda was the first one home. He watched her come toward him from the corner in the hazy golden light. He stood up unsteadily to meet her. "I'm sorry," he said. She was blushing. Or maybe it was the sunset sky. "Don't be," she said. "Come help me cook." He sat in a chair by the window and watched her. He had to leave the room.

When Russell got home, they called him for dinner. He ate without talking. It was hard to listen. He went to bed early and woke up late. His mind was foggy, but his body felt almost good again. He showered and scrambled some eggs and went up to the roof and lay in the sun and baked. He sat up, smoking. He listened to his heartbeat, his pulse. His eyes hurt. The air went cool against his dripping skin. He began to shake, suddenly nauseated by the smell of tar that rose from the roof. He climbed down the ladder and steadied himself, holding the walls. He let himself in. Lucinda was there. His skin went cold.

"I couldn't paint," she said. "I was afraid for you."

He backed up against the wall and shook.

"Get away," he said. "Go away. Paint. Anything. Don't be here. For Christ's sake, don't be here."

She came to him anyway. She touched his wet shoulders. He recoiled. He wanted to puke his guts out. He heaved and nothing came up. She ran a bath. She told him to get into the tub. He obeyed. He couldn't look at her. He wouldn't speak. He willed her not to be there. He went back to bed. He dreamed of snow. He shook all night, from deep in his body. He prayed, *"Nuestro Señor . . ."* He raged. "One fucking night," he said, "less than twenty-four hours." He sat up in the darkness, wrapped in blankets, smoking.

In the morning he heard them. He heard Russell leave. Lucinda tapped on the door. He coughed. He said, "Yes?" She stood in the doorway and looked at him. He lit another cigarette. She asked if he wanted coffee, juice. He shook his head no, then said, "Thanks. Juice." When she brought it, his hands shook. He didn't trust his grip on the glass. She held it to his lips. Her hands shook too. "Don't shake for me," he said. "It was a mistake," he said. "Maybe," she said. He slept. When he woke up he had a few good hours, then his body began to ache. He soaked in the tub. At night the shaking began again. He didn't sleep. He talked to the walls, he unpacked Russell's boxes and talked to the photographs, he talked to Dominique, he talked to God. The shaking sank into his bones.

In the morning Russell was with him, sitting beside him on the edge of the bed. "Okay?" he asked.

"Better." He tried to laugh. "You miss this shit in detox," he said. "They tranq you out. Prevents convulsions. You're walking around but nobody's home. Five days later they tell you you're clean." He laughed. "One fucking night," he said, "and look at me."

"It was more than one night," Russell said.

More than one night. It took him a while to ask, "How long then?"

"Four," Russell told him.

Four. It took time to understand it. "What did I do?" he finally asked.

"Just sat in here drinking."

Vodka. Smoking in the dark. Maybe he remembered. "Yours?" he asked.

"The night you got here."

"After that?"

"You ordered in."

Santana nodded. He had forgotten you could do that. But drinking, somehow, he had known. He shuddered. "Did I piss the bed?"

"Once," Russell said.

"And you changed the sheets." He seemed to remember. "I yelled at you." He wiped his eyes, suddenly full of tears. "Why did I stop?" he asked. "I didn't say anything?"

"You hardly knew we were here."

Four days gone and suddenly it was over and he would never know why. He looked at Russell, asking.

"You pounded the walls," Russell said. "Sunday you were quiet. You wouldn't come out. Then in the night, you were pounding the walls. You cried. You wouldn't let us in. You were shouting in Spanish. Lucinda said you were praying."

Santana stared at the ceiling. "Light me a cigarette," he said. He watched the smoke rise. "My father was a drunk." He dragged on the cigarette and watched the smoke. "I think it's time I checked out of here, Doc."

Russell objected: it was still too dangerous—what if he had convulsions, hallucinations?

Santana reached for his hand. "I'll be all right now," he said. His hands were shaking, his palms sweaty and cold. "I'll go back to East Third Street," he said. "The old woman across the hall will look after me. Let me go now." He held Russell's hand.

9

"This is what I know about desire," Santana said years later. "To know the changes of desire is to know the maya of all things." Russell asked how Lucinda was. "She still loves me," Santana said. She was working as a midwife in El Quiché province. "And you?" Russell asked. Santana answered ambiguously — "We don't get together much." He seemed to live on cigarettes and coffee. He was thinner than Russell had ever seen him, hard and all muscle. He never slept. "Coffee empowers the brain," he said. "Everything else shuts down." Russell thought maybe he was finally crazy. "Liquid hope," he said. Cradled in his hands, the coffee mug became a sacred object. "Poison," he said. "It kills them, it kills us —" He shrugged. "Maya anyhow," he said. "The West as we know and love it —" He tapped the mug, he lit a cigarette. "Funny, isn't it, that they're called the Maya? Words are mirrors that travel like water. And here we are — and I stole your wife. I never meant to. She used to be an artist. Now she's in El Quiché. I'm too confused for her and she loves me anyway. She loves me but I'm too confused. And me —" He shrugged. "In Guatemala they starve, they're slaughtered — the government kills them." He drank his coffee. "I'm not coming back," he said. "It's the last time." Russell refused to understand. "In the center of maya," Santana said — he closed his eyes, looking for words — "in the center of the vision of maya, in the center of the clarity of the world that is maya —" He opened his eyes. "In the center of all things is acceptance. Acceptance: the desire for what is. And out of acceptance comes the possibility to act —

not even the possibility — the necessity: the necessity to act arises from the knowledge of maya — doesn't arise from — *is* the knowledge of maya. Action without acceptance of maya is not action. Action and the center of maya are one thing: action and the freedom to act and the knowledge of life as maya — maya the origin of the world and maya the illusion of the world, maya the one and maya the many — "

He stopped. He looked at Russell for comprehension. "You don't understand," he said.

"I'm trying," Russell said.

"It's in God," Santana said. "It's God's understanding — but not understanding — vision. You ask for it. You pray for it. And if you don't, it comes to you anyhow. It comes to you — someday it will come to you" — he laughed a little — "even to you, Jacks. Let me tell you a story," he said. "I'll tell you why I came back now.

"I had a brother," he said. "Before I went to Vietnam I had a little brother. I walked away from him when I walked away from the war. Two months ago he killed himself. He was messing with his girlfriend's daughter and when the girl confronted him he went out and shot himself. It happened here. At first the girl ran away. Apparently my brother wouldn't remember what he'd done. And then one day he found her. Or she found him. And after he listened to her he wrote a letter to the mother and he went away and died. I read about it in Guatemala — in a *Daily News* stuffing a box of canned goods donated by a church congregation in support of resettled Indians, refugees in their own country. Caucasian male suicide. Unidentified — using a made-up name. But I knew the name. It was one of his make-believe names when he was a kid. I knew it was my brother. It happened right here, in a burned-out building a few blocks from East Third Street. I came up here to find the mother. Her name was in the article. I tracked her down. I had to pay out some cash and lie a little to find her but it wasn't hard. I told her that man was my brother. When I found her she spooked me. She was pale and thin, ashen. Her grief was ancient — the grief I see in Guatemala. That grief was not for my brother.

"She told me the story. She said she wanted to find her daughter. I told her I'd help. She laughed. She said no one could help. Her daughter wouldn't come back now. Never, she said. She wanted me to choose, she said. And now it's too late to choose, because your brother is dead. She'll never come back now, she said. He was trying to help too, she said, and look what happened. Children are unforgiving, she said. She thinks I don't love her. She'll never believe I loved her now. She'll never believe I believed her. Do you understand? she asked me.

"Her eyes swam in their sockets, unfocused and dilated. You can't help me, she said. She said, I'm sorry you lost your brother. He thought you were dead, too. That's what he told me. I remember now he told me. He said you were dead. You know what I mean then, don't you? she said. You love them from the other side of the grave . . .

"Then she sent me away," Santana said, "and I went looking for the daughter. It took less than a week to find her. I told her everything her mother had said. She sat on the floor at East Third Street and drank cider and ate cherries and an orange and listened to me and stared and didn't say a word. When I stopped talking she said could she listen to the tape player now, was I done? and I told her yes and she never said another word to me about her mother."

"How do you know it was the same girl?" Russell asked.

"It didn't have to be. That's the point."

Russell was confused. "You've been back a while then," he said.

"A while," Santana said. "I'm leaving tomorrow."

"For Guatemala?"

"We're married," he said.

Russell didn't hear him. "What about the mother?" he asked.

"I haven't found her again."

"And the girl?"

"She took off."

"I don't get it," Russell said.

"We're married," Santana said. "Lucinda and I are married."

"You married Lucinda?"

"That's the point of the story."

Russell stared. He heard the words again. Santana and Lucinda were married. (The changes of desire, he heard — the maya of all things.) He had been married to Lucinda himself once: once upon a time. And before that time, he had spied on her. He had followed her every morning when she left his bed. He watched the traffic at the door to her building. He knew who belonged there and who didn't. His behavior frightened him. He got drunk one night and confessed it. "I've never been like this," he said. He grabbed her hands across the table and opened the fingers and looked at the lines. "I wish I could read them," he said. "I want to know what the truth is. No matter what you say I won't believe you. I don't know where this doubt comes from. It's fear," he said. "I've never felt like this before in my life." She said she could tell him what the lines in her hand said: "They say I follow my heart. They say I couldn't be here with you if I wanted to be anywhere with anyone else. They say I speak the truth."

"Always?" he asked.

"As always as I can," she said.

"Then marry me," he said.

"You think I won't?"

He backed off. "Are we serious?"

She laughed. "Your face," she said.

"Scared?" he asked.

She nodded.

"All right," he said. "We'll do it."

She was shaking her head.

"Stop laughing," he said.

"Tell me tomorrow," she said.

"You don't believe me?"

"Not tonight I don't."

"You'll see. You'll catch me tailing you."

"That part's not funny," she said.

He shrank. He knew it wasn't funny. It scared him and obsessed him, almost as much as she did — his fear for himself as compulsive as his jealousy. Marriage offered itself like salvation;

for two years it worked, until Santana went back to East Third Street and Russell found himself spying on Lucinda again. He couldn't stop. He willed himself to stop but he was powerless against the fascination. She was his wife. This is my wife, he said to himself. It scared him. The words scared him even while he stood watching her from secret distances. He asked himself what he thought he was waiting for, as if he could pretend that he didn't know. He worried about his job — he called in sick, he took vacation days, he brought work home — he tore himself away from watching her and went in to the office unable to concentrate, thinking only of what she might be doing, alone without him — writing scenes between them in his mind, Lucinda and Santana: sometimes she pursued him, sometimes he pursued her, sometimes they found each other as if by accident; one of them always said, "I didn't want this to happen," after the fact, and Russell was never sure which betrayal hurt him more. The longer it went on the more vivid his imagination became. He saw her breasts, Santana's hands, he felt their kisses in shocks through his body. He was safer in the street, watching her door. He sat at his desk, pounding his pencil from the eraser end to the lead end to the eraser to the lead, until finally he had to leave. Let them fire me, he thought. I'll go crazy if I stay here.

Now Lucinda and Santana were married. He hadn't been wrong.

(His fantasies had aroused him. At his desk, sliding his pencil through his fingers, he was so engorged he had to masturbate. Watching her door he could hardly breathe for anticipation of the night. At dinner with her he had no appetite. In bed he went limp. He brought more work home — to save his job, to excuse himself from her. When she was working in the restaurant he waited outside in the shadows, watching the customers come and go, empty with desire for her that would not be fulfilled, and overcome with sudden memories: that morning in Saigon when Santana walked into his life, the excitement that came in off the street with him, Dominique's hand, so tremulous, holding him just above the elbow, his first impression of Santana's eyes — he saw those eyes again, became Lucinda seeing those eyes, eyes full of truth and loss and desire. He was powerless against it, against them. He remembered the day he took Santana to meet Cheyenne. They had run down out of the hills. In a sweat and exhausted from the acid and the running, they hitched to Russell's mother's and Cheyenne went bug-eyed—Santana was a bedtime story, nobody real. They showered and shaved and, wrapped in towels while their clothes were washing, sat on the back steps drinking quart bottles of beer. Cheyenne ran in the grass in circles, arms outstretched, shouting, "I'm a B-52!" and—roaring, making comic-book battle sounds—"Pow! Zowie!"—flew around the corner of the building and disappeared. He sneaked up a few minutes later and crashed onto Santana's shoulders, and Santana swung him down and doused him in beer. Cheyenne was laughing. Russell had never heard Cheyenne laugh like that. He was a solemn child, skinny and wired, hidden inside—moody and not even seven yet. He read— ads in magazines, words on television, signs on the street. In school he refused. He learned from TV. Santana released him. Russell was powerless. Nothing had happened yet, and already he had lost.)

"I knew," he said to Santana. "Didn't I know?"

Santana didn't answer.

"Have you been happy?"

"Don't," Santana said.

"It's an honest question," Russell said.

"It's one I can't answer."

(A month had passed, two. Russell felt himself get stranger. Lucinda began to notice. She had noticed from the first. "You're doing it again, aren't you?" she said. But he wouldn't admit it and she couldn't catch him. Then Santana found someone to sublet the place on East Third Street and left for Vermont, Lucinda moved into her studio—"I won't live like this another day longer"—and Russell lost his job. He collected unemployment for a while and ended up at Bloomingdale's. Lucinda filed for divorce. In February an earthquake devastated Guatemala, and Santana went back. When the divorce was final, Lucinda joined him. They had not been lovers, he had never even kissed her except that night when he was drunk. He had written to her, she said. That was all. When he left for Vermont he had written to her, and again when he left for Guatemala. She didn't know what she would find with him. Not a lover, necessarily. "I wasn't looking for a lover," she said. "I wasn't looking for any of this. You were looking for it, Russell," she said. "It wasn't me." Maybe it was true. He didn't know, and he didn't care to know. She was going was all. She was already gone.)

"How long then?" he asked.

"Four years."

"She never told me. Neither of you told me." He looked at Santana's face as if he had never seen it. He saw a kindness in it, he saw lines etched around the eyes. Suddenly his face seemed older. And younger too. Both things at once. There was a light in his face, just under the skin. The sadness was gone. Was it? Russell wasn't sure. His heart began to pound. He felt frightened. "Tell me how she is," he said. He got up from the table and poured himself a drink.

"Magnificent," Santana said.

"That's all?"

Santana didn't answer. "Cheyenne called me," he said.

"I see," Russell said. He felt frightened. He couldn't go back to the table. He leaned against the kitchen counter and talked across the distance. "He came here wanting to kill me," he said.

"Maybe," Santana said.

"He blames me for everything."

"Maybe."

"What is he, another one? Are you taking him with you too?"

"He was scared. I came and got him."

"He knew you were here?"

"I talked to him before he left California."

"I didn't know you were here until today."

"He's at East Third Street."

"You mean I'm supposed to go look him up?"

"He's detoxing. I don't know what he'll do after that."

"I can guess."

Santana didn't respond.

"Just keep him out of my life, all right?" Russell said. "Keep him away from me. You're good at that sort of thing. Take him with you. Maybe he'll fuck your wife." When he heard his own words he turned his back and hit the counter. "I didn't mean to do this," he said. "From the minute you called, I never meant to do this."

"It's all right," Santana said.

"When you called, I thought about Dominique. Everything you told me that night in the bar. I sat here and remembered it and remembered her and I thought about Lucinda and I swore to myself I wouldn't do this—"

"It's all right," Santana said again.

"Will you shut the fuck up? Have you got any more surprises? Children maybe? A brat named after me?"

"Jacks," he said. "Come back and sit down."

Russell looked at him amazed. "You have children."

"Not our own children."

"Great—you're going for sainthood together. Martyrs in service to another world? Teach them to make guns, do you? Explosives? And Lucinda, what's she doing, target practice or cleaning corn? What happened to her painting? She was a good painter. Do you remember? But you wouldn't know about that, would you? You never saw her paintings. Not if she told me the truth. You were never in her loft, you didn't know a thing about her—"

"Jacks," he said.

"You're not angry anymore, are you? What happened to your anger, Santana? You used to be in a rage all the time." He emptied his glass. His own anger left him. He went back to the table and sat down.

A few months before, Cheyenne had called to talk about their mother. "She's sick," he had said. "She's real sick, big brother. She's dying. You want to come out and watch her die? It's what she's living for, Jacks. Once you get here, she'll go in a flash. It's what she's lived for all these years. Do you believe that? She's been waiting for you. She's been waiting for you ever since your dad left. You took the wrong side. She tells me all the time, all my life she tells me, Rusty took the wrong side, he trusted his father, if only he'd trusted me. She goes over your life, Jacks. She goes all over your life like rosary beads, she feels it all up and down looking for what she did wrong. She knows all about you. She reads between the lines. You tell her next to nothing but she knows everything anyhow. She's psychic. She goes to readers. She prays for you in church. What do I exist for I want to know? Her suffering, that's all. So she can suffer. It's all she ever wanted me for. Pain. Guilt. But you, big brother — oh, from you, honey, she wants salvation. You gonna give it to her? You gonna get your ass out here and give her that?"

"Let me speak to her," Russell said.

"Sure," Cheyenne said, "you want to speak to her. How often do you speak to her? The longer you stay away the less you speak, you know that, bro? How often do you think? Once a year? Maybe once a year? So what's the point, Jacks? You got no right to be here if she dies. You got no rights at all. I'm the one who treats her like a mother. I'm who comes around here, I'm who sends her money, I'm who brings her flowers and keeps her company and sends her postcards from everywhere I go. You — you stay away is what you do. You better stay away."

"I want to talk to her."

"If you talk to her she'll tell you she's fine. She's going to lie to you, bro. She don't want you coming out just 'cause she's sick and dying. She wants you coming out because you love her, she wants you to forgive her, she wants you to take her in your arms and kiss her and tell her she was right, her whole life was right, everything was fucking right with her — she wants mercy, Jacks — have you got that in you?"

"Is she dying or isn't she?"

"Does it matter?" Cheyenne asked. "Do you really want to know?"

Russell answered automatically: Of course he did. But Cheyenne had hung up the phone. Russell called back but got no answer. For several days he kept trying. He tried his father, who said he'd look into it. A Christmas card came from Cheyenne — it was April: "Disregard," it said, "I was high." Russell wrote his mother a note saying he was worried about her health. She didn't write back. Another month passed. Then Cheyenne showed up in the street down below his window, and even before he yelled up, "She's dead," Russell knew the whole thing.

"I'm sorry," he said to Santana now.

"You have reasons to be angry."

"It's old," Russell said.

"Your mother just died."

"I haven't seen her in thirteen years," Russell said. "I don't know what it means." He had talked to his father. He had had to talk to his father. Nobody knew what to say. "My father never saw her either. At the end he saw her. He got past Cheyenne. He tried to call me. He tried to let me know. I was out, the line was busy, I don't know, he never reached me. Who knows how hard he tried? Who knows what I would have done anyway? We didn't know what to say to each other. Nobody knows anything to say. You—I hardly know why you're here now. I always thought I knew. But I never knew anything, did I? Did you? Know anything, I mean?"

"Maybe," Santana said. "Sometimes. Not here," he said. "Not hanging out anywhere here, I never did."

"She was a drunk is all it was, Santana—her liver, her pancreas. My pious, Catholic mother. Just another drunk. Cheyenne sent her money and she sat home and drank. She didn't wash herself. She wouldn't wash. When he went to see her he had to wash her. She called him Rusty all the time, he'd be there washing her and feeding her and cleaning her up and she'd be calling him by my name. You tell me about that, Santana. You tell me about justice, you and Lucinda down there devoting your lives to it for other people, but what about us? What about Cheyenne? What about my mother? And your own mother too? What about her? You must have a mother."

"I don't know about my mother," Santana said.

The last time Russell saw him they were in Jamaica. In New York he had used one of Santana's contacts to get Isabel a passport, and in Jamaica Santana showed up on the street not far from their hotel.

"I came to meet her," he said. "This isn't an accident."

Isabel blushed, her cheeks already rosy from the sun. She held the shell in her hands—she had bought it just moments before, and while Santana talked she looked at him, then at her feet, at him, at Russell, and back at Santana. All the while she rubbed her thumb against the smooth salmon underside of the shell, and Russell heard nothing else, only her skin, squeaking, as if on glass.

They went to lunch and Santana talked about Guatemala.

"I went down there expecting to die," he said. "I got into it because I had to do something, something had to be done. I knew how to do these things. Over time, things changed."

"Things didn't change," Russell said. "You changed."

"It's true, I did," Santana said, speaking more to Isabel than to him. "I learned the languages of the Indians. There are many languages, and also in their silences and their expressions there is language to learn. I learned their stories. In the language of the daykeepers I learned to penetrate the darkness of time. I learned the stories of creation—how the Quiché gods had given the first four human beings perfect vision—and how, in their jealousy and wisdom, they took this perfect sight away. These are the Mayan ancestors, the founders of the tribes. Before them the gods had made people out of wood—an experiment that ended badly. Those first, wooden people had no heart, no spirit of thanksgiving—no love for their maker, Heart of Sky. The gods sent a great flood to destroy them, and all the tools the wooden manikins had used rose up to attack them, to pound them, the animals they had bred for food, their grinding stones and hearthstones, their water jars and tortilla griddles.

"When I first heard this story I thought that we would end like them, we *norteamericanos* I mean. They were the first people to inhabit the earth and because they were thankless and unfeeling, because they had no compassion, the gods who had made them allowed them to be destroyed by a black rain from heaven and by tools they thought were their own creations, by their clever inventions, by the earth they had abused.

"All this takes place in rain and mist and mud," Santana said, "before the sun has ever moved across the sky. In these creation stories, the coming of the first dawn reunites the tribes, the scattered peoples descended from the first four human beings, whose perfect vision the gods had veiled in fog.

"For the Quiché," he said, "red is the color of dawn. In Guatemala today, the mass organizations act as a red sunrise to gather the scattered peoples together from out of the past. I didn't understand this when I went there. Remember how I was then, Jacks. You can understand. My head full of Fanon and Debray, the cleansing power of violence, *foco* theory, the guerrilla vanguard, revolution in the revolution—I was ready for martyrdom, I expected to die. Nearly thirteen years ago.

"But there they opened my eyes and my ears and everything changed. I built schools with them. I worked in the fields, like a peasant, with oxen. I worked in the mines. I hid myself among them. I didn't change their world. Their world changed me.

"The same thing happened to the priests. The priests went in to bring them to the church, and the people changed the church. Now the generals have evicted the church from Quiché province.

"The language of the generals is a repetition," he said. "Pacification, strategic hamlets, hearts and minds, scorched earth, search and destroy. We have heard all this before. But the dead, the carved-up bodies scattered along the highways, are the Guatemalans' own. Every severed head has its antecedent in ancient lore."

Standing up to say good-bye, he took a spray of small white orchids from the glass on their table and carefully braided the flowers into Isabel's wild hair. "It's hardly safe for anyone," he said. "Lucinda's gone to Nicaragua." Russell nodded. "She took the children." Russell nodded again. "Your own now?" he asked, and Santana said yes, one was. "Not named for me, I hope?" Russell asked, and Santana said no, it was a girl. "She paints, you know," he said. "I wanted you to know she never stopped painting," and Russell said, "Ahh," abstracted, watching Isabel.

10

"Keep her away from me, Jacks," Cheyenne says. "You've got to keep that girl away from me.

"She's taking too long," he says. "Let's go for a walk. She'll be back any minute and I haven't told you a thing."

On the street he says, "Get me some cigarettes," and they walk up Bedford Avenue in the weird wet orange city light past Hispanic kids with boom boxes and old people on stoops and lonely single Polish men gathered on the corner with bottles of vodka and beer. "If we understood Polish," he says, "what do you think they'd be saying? Are we missing something maybe you think? Get me a Rolling Rock, too," he says, "will you? Camels and a Rolling Rock?"

On the street again with his lit cigarette and his open beer he says, "I always thought I was missing something. Like up there at the park, they're playing baseball, aren't they? Maybe not, the rain. But some nights, I remember when I was here before, I'd go out and walk around and in the park there'd be these baseball games, those big arc lights, guys in uniforms, big guys, not just kids, there'd be families out rooting for them and there'd be these teams, real teams, and everybody'd be like watching the ballgame and listening to the music and sitting on little canvas folding chairs and the kids running around and they'd be drinking beer and Coke and whatever and watching the ballgame and maybe the dogs would be running around or lying there and something would happen in the game and everybody'd get excited and cheer and they'd be passing bags of corn chips and whatever. I mean didn't you ever think you missed all that? Or something, anyhow, not that exactly, but something, you know what I mean, don't you? You missed it too, didn't you? I always thought you had it, see, I thought since you grew up when she was married, when your father was there, I thought you had all that I didn't have. But how could you? I mean it was still her, wasn't it, when you were a kid? If it was any different for you, you wouldn't have disappeared like you did. I mean you'd have come around for me. If he'd been around for you maybe you'd have come around for me? Christ, I don't know. Let's go down by the river," he says. "Let's go look at the city. I've got stuff I have to tell you. I don't know how to say it. You have to wait for me, Jacks. I mean you have to just come along with me and wait, I don't know how to get to it, it scares me too much, okay? Can you wait with me?"

They walk out past warehouses and boxcars along loading tracks and weeds to the water's edge, the river breaking in gentle waves against the pilings and concrete. Small boats pass, their lights half-fogged, their reflections rippling out across the agitated surface. Vaguely misted across the water, Manhattan shoots beams of light into the sky. "There's another way to live," Cheyenne says. "She made me feel there was another way to live."

"She?" Russell asks.

"She." Cheyenne laughs. He tosses the cigarette still glowing into the river. "She," he says again. "They, all of them. Haven't you noticed that? How they make you feel there's some other way to live? They always make you feel that? There's something you're supposed to be doing different? They have the secret, they almost have the secret, but you have to guess it, figure it out, it's up to you, you're not worthy of receiving it unless you can figure it out for yourself? Like it's a test. They know it and they're waiting to see if you can find it and win the prize? Another way to live. A better way. And you owe it to them, too. To find out, I mean. If you fail, they won't get free either? Haven't you felt that, I mean? That that's what they want, it's what they're waiting for all the time, waiting and waiting, they make you think their waiting is some kind of favor they're doing you? Don't you know what I mean?"

"Maybe," Russell says.

"Maybe," Cheyenne repeats. He laughs. He empties his beer and throws the bottle into the river. He lights another cigarette. "She used to follow me around," he says. "My little mascot. She showed up when I was at Santana's. I went to Santana's from here. After I freaked out on you. I hated you. Thought I hated you. I was crazy. I wanted you to save me. I hadn't seen you since I was eight years old. You were an idea to me, a fantasy. I remembered you. You were the other half of Santana. But you took off and Santana stayed. I didn't notice maybe. Maybe at first I didn't notice. But later I did. Because of her. Our *mother*. Because she wouldn't let me forget you. Because she always went on about you. As if I didn't exist. Because of you, Jacks. You tell me about that—did you ever know what that was like? I hated you for it. Then I started thinking—maybe Santana made me see, I don't know—but sometime later, a lot later, I started thinking and I understood that what she did maybe wasn't your fault—I told myself that—it wasn't your fault. But I couldn't stop being angry. I didn't come here to be angry. But then when I saw you—" He stops and stares at the skyline.

"Did you ever think how fragile it can look?" he asks. "Sometimes it's a prison, dead power, ugly and solid. And sometimes it looks like that, like it could just—break." He turns suddenly, suddenly crying. "I'm in trouble, Jacks," he says, "you have to believe the trouble I'm in, I can't tell you," and facing him in the darkness, he suddenly sobs and throws himself into Russell's arms.

"Cheyenne—" Russell says, helpless—willing himself to hold him now, to keep him. But as suddenly as Cheyenne came to him, he pulls away.

"No," he says. "I shouldn't have come here. It has nothing to do with you.

"That girl," he says. "What's that girl doing here?" He looks at Russell and away.

"She's who left," he says. "She left me."

He bends down and gathers a handful of rocks and, standing, pitches them one by one out into the water.

"She showed up there at Santana's when I was trying to get clean. Curled in the doorway — like a homeless person, a drunk on the street. I took her in. I took care of her. She took care of me. We took care of each other. We didn't have anything, either one of us. I stole, she begged. I got some kind of job. I don't know. We were poor. She went out and came back sometimes with money. She brought me things." He looks at Russell. "Things like she brings you here — flowers and cards. And food too, cigarettes. She wouldn't tell me where she came from. She didn't call herself Isabel then. She had another name. Maybe it wasn't real either. She came and went. I came and went. And then one day she didn't come back. At first I didn't know it. Then I knew. Santana was here then, for a day or two. He gave me money to clear out. He needed the apartment. Not for himself. A sanctuary, I guess it was. He gave me money and put me on a bus back to Wyoming.

"Santana," he says. He lights another cigarette.

"I always knew where to find him," he says, watching the water. "You didn't know that. He was always around and I always knew where to find him. I mean he left, but never like you. He never left me like you did. I used to think that was some kind of goodness in him. I thought he was what you should've been, somebody I could find — "

"I've been here," Russell says.

" — somebody I could count on. Who cared about me and came around now and then and checked up. He did that with you too, didn't he? That's all he's ever done. He comes around and checks up and helps you out of a jam or whatever and before you know it he's taken over your life. Did you notice that yet? What he's done? Disappeared his own life and taken over yours? Your wife, I mean, your brother? He was in touch with our mother, too, did you know that either? He talked to her on the phone. Talked to her — you know what that means? You wouldn't, would you? What it means is he listened while she raved at him, got on that phone with him and ranted and raved and asked him what in the hell he thought he was doing down there, was he some kind of communist? — and then she'd tell him her theories about who was in charge of what and what was really happening everywhere in the world and he would hang on and listen to her and let her go on and now and then when she'd stop to drink he'd tell her he loved her. I love you, Ma, he'd say, and she'd laugh at that, she loved him to call her Ma, like somebody out of Steinbeck or something, that was her country, that displaced California agricultural country, and she'd get all teary-eyed when he talked like that and she'd say you know, it's okay, sonny, you're a communist or whatever, I know you've got a good heart, you love your mother. She'd forget it was him, I think — like she thought it was you, and when she'd get off the phone if she could still talk she'd call me to her and tell me about you — as if you were still a kid, still hanging around the house. Or sometimes she'd remember and get angry and throw things and cry. I told you all this, didn't I?"

"Some of it," Russell says.

"All of it. I told you it all. Verbatim, probably. I don't remember. Did I run around throwing things, or what? I must have told you everything about her that week after she died. Didn't I? Did I do that?"

"Not about Santana you didn't."

"Whatever," Cheyenne says. "It's the same story. He gave up his life and he took over yours. You didn't notice that?"

"I wouldn't have put those words on it," Russell says.

"Words," Cheyenne says. "Fucking words. It's the same story. It's always the same story. I ran into this woman," he says. "I need a change of clothes," he says. "A shower. Something to clean up these hands. Let's go back."

At Eighth and Berry he stops. "Buy me a drink," he says, and Russell follows him into the red-lit bar on the corner. "Jack Daniel's," he orders. "Pool?" he asks, but the table is taken and by the time it's free he's forgotten he wanted to play.

"Cheyenne," Russell says, not knowing how to slow him down. He's seen all this before. It's a moment of déjà vu: the two of them together leaning into the bar at Teddy's, Cheyenne drinking and smoking and talking nonstop, Russell silent and waiting. A second more and Isabel will walk in, make a scene at Cheyenne the way abandoned women do, tear her hair and cry, order a drink and age in front of Russell's face and die away from him into a stranger.

"You wanted to leave," Cheyenne says. "You had to leave us. I understand that. Maybe I always understood. Maybe it's what I hated, that I was part of what you had to leave. But you know, Jacks, I come to you, came to you, back when she died—" He stops, suddenly mesmerized by the television over the bar. "Listen," he says. "Listen to this story."

But the bar is too loud, Russell can't hear it. What he sees is a Hispanic kid getting interviewed by a local newsman, then the police sketch he and Isabel had seen earlier.

"Well?" Cheyenne says.

"I couldn't hear," Russell says. "What's the point?"

Cheyenne laughs. Distant thunder rumbles. "So you had a father," he says. "Did he play catch with you? Was he, like, you know, a real dad, bro? One more here," he says to the bartender. "What do you think, Jacks? Was he good to have around? Did he teach you how to live in this world? Would everything have been cool if he'd just stood by the old lady? I mean, do you blame me, bro? If I hadn't had to be born, maybe things would have been different."

"He left her first. You know that."

"Oh, I know, I do know that. But that's not what I mean. What I mean is, if I had to be born—*had to be*—cosmically, you know?—take the God's-eye view, like those psychic readers of hers, try looking down the wrong end of the telescope, field glasses, whatever, get some distance on it, bro. What I'm saying is there I am somewhere in the future—you know, out in the future, waiting to be born—to be born in just this way, in just this time, to just this woman—you follow? So I'm out there waiting and time's passing, until maybe it's necessary for your old man to leave her because otherwise there's no way she'll get it on with this spic or whoever my dad was from down at that Oakland church.

"I used to look at those guys, you know? I used to eye all those guys and wonder which one it was. You weren't wrong to name me Cheyenne. You knew that, didn't you? A little bit of Injun in these cheekbones maybe, what do you think? I mean maybe not Cheyenne—maybe, you know, Aztec, or Mayan like those guys down there in Guatemala Santana's so tight with, but you got the idea, didn't you? I mean you knew I was no brother of yours. You always knew it, didn't you, bro? You knew I came from somewhere else. Another planet maybe. I always knew. I used to look at those guys, trying to figure out which one it was. I'd stare at them and wait for them to look guilty and look away. Most of them never looked at me long enough to look away. Who ever looks at a little brat anyhow? For a while I even thought it was the priest. The young one. There was this young one. From Salvador. Too young for the old lady, I thought, until I saw some photographs of her from that time—I mean forty maybe she wasn't so old, maybe this guy he liked her, who knows?—maybe he broke his vows, maybe it was a fucking immaculate conception."

"You're too fair-skinned to be an Indian."

"Why shouldn't I be an Indian? You named me Indian, didn't you? Did you ever look at a picture of me in black and white? In black and white I look like my Indian father. My eyes look black. They're so dark they look black. And I have all this straight black hair. My bones show. You should see the photograph of my confirmation day, all dressed in white, my shoes, my socks, my tie, my little white suit and my hair slicked down, grinning and standing there next to Father Torres, and if he wasn't a damn priest he'd be my father. I have the bones.

"But you got me hung up here, big brother," he says. "You missed the real point, Jacks. I'm out there in the stars waiting to be born by the pure spiritual union of your mother and this *ladino* priest from Salvador, and what after all can your father do but leave her to make way for me? Did you ever look at it like that? I'm asking you. Because if you did I could understand why you always left me alone, why you went cold on me. You always went cold on me, except for that little while when you came back from Vietnam. For a while I thought you loved me. But that was an illusion. It was meant to be an illusion. I was supposed to taste the illusion. I was supposed to know what was missing. What I had always been missing. Let's get out of here."

On the street he says, "That girl. When that girl was with me, I got it too. I thought that kid loved me. I had such a jones for her. I'd put everything down, like Santana told me, and then this girl came along and all the wanting I had for everything else turned into wanting her. I wanted to hook into her, hold on to her, hold her forever. She was so young, so fragile, so almost broken. I could hardly touch her. I kissed her cheek maybe. I couldn't stand it, I shook inside for her all the time. I never hurt her. I never touched her, I died for her, all the days and all the nights and then when she disappeared on me — " He stops.

"I don't want to tell you this," he says. "I don't want you to know this. She wasn't supposed to be here. I'm trying to tell you something different. We've got to go around the block again. Come around the block. I have so much to tell you. I can't tell you back there. She's in there. She lives with you. Is it true what she said, she was never your lover?"

"She was never my lover."

"But you want her."

"For a while I did."

They fall into a silence then, walking up Bedford Avenue toward the park.

"I didn't mean to leave you," Russell says. "Not you, Cheyenne. It was me. The way I am. I've left everyone. It isn't personal."

Cheyenne laughs. "What is?"

They walk on in silence. The orange light goes misty in the steamy air. Salsa music comes dancing from a distant boom box, and when thunder cracks, kids hanging out on porches shriek and laugh and shout and run in the street.

"That morning on the mattress," Cheyenne says. "I wanted to die. I wanted to kill you and I wanted to die but most of all I wanted to — live some other way. That's what I wanted. Some other life. I was sitting there imagining snow. Remembering snow. In the mountains, in Wyoming, sometimes alone in the mountains I camped in the snow. It was clean. You don't know how snow can be clean, you live in the city, you can't feel how clean the cold is, how white and clean and light the snow is, how free. Up in the snow was like being in the stars again waiting to be born. Can you know that?"

"Yes, I think. Maybe," Russell says.

"Maybe," Cheyenne repeats.

"When she died," he says, "the first thing I did was I rented some drums. I went to this music outlet and I rented a big set of drums. Like a rock-and-roll musician." He laughs, remembering, and suddenly walking faster, ahead of Russell, turns and walks backward, miming drumming while he talks.

"I sat there in her place on Kains Street," he says, "drumming and drumming, day and night, drinking up her liquor stock and drumming — rumming and drumming I kept saying to myself, a little song as if I was writing it, no melody, just this beat, this constant changing beat beat beat, rumming and drumming." He shrugs and falls back in step.

"The neighbors didn't complain or bother me or anything, like they understood maybe, for a while anyhow, and then one day they stopped understanding, they sent a cop around, he said stop, you know. He commiserated. But a week was long enough, he said. I had to show some consideration for other people now, didn't I have anyone to go to, any other family, a father, a brother?

"I laughed in his face. A brother. I was twenty. Plenty guys lose their mothers at twenty. What do I need with a brother? I asked him. I'm just drumming my mind out. But I cooperated anyway. I let him take the drums back to the store. He offered, I let him. Nice of him, hunh?

"I went around the place then looking at all her stuff, looking at everything, one thing at a time, piece by piece. I found all these notes. You believe that? Notes, I mean. To remind herself what was happening I guess. A record. Drunken notes on phone calls. So she'd know the next day what she'd said the night before. Maybe that was it. I don't know.

"Then her brothers showed up and told me I had a week to get out of the house. The brothers from Fresno. They were taking her back. Maybe that's what a brother's for — someone to bury you — what do you say?" He grins and gives a little drumroll, rat-a-tat-tat.

"I made a box of her things," he says. "She had a cigar box with things of yours. A spelling medal. A handmade valentine card. Old report cards. All this shit of yours. A photograph with a little dog. And that photograph of me, too. The confirmation picture with Father Torres. And my white rosary beads. The brothers took everything, but I had my box. I went out and buried it in the backyard. I didn't tell you that, did I? I buried the box of you and me and her and a picture of her in it, too, and a love letter from your father. One letter. I buried it out in the yard and I planted flowers over it and I even, I don't know, maybe I said a prayer. It was like it was her there. I never told you that.

"I didn't go to the funeral. The brothers took care of it. The brothers took care of everything. I stayed away. They gave me the creeps, the brothers. You stay in this family long enough, what you get is to fail at life.

"But you," he says, stopping suddenly. "Look at you now. You got out and you're not any better off, now are you?"

Russell has seen this act before. "I think I've had enough tonight."

Cheyenne laughs. "Same old thing, isn't it? Nothing changes? You. Me. All the same."

"All the same."

"All these years I wanted you," Cheyenne says. "Ever since you left the first time. I remember you even then. I always remembered you. I loved the war because of you. I watched it on TV, I watched it watching for you, I prayed to it for you. I loved you and prayed for you and asked God what I ever had done wrong that you should die because of me. I was afraid you would die in the war and it would be because of me. I was five years old, Jacks. And then you came back, and you loved Santana, and loving Santana you even loved me. For a while I knew everything about you. Even when you disappeared. In church I prayed for you. In my white communion suit I prayed for you. I dreamed in your dreams. I wanted you. When she was sick and dying I wanted you. When she was dead I wanted you. When I drummed all that week drinking and drumming I wanted you. Then I buried that box and I buried you with it. I buried you, Jacks. I didn't want you anymore.

"I wasted all that time and all that pain waiting for you to forgive me. To forgive me. Do you know for what? For being born. Well fuck that, Jacks, it's over." Suddenly he stops. Thunder is rolling in closer now. Lavender lightning flares in the sky.

"I'm turning back," Russell says. "Are you coming?"

Cheyenne stands on the corner, watching the sky.

"That morning on the mattress," he says. But Russell is already walking away, and he has to run to catch up. "On the mattress," he says. "When I couldn't move, when I couldn't kill you? That snow," he says. "It was the snow that kept me sane — the snow, the cold, the feeling of the purity of the snow and the cold that kept me from killing you. But you know, lately," he says, "it's been so hot.

"It's been so hot," he says. "I don't always know what's happening. Do you ever feel that? It's so hot you don't know what's happening?

"Because something happened like that. I was with this woman. I met this woman. Our bodies — I don't know — we were like hypnotized. It came to us. From outside. It took over. Not desire, I mean, not just sex. It was so strong — and then sometimes she'd go off. Just go off. But I knew what that was. From our mother. And from myself. I knew from myself what it was to go off like that. I stayed with her anyway. I loved her maybe, I don't know. Whatever it was, I stayed. And it was always so hot and we stayed in there and we stayed.

"I got all scratched up," he says.

"She'll be there, won't she?" he says. "When we get back? That girl?

"She left me, you know. I couldn't take it when she left me. And now she acts all — what does she want acting the way she did in there? She has to stay off me, she can't come near me. Don't let her come near me. We have to go back and wait for Santana. Maybe he called. Would she tell us if he called? You don't trust her. You said that. You don't know you said it, but you did. I heard you say it. She lies to you, too. She was always full of lies. Then Santana showed up and she disappeared. It was in the fall, I think."

"In October."

Cheyenne stops walking. "She went straight to you?"

"Come on," Russell says. "Keep moving."

At the door he turns and waits, watching his brother come slowly, brooding, up the street.

"She must have talked to Santana," Cheyenne says when he gets there. "Santana must have told her. I didn't put her on to you. You believe that, don't you?"

"Why not?" Russell says.

Cheyenne laughs. "You'll believe anything, won't you? Believe anything, say anything, do anything? What ever happened to you anyhow? I used to idolize you. And you turned into nothing, nobody. You're air. There's nobody home."

"Are you trying to provoke me to fight?" Russell asks.

"To fight?" Cheyenne asks. "I guess I'm in no condition to fight."

Under the bright porch light Russell can see how flushed his face is, how distracted his eyes. "You should rest," he says, thinking how pale-skinned Cheyenne is and wondering how the Salvadoran priest came to live in his fantasies.

"Rest?" Cheyenne repeats. "How can I rest? I'm all cut up. Look at my hands. Look at my chest." He opens his shirt: fingernail scratches and long cuts from a knife maybe or glass, old cuts, scabbing and crusty, and fresh ones, red and jagged, possibly deep. "She's up there," he says, "isn't she? Can she hear us?" He leans closer to Russell and whispers: "I hurt somebody. I think I hurt somebody."

11
___

"You get close enough to anyone they turn out to be despicable," Cheyenne had said once, back on East Third Street. She wanted to argue when he talked like that, wanted to prove it wasn't so, wanted him to admit kindness, affection, wanted him to trust her. He was damaged, broken in spirit. She was a little girl on the run (so far from herself now, she thinks), but she knew that hopelessness he wore was a lie, that refusal to love; all that time with her mother, she had never stopped loving; but the word, even thinking the word, makes her cry. Love. Love feels like this: staring at the ceiling in a dark room, a lightning storm outside, rolling thunder and no rain, alone in a dark room listening for the others, the other — for anyone, anything, waiting for the change to come, for the love to be set free. A child's love, she thinks, the love of a little child, locked up in the night, surrounded by whispers and a world too big to speak to.

Her mother, the last time she saw her: at an outdoor café on Broadway across from Lincoln Center, in October, one of the last days warm enough for sitting on the sidewalk. The light was bright. Yellow and brown and orange leaves skittered along the pavement and caught in the gutters. Traffic was loud. Her mother wore dark glasses, so blackish blue Isabel could hardly see her eyes. She seemed to stare at all the hip, stylish people passing by. She was very thin. Isabel had never seen her mother so thin. She smoked Lucky Strikes. She drank cassis, sipping it slowly. She said she was glad to see Isabel looking so well, she said it was good she had found a home for a while at last. She took her hand and tried to look at her. "You're happy, aren't you?" she asked. "You are happy?" and Isabel said yes, she was happy. "But will you be as happy," her mother wanted to know, "when I tell you the truth?"

Her mother: on the beach in Santa Monica. They lived in a little rented house, painted red, a block from the sand. They swam, they browned themselves in the sun. Isabel imagined she could stay there forever. But her mother got restless — with her job, with her boyfriend, with the sunshine, the palm trees, the brilliant flowers, the beauty of it all, the beauty of the people, the visible happiness: the sheer happiness drove her mad, she said. "Nothing is true here," she said. "Just look at everyone smiling," and she pitched a bottle through the window that faced the sunny street. Glass shattered, she sobbed and hid her face. "I'll clean it up," she said. "It's nothing. A new window is easy. It's nothing. There is too much peace here," she said. "There is too much peace."

When Isabel was a child, sometimes Santana read her bedtime stories; he sat on her mattress with her in that apartment where her room was painted green and they watched *Star Trek* together, not really watching maybe, just sitting together sometimes, but most of all he took her out alone, nowhere special necessarily, sometimes to the park or the zoo or the beach or for ice cream, but mostly just out, on adventures, riding buses, cable cars, walking, going along with him, anywhere he wanted to go, looking at people and at the streets and at the bright white sunlight she could see on the water when they walked on the bridge or looked down from the top of a hill. She rode on his shoulders. She remembers his hair in her hands and his hands on her thighs, holding her safe and taller than anyone.

She remembers him later, in Houston, bringing books for her, bringing food. He took her out to buy shoes once. She remembers the shoes (silver sneakers with blood-red laces). In New Orleans he cut her hair.

In L.A. he borrowed a car and took her to a Dodgers game. He talked about Guatemala, about the Quiché and the stories of the

Popol Vuh, he talked about her mother. "Don't let it hurt you," he said. "It isn't your fault."

"She says that too," Isabel told him.

"But you don't believe her."

"Maybe," she said. "It's all right, you know, with her—most of the time it's all right. It's just that sometimes I think I'll have to stay with her forever—if I don't stay with her she'll get worse and worse."

"She'll get worse anyway, whether you stay with her or not."

"I don't know," she said. "Maybe that's how it was with you. Maybe it's not the same for her."

"It is the same. You can't make it better for her and you can't make it worse. But for yourself—it will get too hard for you someday. Too hard for her too maybe, having you with her."

But Isabel didn't believe him.

On the run, curled up in Santana's doorway: it was Cheyenne who found her, Cheyenne who took her in. He made her a bath, he brought her lemonade. It was hot in the apartment. She wrapped herself in a towel. They sat on the floor next to a fan and drank cold lemonade and ate popcorn and watched a Japanese monster movie on the little black-and-white TV. She wouldn't tell him who she was, where she had come from, why she was running, didn't tell him she knew Santana, had known him all her life. She was keeping her mother's secret. She asked him could she stay, could she help out somehow and stay, knowing that sooner or later Santana would show up. Cheyenne was noncommittal. He asked her age. "Fifteen," she said. "You look younger," he said. She was skinny then, she'd been on the road a while, all the way from California, and hardly eating before that. He put his hand on her face. He looked at her, close, in the eyes. "You're a lost little thing," he said, and his eyes teared up and she thought he was going to kiss her. She turned away to look at the movie. "What's your name?" he asked, and she whispered, "Sophie," hiding in her hair. He asked where she came from and she said she didn't want to tell him. She didn't want to tell him anything, just wanted to sit with him in the breeze from the fan eating popcorn and watching TV. He made her feel safe, as long as he didn't ask questions, as long as he didn't look so closely into her eyes. That scared her. He scared her from the beginning. She got used to him, she forgot he scared her, she grew fond of him and she forgot, when she left him she forgot, and later when her mother sat with her on the sidewalk across from Lincoln Center and told her the truth, when she began to let herself remember, to long for him, all this time while she's called it love, while she waited here (secretly even sometimes from herself) for him to come, for tonight—until this moment she forgot.

"Don't think," she says out loud. Don't ask questions. You can't figure anything out. You don't know anything. You don't know anything to figure anything out with. But: Oh no, Cheyenne seems to say, his voice as if from outside her. You know plenty. You know more than anybody, you have all the secrets. "No," she says. They're not my secrets. In the lightning and thunder Cheyenne seems to laugh.

Santana: "You have to get away from him now. You can't even tell him you're leaving. Isabel, you know I'm right." She knew he was right.

Cheyenne's face tonight when she opened the door: bloodless, terrified. He held on to the frame and pulled himself in. "You," he managed to say. His body looked wasted, he smelled bad, his hands shook. He was holding a brown paper bag. She could see from the shape it was booze. "You're all wet," she said. "What's wrong with your hands?" They were cut and scratched, they looked bruised. "What're you doing here?" he said. "Why are you here?" The door stood open beside him. In the street a playing card caught her eye. "Wait," she said. She came back to him laughing. She was trembling. There was nothing to laugh at. "Let's go up," she said. "We have to go up now." She looked into his eyes, so dark and dilated in the gloomy hall. "Chey," she whispered, but he turned away from her suddenly and she followed him up the stairs.

"After so many stories," Russell said, "what's one more?"

For two years she had believed he was her father. She had lived with him believing it.

From L.A. she had called her mother: "I can't stay here. I'm going to New York, to Santana."

"Promise," her mother said. "Make me a promise."

"I cry for history," her mother said that day on Broadway. "Santana also cries for history. That is what I have loved about him. He lives in history without a skin. He lives in time — " She shook her head. "You're too young," she said. "You can't understand. God protect you, maybe you will always be too young." She took Isabel's hand. "But you must promise me — "

(On the phone from Rome: "Tell no one you meet there who I am.")

"I already promised," Isabel said.

"Now more than ever," her mother said.

"I've kept my promise."

"Keep keeping it."

"I am," Isabel said. She wanted to cry. "I was angry when I went to Russell. I didn't want to go to him, I didn't want him to be my father, I didn't want a father at all. But he was good to me. He's been good to me."

"All the more reason to keep silent."

"What shall I tell him then?"

"Whatever you like."

"Except the truth."

"The truth," her mother said. "The virtue of truth-telling is overrated. An invention of — I don't know, some philosopher probably, some logician who couldn't read poetry. Your Russell — he is the opposite. He lives in a dream. You live in it with him — that is all, he needs nothing more."

"I don't like to lie to him."

"My darling, you are not lying to him."

"I'm withholding."

"A fact. What is a fact? A fact is nothing. The truth is not a fact or an aggregate of facts. You are withholding a fact because I tell you it is an act of love to withhold it, and because I am your mother, you will believe me — you will withhold my fact as an act of faith and love, and if that isn't enough, then you will withhold it as an act of obedience."

"And contrition," Isabel said.

"Don't tease me."

"I'm not."

"You have no cause for contrition."

"I left you."

Her mother shrugged. "And someday you will come back. You have a home for a while at last. I rejoice for you. Why do you grieve?"

Isabel couldn't answer. "I love you," she whispered finally.

"Then out of love for me you will keep my secret," her mother said.

"I have kept it," Isabel said. She couldn't hold back her tears.

"Listen," her mother said. "I can't bear it if you cry. You must not cry now. Listen — I told you — he is not your father. Do you hear me? — you owe him nothing, he is not your father. Tell him this or not. As you wish. But he is not your father. He has no right to know anything about you that you do not choose to tell. You are not lying when you withhold me from him — do you hear me?"

"Yes," Isabel said.

"Good," her mother said.

"But why does it have to be such a mystery?"

"Because I do not want him in my life. It is bad enough that you live with him. I will not have him in my life."

"But — "

"No more discussion. You will not betray me. You would break my heart. It is the only loyalty I have asked of you. You can love him, keep him as your father, or not, however you choose. But do not tell him who I am. I am older than you are, wiser. Believe me. Knowing that I am your mother, that I am in your flesh — this would hurt him, darling, whether he thinks he is your father or not — to see me in you will hurt him. And if he knows that in you he has me with him — this would hurt me. Do you understand? Knowing will hurt him, and his knowing will hurt me. Your betrayal will hurt me also, and because I explain this to you now, to betray me will hurt you as well. It will hurt you. You cannot tell him. For two years you have not told him and you cannot tell him now."

"No," Isabel said. "I can't tell him."

"Good," her mother said.

"But what about Santana?" Isabel asked.

Her mother smiled. "He has always known how to love and to keep counsel."

"Is he my father then?"

Her mother didn't answer.

"You never told him? Doesn't he know?"

"He had a different life to follow—"

"And you keep a different secret from everyone?"

"Not from you."

"My father wasn't a secret?"

"Only moments ago you said you didn't want a father. You never wanted a father. What would a father have been to you? A father," she said, "what's a father, darling? I had a father—a father is only for breaking your heart. You don't need a father. You never did. You are better as you are. Your Russell too—release him. He doesn't want to be your father, I don't think. This is my instinct. You will both be happier. Maybe then you will understand why I insist you make this promise. Maybe then you will forgive me for these secrets.

"It is not for want of loving," she said. "You do believe me in this? It is not for want of love.

"You know what a father is?" she said. "A father is that dirty old man in a bathrobe who scared you out of L.A."

In L.A. she had said, "I can't live here any longer." But Isabel hadn't wanted to leave with her on another search for a new perfection. "What happens when you find it?" she asked. "You find it and then this change comes again but I don't want to leave anymore. I don't want any more leaving." Her mother had not been surprised. They seemed to have collaborated in reaching this silent agreement: she would make the impossible claim, Isabel would refuse it—as if they had been working throughout those years to arrive at this good-bye. On the sidewalk on Broadway while her mother drank cassis Isabel suddenly knew this. At the time she had felt only free, and later guilty, and frightened for her mother, leaving alone for Europe, while she moved in with an old couple who lived up the block. Her mother sent them money for food and rent, an allowance for Isabel. Some months, she didn't have it to send. Isabel got an after-school job selling hot dogs at the beach and stayed away from the house as much as she could. She didn't like the way the old man looked at her. He came up behind her sometimes at night when she was washing dishes and tried to put his hands on her hips. She felt his breath at the back of her neck and turned around and stopped him, speaking loudly and walking away. His wife was frail but energetic — she played bridge and did volunteer work and shopped and went to church and to the beauty parlor and to museums and musical matinees. The old man sat around the house most of the day in a dirty T-shirt and baggy pajama bottoms, tied with a drawstring, hanging half open. Isabel tried not to look and then he'd come up behind her and brush himself against her. She pushed him away and he said *shhh* with a finger to his lips. "I can get you in trouble here," he said one afternoon when they were alone. "You want me to get you in trouble?" and she knew she had to leave. She packed the things she cared most about into a box and took them to her girlfriend Sophie, who asked, "Why can't you just stay with me?" But they had tried that in the first place, Sophie's mother wasn't willing. "It isn't wise, you know," she'd said to Isabel's mother. "Surely you under- stand, a woman like yourself. To bring a young girl into the house, a girl so pretty, not his daughter — I couldn't live with it," she said. "I'm a jealous woman." Isabel's mother came home and told her everything: "*A woman like myself,*" she repeated. "So it's the old people, darling. It will have to be the old people." Less than six months later, Isabel ran away. "You want me to get you in trouble?" he'd said, loosening his drawstring at her. She wouldn't look. "Just touch me, honey, just touch it a little, that's all I want," and she tried to scoot past him, but he grabbed her around the waist and pressed her up against himself, his other hand hard on the seat of her jeans. She bit him, but he pushed her harder, backing her up against the wall. "Don't be afraid, honey," he said, "I can't hurt you, can't you see? Look down there, honey girl, it's just an old useless thing, limp as a wet dishrag, it can't do you any harm, just touch it a little for me, that's a good girl, that's all I want, just open your blouse a minute and show me your pretty little girl breasts. Show an old man your pretty little breasts — without fighting, girl, I'll let you be. I won't touch them, if that's what you want, I won't touch, just open that little blouse for me and let me see. Or I will touch, is that what you like? You want me to push my face in there and scratch your skin with these old whiskers, you want me to bite your hard little tits? Come on, girlie, I'm in a hurry now, open that blouse up. I'll stand back. I promise. I'll stand back here and just look at you, I'll put my hands on myself myself if that's what you want, you want to see that? Why won't you look? It's not so ugly, it's old but not so ugly. An old bag of flesh is all, a man gets lonely here, you can understand, can't you? You don't have to be scared of me, girlie, honey, I'm a useless old thing," and he went on talking like that, pressing against her more and more gently and crying against her shoulder, trying to feel her breasts in her blouse and letting her push his hands away, until she slipped out from his grasp and left him leaning there crying against the wall. She phoned her mother in Rome. "I have no money to send you," her mother said. "It's all right," Isabel said, "I have enough money." She didn't have. She hit the road anyway. She hitched across country without incident — tired, hungry, and dirty, constantly helped by strangers. She kept her face and hands clean and changed rides in truck stops and diners. When cops anywhere made her nervous she pretended to make a phone call (see? — I'm not alone in the world . . .) and sometimes she got on a bus. In New York, on Santana's doorstep, it was Cheyenne who found her.

Cheyenne.

She ran away from Cheyenne too. The first time he touched her, she smelled that fat old man. But Cheyenne was gentle. He touched her gently. He kept a distance from her when she was scared. She stopped being scared. He kissed her on the cheek. She curled up with him and they sat huddled together, watching television, like kittens curled up sleeping, for the sound of another heartbeat, for animal heat. He made her cry, not from anything he did, from the gentleness in him; whenever he was out, or when she was, when she sat alone anywhere without him, tears came to her eyes. He was kind to her and she could see he didn't always want to be kind. She could see he wanted more from her and wouldn't take it. She saw it all, but understood it only later—only tonight maybe, seeing him now, returning.

What she saw then: does she remember? Helplessness, his and hers. And waiting. And then one night, his drinking. He sat with her, talking at her, about her, about his mother, about his brother, about women he'd known, about Santana, and always back again to her, Sophie, Sophie, and for the first time, sitting there with his drunken ramblings, she regretted having lied about her name. The more he drank the angrier he got, angry that he knew nothing about her, angry that she wouldn't tell him, so she began to make up stories about herself, but he saw she was making them up and got angrier and came at her and almost hit her but didn't, stood there facing her and cried. She touched his tears and he kissed her, kissed her violently, the way he would kiss a woman, she thought, and she held on as if she knew what to do but she knew nothing, she was terrified and hungry for him all at once and kissed him fiercely and ran away, out into the street. When she came back a few hours later he was passed out in front of the television. She covered him and went to take a shower and came back and lay down beside him and fell asleep. In the morning he was gone. A few days later he came back and wouldn't look at her. They circled each other and kept a distance. He didn't drink again, not that she saw. But they had lost something. They looked at each other in fleeting moments, with fear, with doubt. They couldn't speak. When she was alone she saw his face behind her eyes. She tried not to cry. She lost her appetite. The tears filled her stomach and felt like hunger but she didn't want food. Santana came. She had forgotten she was waiting for him. He told her Cheyenne was her uncle, and the tears inside her turned to rage.

"Oh, my darling," her mother said to her that day in October. "Is there still enough time for us both to be happy?" She sipped her drink and ordered another and lowered her dark glasses a moment to press her fingers against her eyes.

"Are you happy?" Isabel asked. "Have you ever been happy?"

Her mother shrugged, said "Happiness?" and waited for her drink.

"We must submit to the future," she said. "We must abandon the past. The past lives only if we let it in the present. We must abandon the present. The present is doomed. No loyalty requires us to defend what is doomed. We can move on. We can move away. The future is written. We need not wait to meet it fearfully. We can join it now. The future is," she said. "But the future is elsewhere." She was staring at the people passing by, at the traffic in the street. "It is not here," she said.

"Happiness?" she said again. "I don't know what I mean by it. But maybe you do. You there, darling, with your Russell who is not your father — maybe you do."

Russell.

She was angry when she came to him — she was hiding, she had learned to protect herself, she played parts — but most of all she was angry. Santana had told her to go to him. "He's gentle," he said. "I can't keep you. You'll hurt yourself here, you can't stay with Cheyenne," and she was angry because it was true and angry at Russell for being Cheyenne's brother, angry at Russell for everything, for his kindness, for his tears, for the love she saw in his eyes or the pity, whatever it was, for the sorrow, for the tenderness, for the loss — she wanted to kill him for it, she wanted to kill him for all of it. She was as cruel to him as she knew how to be. She wanted to rub his face in it, in herself, in her scrawny body and her hunger, she wanted to give it back to him, a despair she didn't know she lived in until she stood in the rain outside that restaurant and willed him to see her. Then he brought her home and gave her air and space and light and room to breathe in and when she was alone she lay down and cried for relief.

"Is it over now?" she asked Santana on the phone. "With both of you coming now, is it finally over?"

12

"Do you want to tell me about it?" Russell asks, and Cheyenne goes blank. "Tell you?" he says. "You said you hurt someone," Russell says. "Did I?" Cheyenne says. "No," he says. "I don't know. I don't think so. I'm hungry," he says. "I thought we were going for food. Weren't we going for food? I need to eat."

Russell has seen all this before, the changes of mood, the sudden stops of mind. Under the porch light, he looks at his brother—his face drained of color, his eyes dark and dead. The steamy air carries the smell of him, the smell of the street. His hands shake, lighting a cigarette.

"We have to go up now," Russell says.

"On your nerves already, am I? Know why? I know why."

"I've had enough," Russell says. "I'm tired."

"Tired?" Cheyenne repeats. "I didn't sleep for a month until I fell asleep on that train from Belmont and you're telling me you're tired?" He stops, forgets him. "That dream's what brought me here," he says. "I didn't know I was coming until I had that dream. I never thought about you today until I had that dream. Did I tell you about that dream? I was coming to you all day and didn't know it."

"I'm going in," Russell says.

"You do that then," Cheyenne says, but he follows. "I need a shower," he says. "Maybe some clothes. You have clothes for me, don't you?" he says on the stairs. "I'm a fugitive. These things are evidence. I have to make some kind of disguise." When Russell turns to unlock the door, Cheyenne pulls him back around. "I'm not kidding," he says.

"Come inside," Russell says.

"Fuck," Cheyenne says and slams his fist against the wall. "Open the door then, why don't you? Maybe she wants to listen. Maybe you don't want to listen, maybe I should talk to the fucking girl."

She is standing at the sink: dry now, hair dry, she's changed her clothes again, a big pale yellow shirt now and her favorite old worn blue jeans with the rip in the knee. Only her eyes move, watching them come in.

At the table Cheyenne pours himself a drink.

"Give me that tequila," she says. "I have a few things to say."

"No kidding," he says. "Me too." He hands her the bottle. Outside the rain begins, dense and sudden. He lights a cigarette at the stove. Isabel holds the bottle and doesn't drink. "All grown up now, aren't we?" he says—desire palpable in the air between them, in the steamy heat of the room.

"Not really," she says.

"Been to school. Been reading Jacks's books."

She shrugs.

He watches her, smoking. "I thought you wanted a drink," he says.

"I want to talk," she says.

"I'm sorry to hear that," he says. "I thought you were planning to drink with me."

"I see you dying," she says. "I see you killing yourself."

He walks away from her.

"You turn pale whenever you look at me."

He keeps his distance. "I'm in trouble," he says. "I told you."

"That's not the reason."

"Believe it," he says. "It's the reason. If I'd known you were here I wouldn't have come."

"You did know," she says.

"My mother was the psychic."

"Santana told you."

"He didn't."

"He told you," she says.

Cheyenne goes white and stops arguing. He paces, smoking, hugging the walls. "A card," he says. "The three of clubs. Quick," he says, snapping his fingers.

"Uncertainty," she says. "Confusion. A person who can't tell reality from fantasy, truth from falsehood, right from wrong."

"Excellent," he says. He pulls the card down from the wall and throws it on the table. "Can you divine from flowers too? If we took all these dead flowers and scattered their petals would you know how to read them? Is there a soothsayer in the house? I need some help here," he says. "You," he says to Russell. Suddenly he stops. He sits down, collapsing.

"You need a bath," Isabel says. "Food. Sleep. You need to let us clean up your shoulder. I bought peroxide. Bandages."

He doesn't answer. He won't look at her.

"I'll run the bath," she says. She glances at Russell and leaves them.

"I don't want this," Cheyenne says when she's gone. "I don't want her taking care of me."

From the bathroom they can hear her washing out the tub.

"I shouldn't have come," he says. He looks up and locates the bottle, on the counter where Isabel left it. He nods at it. "The bottle," he says. "Jacks? Please?" and Russell gets it for him.

"I was in jail a while in Texas," he says. "I don't want to go to jail again.

"Maybe it wasn't Texas. Maybe it was Wyoming," he says. "You always wanted me to be a cowboy, right?" He drinks from the bottle and holds it, staring at nothing. "I was in jail once, for a while. In jail for a while I was clean. You know that? There's a clean life. There's life. It starts in the morning and ends in the evening. You know about that? It was never like that for you, was it? You don't know what I mean. I don't either. We never had it. That little girl didn't either. With her crazy mother. Let's drink to all the crazy mothers, what do you say? Drink with me. Fuck it, I don't care. I miss you. You and your Billy Santana. You want to know about your Billy Santana? Let me tell you about Billy Santana."

But instead he splashes tequila into his glass and Russell walks away. He doesn't know what to do with himself. Hide in the darkroom maybe. The loft, so large, suddenly closes in on him, dominated by the insanity of his brother. He has felt this way before, when he was a child. For an instant he almost remembers what it was to be himself then—what he had escaped, what Cheyenne hates him for escaping. But only for an instant. Isabel comes back into the room.

On her knees in front of Cheyenne, she whispers his name. "Give me your hand," she says, and he obeys. "Your bath is ready," she tells him—holding his hands, examining the cuts, the dirty nails. "Let Russell give you your bath now," she says. "Let him clean you up and then go to bed."

"I'll need your help," Russell says.

"Okay," she says. She's crying. Tears are running down her face.

Cheyenne looks at her tears. He reaches a hand out to touch them. "Why?" he asks her. "What do you care?"

"I care," she says.

"You left," he says. "You disappeared."

"Santana made me."

"Santana couldn't make you."

She glances at Russell. "Well, he did," she says. She tries to wipe her tears away. Still on her knees, she is taking his boots off, his socks. Cheyenne looks at her, blank, uncomprehending. "I stink," he says. "I know I stink. The room people gave me on the train." He looks at her, at Russell over her shoulder, at her again. He leans forward and looks at her hard, one sock still in her hands. "Who are you?" he asks.

"Hush," she says. "Are you going to help me or not?" she asks Russell, and together they half carry Cheyenne to the bathroom. They peel his shirt down slowly where it sticks to the wound in his shoulder. They loosen it with warm water. In tiny glittering drops the wound begins to bleed. Together they lower him into the water. The water is hot. He is naked under their soapy hands. A little boy-child. They lean over him and wash him and wash his cuts and scratches. They pour peroxide into the shoulder wound.

"It's deep," Russell says.

"A knife?" Isabel asks.

"Looks like."

"Infected?"

"I don't know," he says. "It looks clean to me."

He watches her then. She asks Cheyenne for his hands. She pours peroxide over them. She washes his chest in peroxide. She shampoos his hair. Russell watches her hands — covered in lather, working into Cheyenne's hair, sliding up and down his pale skin. She lowers him into the water to rinse. Blood from his shoulder runs into the water. When she helps him sit again, he sees it. Gooseflesh rises all over his body. His skin goes gray. Blood still trickles down his back, and, looking over his shoulder, he stares at the blood fanning out in the water.

"Chey," Isabel says.

He turns to her, frightened. They lift him, they wrap him in towels. They seat him on the toilet and dry his arms, his chest, his back — so much skinnier than Russell would have imagined, almost frail, the rib cage visible, bone by bone. Russell pours more peroxide into the shoulder wound and makes a bandage of gauze and tape, while Isabel, sitting on the floor, holds Cheyenne's hands. Cheyenne looks at her hands in his — his ugly wounded hand. He opens his hand and looks at the gash in the soft flesh between his thumb and forefinger. He looks at her face then and shivers. "Go away," he says. "Get away from me." He isn't angry. He's frightened. He turns to Russell for help. Isabel turns to him too. She stands. "I'll make him a sandwich," she says. Together they watch her leave.

"I'll hurt her," Cheyenne says. "Don't let me," he says.

"You won't hurt her," Russell says.

"You don't know."

"I won't let you," Russell says.

"Don't let me," Cheyenne says again.

"No," Russell says. "I won't. Wait here," he says. "I'll get you some clothes."

But Cheyenne is incapable of waiting. When Russell comes back around the partition with a pile of clean clothes, he is already at the table, bare-chested, dressed in his own dirty blue jeans. "I don't want this," he says, indicating the sandwich Isabel's put in front of him. "I want the bottle," he says. "Tell her not to hide it from me."

"Tell me yourself," she says.

But he won't look at her. He takes the shirt from the pile of clothes and pulls it on. He fumbles with the buttons.

"He might as well drink," Russell says.

"Until he's dead?"

"Isabel—"

"He wants to die. You want him to die. Well, I don't want him to die."

"You can't stop his drinking."

"Maybe," she says.

"You know you can't."

Tears fill her eyes. She opens the cupboard under the sink and pulls out the bottle. "You're not my father," she says.

"I know that," he says.

"No," she says. "You don't know it. My mother—" she says. She stops. She looks at him suddenly. "You're not alone here," she says.

"I know," he says.

"No," she says. "You don't. You're just like him. You may not be drunk, but you're just like him."

Cheyenne giggles, still fumbling with his buttons. "What an awful thing to tell him," he says. "That's not a nice thing to tell him."

"Hush," she says. She looks at Russell. "You know my mother—knew her—" She stops. She turns and puts the bottle on the counter and turns back around. She hesitates. "She made me promise never to tell you. All along she made me promise. When I called her in Rome, when I came to New York to look for Santana . . ."

"To look for Santana?" Russell repeats.

"I know Santana," she says. "I've always known Santana. From the beginning. In San Francisco."

"You knew Santana first," he says.

"Just like my mother."

"Who is your mother?"

She sucks her breath in. "Dominique," she says. "My mother is Dominique."

"Don't lie," he says. "Don't lie this time."

"She said it would hurt you. It would hurt her, it would hurt me. Last year she sat with me in a sidewalk café on Broadway and made me promise again. She was wearing blue-black glasses and drinking cassis and she sat there smoking and talking, endlessly, asking me to promise. *Promise me, darling,* she said, over and over. I wanted to tell you, I wanted her to let me tell you, but she refused, she made it harder. That was the day she told me you're not my father. A few weeks later I told you.

"You're not my father. That's why I'm telling you now. Cheyenne's not my uncle. I want him to understand. I never wanted to leave him. I wanted to hurt you when I came here. Because Santana told me I was your daughter and sent me away from Cheyenne. I was fifteen then, I'm eighteen now, I'm already eighteen. My birthday was in June. I wanted to punish you when I came. I wanted to hurt you. But even when I stopped wanting to hurt you, I still had to lie. For her. I couldn't let you even begin to guess who I was. I lied about my age, I lied about my birthday, I lied about everything. I'm in love with Cheyenne."

At the table Cheyenne laughs. "All I want," he says, "is the bottle." He tries to stand up and his chair falls over. Gripping the edge of the table, he looks at them with frightened eyes. In the sudden silence he is a stranger, an intruder.

"I'm sorry," he says. "I just need a drink."

He rights his fallen chair and stumbles into it, and Isabel sobs and runs from the room. Behind her, Cheyenne laughs. "She may look like a woman, but she's only a child at heart."

"Leave her alone," Russell says.

"She doesn't want to be left alone. You heard her. You know what she wants. I mean you can see it can't you, what she wants?"

"I'll kill you."

"No you won't."

"If you touch her."

"Not even then." He laughs. He coughs, choking. He points at the bottle. Russell brings it to him. He drinks. He waves his hand, erasing her. "She's a kid," he says. "A girl, it's nothing. You know what she needs, don't go righteous on me." He picks up the sandwich and begins to eat. Eating, he says, "She's got the hots for me, for you too, for God knows who, some pimply boy with dyed-black hair, she's hyped up, it comes naturally, you know what girls are like, even when they get older they're like that you get a little booze in them. It'll pass, it'll all pass, those tears, that crying, that carrying on, she's a sexual powder keg but it passes. I have something to talk about that doesn't pass. It isn't going to pass, Jacks. It won't just go away like love and sex and boozing, it doesn't end in just some hangover. Some things are final, terminal, no more. *Nada, nada* — you know what I mean? And don't come back at me with any fucking *maybe* either, and don't interrupt. I have something to tell you, don't walk away. Don't leave me sitting here for some hysterical little female. I have a story to tell. I don't know how to tell it. I'm drinking my way to it, is all, drinking my way to what's real. I'm scared, Jacks. It's too real to talk it."

Russell walks away. He knocks at Isabel's door. He knocks again and pushes the door open. The room is dark. "Isabel?" he says, blind in the sudden darkness.

"What," she says — a flat, small child's voice, muffled in a pillow.

"Can I come in?"

"I guess," she says, and rolls over in the unmade bed. When he sits down beside her she buries her face in his lap and cries. "I'm sorry," she says through her sniffles. "I'll show you my birth certificate, my passport, the real one. It's the truth," she says, and he strokes her hair and her sobs get quieter.

From the doorway Cheyenne says, "I told you not to leave me, Jacks" — holding the tequila bottle, smoking a cigarette, dropping ashes on the floor.

Isabel sits up suddenly, wiping her eyes. "Come in," she says.

"I am in," he says.

"Come lie down," she says.

"Isabel—" Russell says.

Cheyenne laughs at him.

"Stop it," she says. "Both of you. You need to rest," she says to Cheyenne, and he comes forward, eyeing them. He hesitates at the foot of the bed, then sits, drinks, drops back on the bed, behind them, legs dangling down. He smokes and lets the ashes fall.

"You can't do this," Russell tells her.

"Do what?" she says. "What exactly do you think I'm doing?" He can't answer.

"You have no rights," she says. "You're not my father."

"Tell me the truth," he says.

"I told you the truth. I'm Dominique's daughter."

"And your father?"

She shakes her head.

"Santana?"

She shrugs.

"And I don't have a daughter?"

"You never had a daughter."

He listens to the sound of that.

"And Dominique?" he says. "Your mother—the stories you told me about your mother?"

"True stories. Most of them."

"Yes," he says.

"You do understand?" she asks. "You believe me? You recognize my mother now?"

"I recognize her."

"And you're not surprised."

"No," he says. "I'm not surprised."

Behind her, Cheyenne laughs.

"Maybe it's over then," Isabel says. "I asked Santana on the phone, with both of them coming—" She interrupts herself. "Russell, please, go now," she says. But Russell doesn't move.

"It's not about me," she says. "It's never been about me."

He looks at her in the darkness. In Saigon they had stood at her window and watched the war—the pretty war, the show war, the psychedelic war—the dance of peacocks, she said—the movie. They stood naked at her window and watched it like a movie. They smoked and the fans blew their sweat dry. While Isabel spoke, he had seen her—wearing blue-black glasses and drinking her blue-black drink, her face tanned and finely lined, eyes hiding while she called Isabel *darling*—running—after so many years, still lost behind words.

"All right," he says to Isabel. Slowly, he gets up from her bed. He leans down and kisses her cheek. He closes the door behind him. He takes his place at the window. In the street three men come out of the bar on the corner, yelling loudly in Spanish, arguing, he thinks, but they're not, they laugh. They race each other through the rain up the street. A car passes under the window. A taxi pulls up, a man gets out. It isn't Santana.

"Dominique," he says to the rain. He doesn't believe that Isabel isn't his daughter. "Nothing changes," he says out loud. Least of all you, he says to himself, the voice from outside inside him. He agrees: Least of all me—paralyzed here at the window while Isabel, who might be his daughter, takes his brother to bed. If not now, later. Cheyenne was right. Cheyenne had missed something, though—what she wanted: not his body, but his soul. She means to save him. She lusts for salvation, just like her mother. Russell is as unsurprised as if he had known Dominique in her from the start. And, after all, maybe he has known. From the first time he saw her, calling him out of the rain. "Yes," she said. "What?" he said. "I'm hungry," she said. Yes. I'm hungry. Fatal first words. Hungry, just like her mother. Not for food. Not for sex. Not even for love. For something nameless and eternal and always already out of reach. Hungry for it in Cheyenne the same way Cheyenne was hungry for it in the bottle.

He holds on to the image: Isabel's face that night in the rain. All this time he has known her as if her life had begun in that moment. She has told him her stories, he has listened to her stories, and still he has believed that she had no life before him. Now suddenly her life before is his life, and his own life is the life that didn't exist before she came. He would like to be able to laugh at this thought. They were all of them gone until Isabel brought them back: Cheyenne was gone, Santana was gone,

Dominique was gone — now here they were again, standing in for each other. Nothing else had ever mattered. No one else was ever real. They lived in a closed world. It is nightmarish to see this. It scares him and fascinates him, the way the sight of blood in the bathwater scared and fascinated his brother.

There is a word for the state of his mind, he thinks. Adadonia. The inability to feel pain. If you looked hard enough you could find the word for anything. Not always in your own language. Even for the nameless thing, absent, eternal, and out of reach. Adadonia. If he can't feel pain he can't feel anything. In the next room Isabel is alone with Cheyenne. Is he supposed to feel that? What he feels is Cheyenne's face, inside his own face, inside his skin: Cheyenne's face, and Isabel's face close enough to catch the breath of her voice — in the lavender light, skin pale, her blue eyes black in the darkness, wet with tears. What he feels is Cheyenne's mouth, the taste of tequila in it, the thirst for Isabel. What he feels is the silence when they stop talking. What he does not feel is himself. Only Isabel and Cheyenne, alone in the bedroom. She has kissed him now, gently, very gently. They are lying down and she is kissing him and crying and whispering to him while she kisses him and the violence has gone out of him but not the fear — when he lets the anger down, the fear grows. What a mystery Isabel's heart is. But so familiar suddenly, so much like her mother's: he takes the kisses, she lies with him and for her kisses takes the anger and the fear, offers herself in exchange, a medium, inhabitant of the psychic land between life and death, as if on the other side of her body Cheyenne will have passed through her to deliverance. But it won't happen. Nothing happens. Cheyenne rejects the promise. He refuses. He drinks. The bottle is almost empty. He laughs and falls into the pillows. He rolls his head from side to side. Maybe he isn't laughing. He reaches for Isabel and pulls her to him, he holds her against his skin. Their hearts beat together. No more stories now, no more speaking, no kisses either, just two warm animal bodies, small and frightened in the night.

Standing in the window, keeping watch like a sentinel, Russell tells himself he feels nothing. In the street the rain comes down, hot and tropical, the orange glow like science fiction, airplane lights in the sky. It wasn't always like this, he thinks. He hasn't always been like this. He was in love once. At some time in his life he must have been in love.

13

In the darkness somewhere a woman was sleeping. He
lived with her. She took him home and he lived with her. For a
while he loved her. Wanted to love her. She wouldn't let him. She
tried. They both tried. But she was a woman who wanted to die.
He woke up on the floor, with blood on his hands. He was afraid.
But not anymore. He is lying in bed with a girl now. Shaking,
and lying in bed with a girl. She's wrapped him in blankets and
pulled them tight around his shoulders and she whispers in his
ear. Don't whisper, go away, don't talk — he rolls his head free and
moves away from her, curling into himself, and she curls herself
around him. It is night. Thundering. Outside he hears rain. The
rain comes down. He knows who he is. William Henry Jackson,
a.k.a. Cheyenne. Born in Alameda County, California, July 17,
1961. Mother: Lorraine. At his back he can feel the girl, around
his body, her hands at his chest, over his heart, feeling how his
heart beats, feeling his breathing. He touches her hands. He likes
her hands. He is too hot. Her hands are like ice. Who is she? A
girl. The girl. He is alone with her now. In the dark. Alone in the
dark with a girl with hands like ice. Isabel. She is Isabel. She used
to be Sophie A lost stray thing, a wandering girl. As Sophie she
tormented him. But now she is new again. How did he get here?
Isabel, he says. He moves away from her hands and opens his
arms for her — her head on his chest, on his heart — he kisses her
hair. She raises her mouth to his. She unbuttons his shirt, she
kisses his chest, the scratches, she kisses his hand, the wound,
she kisses the wound and folds her hand around his hand, her

151

fingers closing his fingers, she kisses the shirt off him, he touches her hair, he wants to stop her. Stop, he says, but she doesn't stop and he holds her hair tighter, her head, saying stop, stop, but maybe doesn't say it, doesn't say anything, where is his voice now? He doesn't know.

He sits up from under her kisses and finds his bottle on the table at the head of the bed. He swallows. "There was a woman," he says. He leans against the wall. He drinks from the bottle. "We met in a bar," he says. She was older. She was beautiful. She had — eyes. She saw things. "I loved her," he says. "I did love her. But love isn't what you think it is. It's not what you think. This woman . . . I don't know, I loved her, but not for long. It wasn't long. But it was forever. And then one morning I woke up on the floor with blood on my hands." There was blood in the room. Everywhere there was blood. He didn't see the blood at first. "It was today, I think," he says. "Or yesterday." The blood surprised him. "I didn't hurt her," he says. "I couldn't do anything to hurt her. I loved her. Wanted to love her. I wanted to take her away." He drinks. "Isabel?" he says.

"I'm here," she says.

"I couldn't have hurt her."

"I believe you," she says.

In the darkness he can see her. He drinks and pulls her head down into his lap and lets it rest there like a cat. Like a cat, he says. Be like a cat, be still, be still now. He pets her hair and drinks tequila. The night is dark, and outside the rain. He has to think. He has been running all day. At last he has time to think now. He is safe here in the darkness, safe here with this girl. Santana is coming. Santana will help him. He didn't see the blood at first. First he called the liquor store. Every day they called the liquor store. When he woke up, the phone was already in his hands. The blood surprised him. On his hands, on the floor, on the sheet. There was a sheet. There was a knife. There was a mirror. Broken glass was everywhere. He tried standing up. He had already made the phone call. The woman was on the floor. The blood scared him. He drank from the shower and heaved, but nothing came up. He watched the blood wash away.

He put on his clothes. He knew where to find them. From the beginning he had been careful to know where he put them, careful so he could clear out at any time. He kept a stash with them too, a little money and the last of a bottle, which he drank. Then the bell rang. The boy from the liquor store. He listened to the bell while he looked through the woman's desk for anything that might help him leave her. He took the army jacket out of her closet, thinking it was big enough to hide him. He stuffed papers and earrings and change and letters and her used-up wallet and passport and checkbook and credit cards and their last bottle of vodka, which was almost empty, into its pockets. The bell stopped. He took a cautious look out the window and watched the boy go. He slipped out into the hall. The door locked behind him. With his hands he combed his wet hair back while he ran down the stairs. Nobody saw him. Nobody knew him. Not even his face on TV.

Now Santana was coming. To help him. He's shaking again. He takes another drink.

Everything is vivid. Moment by moment, each moment is suddenly crystal clear. Illuminated by lightning, she sits ghostly before him. So young. So pale. Not a woman. A child. Not even a child. Disappearing. Already gone. He reaches a hand out for her. He sees her eyes. He feels her hair in his face, in his mouth, her mouth in his mouth, the taste of tequila, her hungry little breasts naked under her shirt, her hands on his face, her fingers, her eyes in his eyes, her eyes wide open, black in the darkness, her mouth in his ear: Cheyenne, Cheyenne.

Suddenly he is cold. He pushes her back. She comes at him, holding a knife. Tell me the truth, she says. White light gleams off the blade. How many times, Daddy? He thinks she's kidding, playing around. What did you do to me? she asks. Tell me what you did, I have to know. Why are you frightened? she asks. Come back, Daddy. Tell me the truth now. I want to know the truth. Talk, she says — the knife blade pointed at him, her eyes wild. *Talk to me*. He doesn't know what she means.

He is cold, wrapped tight in Isabel's blankets, her hand on his forehead, his head in her lap, his face in a sweat underneath her hand, the sweat cold, her hand cold. He was kissing her and suddenly he was cold. But he wants her now, swollen inside his jeans, wants her and can't have her. He stops her hand. She is naked beside him. How did she get naked? With will and concentration he can stop her hand. But her hand keeps wiping his brow. Stop, he says, but she doesn't hear him. She shouldn't be naked. Naked, he will hurt her. Lightning flashes, and above him the knife blade. Stop — and his hand moves suddenly, stops her hand, holds it, and he squirms up her naked body to kiss her up against the wall, with sudden strength to hold her there, to press himself chafing inside his jeans into the heat of her thighs, her belly. He wraps his arms around her and holds her neck, her shoulders, and instead of her body feels the knife. His shoulder bleeds. Stop, he says, but he has the knife now. She tugs at his belt, she pulls at his buttons — this virgin, this girl. Isabel. She will make him clean. The knife disappears. He falls back on the bed and lets her take his jeans off. He reaches for her and pulls her up to lie beside him. He holds her still, her hair, her hands. He looks at his hands. His hands are shaking. Even tequila won't stop them from shaking now. The knife was in his hands. They felt the knife bite into her skin.

"What is it?" she asks.

"My hands," he says.

"They're shaking," she says.

"They're evil," he says.

"No," she says. "I know your hands."

"They'll hurt you," he says.

"No," she says. "They're kind. They've always been kind. I remember how they touched me. We walked in the park and sat next to the water. We were laughing, the sun was bright, you touched my hair — just for a second, you put this hand on my hair — here — and held my head against your chest. You kissed me. You kissed the top of my head. So gentle you thought I didn't feel it. But I did feel it. They are good hands. Your hands are innocent," she says. "Innocent."

He looks at his hands. Covered with cuts and scratches, a gash that won't heal. He shows her his hands. She kisses them. I felt the knife, he says. I felt the knife sink into your body. Don't move, he says. He lies still beside her and wants her and doesn't move. Don't, he says, but she's already moving, he stops her and rolls her away from himself but already he's going with her, following her, this girl, this little girl, and she has him now, what she wants, it's too late now, everything is too late, she has him and thunder fills his body and there's blood on his hands, and kisses, and his hand hurts, he's bleeding again, this old wound, and she kisses his blood and he kisses her kisses and the thunder gets louder and he holds her still again and looks at her face in the light-ning—Isabel—and her body comes apart in the darkness under his hands, under his mouth, she slips away from him, farther and farther, he'll never find her now, she'll never come back, lost—he holds her—stop, he cries, but there is no stopping, everything is too late now, she's gone and holding her hair, his head, his face against her breast, her heartbeat, her heart beating, her heart. She pulls the sheet up around him. He shudders. The sheet. The sheet is death, sticky and cold. His skin hurts. He listens to her heart. He is frightened. He gropes for her hand and holds it tight. Shivering, he kisses her breast, and the taste of her skin and his sweat turns his stomach. He rolls away from her, curling up like a baby. She follows. He shakes and listens to the rain. She squirms behind him, runs a hand through his hair. Enough now, he says. Be still. But even her breathing against his back is too much movement, her breasts and belly and legs too much skin. Get off, he says. He pulls himself away from her—gently, trying to be gentle. He holds her hand. Tries to hold it. I'm sick, he says. Don't mind me, Sophie. I'm sick. But she doesn't hear him. He can feel her sadness in the dark. It fills the night. Isabel, he says. Isabel, Sophie. I killed that woman. I killed her. I don't remember killing her but I killed her. It's why I'm here. It's why Santana's coming. To help me. I killed that woman. I killed, I killed, I killed—in rhythm with the rain and their heartbeats, until she says but Santana won't help you. He wants to put you in a detox. It's what he's coming for. Not to take you to Guatemala. Not to give you money and get you out of the country. He wants to lock you up in some detox. He wants you to turn yourself in.

"No," he cries.

She takes his hand. "What is it?" she asks.

"Santana," he says.

"Bad dreams?"

"I wasn't asleep."

"You cried out," she says.

"You weren't talking to me?"

"No," she says.

"Are you talking to me now?"

She smiles. He can feel the smile in her hand. He doesn't mind her hand now. He takes her close to him again. I'm in trouble, he says. I know, she says. She waits. It's that woman, she says, isn't it? Is it that woman who's dead? That woman who's dead. But she isn't dead. She's laughing, counting her toes. One, two, three, three-and-a-half, four. I had nine toes, she tells him, when I was three and a half years old. Three and a half was an integral age. I sat on my parents' big bed and counted my toes. One. Two. Three. Three-and-a-half. She laughs. She is right here laughing. Hiding inside her straw-colored hair. This little piggy went to market, she says.

I killed her, he says. I don't remember. But I killed her. You don't know, Isabel says. Aren't you afraid? he asks. No, she says. What will you do? she asks. Run away, he says. I'm going with you, she says. No, he says. I have money, she says. I have a passport and I have money. Do you have a passport? she asks. Yes, he has a passport. He went to Guatemala. He saw blood in Guatemala. He saw so much blood in Guatemala that blood didn't matter, it wasn't even a color, it wasn't life or death, it was more like puke, the puke you see on subway stairs, the trace of somebody else's already old bad luck. When he was a kid he thought he'd never be afraid, he would grow up to be a man and he would never be afraid, and so he grew up that way, master of himself, held all his fear inside and pushed his body out beyond it and drank all the time to keep it that way. He went out among men, he worked ranches and rodeos and went into the mountains with cowboys like Nazis and learned to fight with his body and guns, and all the time the fear got bigger inside him and he drank, and drank away from himself, until he went to Guatemala and Santana turned his head around. Santana. Santana won't help you, she says. Santana wants to put you in a detox. Did you say that? he asks her. I have money, she says. You don't need him. Don't wait for him, she says. We should go now, without him. Without him? he asks. Why wait? she says. It's dangerous to wait. I was in jail once, he says. For what? she asks. A few days, he says. Just a few days. Drunk. Disorderly. Criminal mischief. Reckless endangerment. I don't know. A few days. Only a few days. I won't go to jail again. *Isabel,* he says.

"Are you all right?" she asks. "You were talking in your sleep."

"I'm not asleep," he says.

He goes on like this, with her and not with her. With his mother on a beach in San Francisco—a deserted, windswept, cold-weather beach, high rolling gray-green waves, a gray sky with rainbows hovering behind it—he's standing in the sand staring at the horizon, waiting for something to appear—a ship—their ship to come in: a Spanish galleon, with square white sails and red-and-yellow pointed flags, gold coins and *conquistadores* in pantaloons, their ship, their future, a ship from out of the past arriving from Vietnam with Russell and Santana, the future he hasn't met yet, Santana and Russell arriving from out of the centuries, from across the Pacific to save him, to change his life, to turn everything around. He hopes—he doesn't know what he hopes. He digs his toes in the sand and stares at the sky and the water. Seagulls glide on the air and cry and watch him like hungry dogs. A fog rolls in, he watches it come. His mother is calling. Cheyenne, she says. Listen. Santana won't help you. Santana's not coming to help you, she says, and she's kissing him, but he hardly knows she's there, he's remembering Santana, who took him out of his world when he was a boy, away from his mother, who took him to the zoo and to see the buffalo in Golden Gate Park, who took him to ballgames and movies, who did magic with cards and pulled dimes from his ears, who told him fairy tales and ghost stories and stories about children he had known in Vietnam—Santana, who helped him with his mother one night when they came in from Tilden Park and pizza on Telegraph Avenue and found her on the living room floor and had to clean her up—his mother in the bathroom naked, old worn-out flesh, Santana helping her into the shower and scrubbing her down, drying her with a big purple towel, wrapping her in her frayed flannel robe, and walking her to bed. Santana, Isabel says, who sent me away from you, who wouldn't let me explain why I was leaving or tell you good-bye, who won't admit that he's my father. Santana, she says, is not here to help you. We don't know, he says. Be still, he says, and she holds him, still, but moving so quietly, she breathes in his ear, you want me, she says, I know you want me, you've always wanted me, tell me the truth now Daddy, I love you Cheyenne, and the rain coming down and his bottle of tequila just out of reach. My bottle, he says, and moves to get it, and she moves with him. Get back, he says, and his eyes are used to the darkness now, he can see her clearly, etched on the night, a ghost figure, wreathed in black hair—like leaves, her hair comes down like leaves, he watches them grow, her hair grow, down her back, her shoulders, her breasts, down in between her legs, her legs open up, she is bleeding, blood all down her legs, it beats like her heart, their hearts beat together, their bodies, he's buried deep inside her, covering her mouth with his hand and watching her eyes die, she kisses his hand, and he cries no and bites his lip and buries the word in her hair, in her hair he says yes, all right, yes, Isabel, and he's terrified, shaking again.

"I have money," Isabel says. "We'll go to Spain. To Barcelona. To my mother. My mother will help us. My mother will like you. She knows you. She knows you already. Come with me," she says. "Cheyenne."

"But the blood," he says.

"What blood?" she says.

He looks at her body. There is no blood. She is clean and glistening, like a runner, a swimmer rising from water.

"I'm afraid," he says. He looks at her, her long naked legs. He needs her. He is terrified to need her. He drinks from his bottle. Isabel, he says. But he has no voice. His voice is all used up. He is all used up. He drinks. He leans back against the wall and looks at her and drinks.

"We can't leave until morning," she says. "All my money's in the bank."

He shakes his head. Nothing he can say will stop her. He can't let her help him. How can she help him? He thought he could run until he heard the words come out of her mouth. There is no running, never has been any running, never will be. Even when he was a child, he knew this. When he drummed his mother's death, he knew. When he came to kill his brother. To kill? He never meant to kill him. It was only a word.

"Sleep," she tells him. "Lie down and sleep." The rain stops, and he's closed in silence and the heat of his body, his stale breath. His heartbeat races, his skin goes cold. Hail Mary, he says. Full of grace. Blessed art thou among women. A picture from his childhood, a woman draped in red and blue, kneeling in front of a white-robed angel — shining, neither male nor female — both — beautiful and handsome, with bright black eyes and golden wings. Golden wings, he thinks, and hears them beating, the air opening, closing. The silence of them. Mother of God, he thinks. Full of grace. The wings soothe him. An angel is on my side, he thinks. One angel. What angel are you? he asks, and the wings beat and he hears crying, children crying, he has to fight them for breath, he has to sit up. Sit up, he wills himself. Breathe. The dream stops.

Was it a dream? He is in the dark. He's alone here. In a moment or two he'll know where. Maybe. He feels around his body. Entangled in a sheet. Naked in a bed. In a room then. A dark room. Somewhere there's a woman. Lying beside him. He can hear her breathing. He looks at the ceiling. Unfamiliar. He spots the bottle. Not quite empty. He listens. Silence. But everything is voices now: *You're not my father. Why are you here? How many times? I want the truth.* He almost knows it. He was on a train. He was at the races. There was a woman. When she was a child, bougainvillea grew all over the front of her house, paper-petaled magenta flowers. Sometime or other her parents took the bougainvillea down and put two twisting cypresses in its place.

She missed the bougainvillea. No one asked me, she told him. No one asked me what I wanted or what I thought. It wasn't my house, she said. It never was my house. (Mine either, he said. Mine wasn't either.) When she was a teenager her father began growing orchids and built a greenhouse in the backyard, Spanish moss grew in the greenhouse, and when she stepped inside it she pretended to enter another world — a world of primeval forests, swamps and bayous, ghost plantations — a past of the imagination, she said. Sometimes she hated the orchids, the heavy air they grew in. They were strange, fleshy flowers, even the most delicate looking. She yearned for Hawaii, the tropics, palm trees on white beaches. She came east instead. To get as far away as possible, she said. Her father drank bourbon. And then he stopped. He was still crazy, she said. He was crazy anyhow. (My mother too, he told her. She didn't stop until she was dead.) It isn't necessary to live like this, she said. Sometimes he almost believed her. She didn't believe herself. He looks around now, at the room. Not this room, he thinks. Not this woman. What woman was this, then? He listens for voices. He drinks what's left in the bottle. He listens to the night sounds. A car passing. A distant siren. Long silences. A footstep in the street. He remembers it was raining. The rain has stopped now. He remembers where he is. The room gets lighter, on the verge of going gray. He hears a bird. He remembers where he is and who the girl is in the bed beside him. He looks at her for the first time — her black hair tangled across her cheek, her back so bare and vulnerable beside him. He would like to touch her. But he is afraid. She breathes so quietly beside him. So serenely. How is this possible? She's in danger. He can feel her danger. Looking at her he can see it. Anyone could see it. He would like to warn her. In the street he hears a car. He hears another bird, birdsong, a chorus of birds. Isabel's fingers curl in her sleep. He should leave her. Disappear. He only half remembers why. But he knows he is afraid. No one can help him. Not even Santana. He's too late for helping. The rest will come back. A little more daylight, a cigarette, a cup of coffee. A few words spoken. The looks on their faces. A drink. Then he'll remember. Whatever it is he needs to know. Or not.

There's no guarantee. There's nothing. Just this moment, this almost-morning, Isabel in the bed beside him, the singing birds, and himself shaking here, pressed against the wall. He is shaking. There's not a drop of tequila now and Jacks doesn't drink. He watches his hands shake. Maybe they're not tequila shakes. Maybe it's the other thing. The fear. That woman is dead. That other woman. He thought he must have left her. He didn't remember why. But then at the racetrack he saw the newspapers and read that she was dead and he remembered—began to remember. Just like now. Now he remembers his picture, the police drawing that doesn't look like him. He remembers the liquor store boy. He liked that boy. He thinks maybe that boy will feel sorry for him. He imagines himself in court. Dressed in a suit. Hair cut short. Some kind of lawyer at his side. Maybe a woman. And the liquor store boy on the witness stand. The liquor store boy will wear a suit too. A shiny suit. He can see it— almost metallic, gleaming—and a red leather tie and black shiny shoes. He'll be wearing cologne. He can smell the cologne from the table where he sits with his lady lawyer. The liquor store boy points at him. It's the biggest thing that has ever happened in the liquor store boy's young life. It's the biggest thing that will ever happen. Who is he to deprive him of his moment? Who is he to run away?

A loud, ugly electric noise—with half his mind he knows it is the door, it is Santana—breaks into his imagining and, echoing down empty prison corridors, leads him past steel bars, down clanging metal stairs, through guarded gates: sounds and pictures from the movies. He is on his way to the electric chair. A priest walks beside him, Father Torres. Pray, the father says. Ask forgiveness for your sins. Pray for God's mercy, my son. Outside the birdsong gets louder, repeating Father Torres's words. Isabel stirs beside him. From the next room he hears footsteps, voices. Isabel rolls over, stretches her arms, and half sits up.

"Was that—?" she begins. She stops, interrupted by sudden light from the opening door.

Santana stands on the threshold, the loft bright at his back.

"Get up," he says. "Get out of that bed."

Nobody moves.

"Now," he says, and closes the door and waits for them on the other side.

14

His face older, his body heavier — in Santana's black hair now Russell sees strands of gray. At the door Santana hugged him, every move slow, too long enduring. Russell felt like a child in his arms, something so old and motionless resided in his body. His weight and stillness made themselves the center of the room. He had spoken only to ask, "Where's Cheyenne?" and when Russell told him, he had gone to Isabel's door. He stopped before he opened it. "He killed a woman," he said. "He was drunk and he killed a woman." Russell would like this fact to have surprised him. "You knew," Santana said. "Apparently," Russell answered, grateful for every word that broke the silence. The silence had been dangerous. In the silence alone with Santana — alone with anyone — he might have had to feel.

Now, an hour later, Dominique is on the phone: "You call to me as to another world," she says, "asking for a sign. Who is calling me? Not you, Jacks?"

"It's about Isabel," he says.

"I knew it must happen, sooner or later."

"She's leaving with my brother. She's running away with my brother."

Dominique laughs. "You are concerned," she says, "with the question of her paternity."

"He killed someone. He's a fugitive."

"Oh so. You want me to stop her."

Stop her? he thinks: In the doorway Isabel had tied her

163

kimono around her naked body and aged before his eyes. She had been in bed with his brother.

"Do you know why he's here?" Santana had asked her.

She raised her chin at him. "He's stabbed too," she said.

"Seventeen times," Santana said.

She tied her kimono tighter and didn't answer.

"The body had seventeen stab wounds. Isabel," he said.

Cheyenne appeared, bare-chested behind her. Russell couldn't imagine the violence of it, the violence of his brother. All he could see was the frailty, the fear. Poor children, he thought: Isabel and Cheyenne.

"Did you understand?" he asks Dominique now.

"Perhaps," she says. "Perhaps. Let me speak to her."

He takes the phone to Isabel's closed door. He knocks. She doesn't answer. He knocks again. "It's your mother."

She opens the door a few inches and stares at him through the crack. She takes the receiver without leaving her room. "Hello?" she says — "Mama?" — her voice like a child's. She takes the phone from him and pulls it in with her, closing the door.

At the stove Santana measures coffee, puts water on to boil. Cheyenne is in the shower.

You call to another world, Dominique said.

"It was a mistake to call her," Russell says. "What time is it in Barcelona?"

"Noon," Santana says.

Time she could be drunk in. "It was a mistake," he says again.

"Take me to Guatemala," Cheyenne had said to Santana.

"I'm going with him," Isabel said.

Santana ignored her. "Seventeen times," he said to Cheyenne. "Look how your hands shake." They were sitting at the table. "Give me your hands," he said, and Cheyenne obeyed.

"Take me to Guatemala," he said again.

"There's no place for you in Guatemala. There's no place for me in Guatemala now. The generals kill Americans in Guatemala now. Even a priest."

"Take me."

Santana. Like a rock. Some ancient tree. He gets older and imperceptibly grows. Santana — who has never stopped touching his life.

"You were free, I thought," Russell tells him. "You lived in a world more real than this one, a world with its own logic of violence, out the other side of some general's wall of terror. A world unlike my own, I thought. Mine was the world you left behind. But you've been here all along, with everyone. How is it possible that after all this time you're still here?"

"They're the same world," Santana says.

"I want to know how it's been possible to live in so many lies." How was it that in the lies he had been alive and in the absence of the lies or the collapse of the lies or the withdrawal of the lies, faced with the truth, left alone with the truth, living in the truth, he'd shut up and died? "Do you know how many stories I've lived in — Isabel's stories, your stories, and Dominique's now suddenly too? Not even Lucinda broke through the stories. Do you understand me? She wasn't real either until she was part of the story and she wasn't part of the story until she left with you."

"You were the good son," he says, "the good husband, the good brother, the good father. While I lived apart, hermetically sealed."

"Hermetically sealed is the national condition."

"No," Russell says, "I'm a fool" — and shrinks from the understanding he suddenly meets in Santana's eyes.

Cheyenne also shrank from those eyes.

"You can't escape that woman's death," Santana told him. "You can't escape her death, but you are not guilty of murder."

"Who made you a priest?" Cheyenne demanded.

"You are not guilty."

"Did God tell you that? Are you still talking God stuff?"

"Yes," Santana said. "Sometimes I am." And then he had fallen silent, looking at the two of them, Isabel and Cheyenne. They waited, awkward under his scrutiny, glancing at each other, at the table, at Russell across the room, until finally Santana spoke again: "In Guatemala they say God blinds those who do not love."

The water boils. Santana pours it.

"Are you her father?" Russell asks him.

"Does it matter?" Santana asks.

The smell of coffee fills Russell's mind, and for a moment coffee, he thinks, will fix everything. "Tell me how it was," he says. "When she was born. Tell me about Dominique."

Santana hesitates.

"You were there," Russell says. "You must have been there."

"I was there," Santana says, and Russell, looking at him, at the graying shadow of beard beginning to show at his chin, thinking he needs a shave, wants to reach out and touch him, to ask is he real.

"What do you think I should do then?" Cheyenne had asked him at the table. "You and God, I mean?"

"You know better than I what to do," Santana told him.

"I thought you came here to help him," Isabel said.

"Stay out of it," Cheyenne said. "You don't know anything."

"I do know." She touched his bare shoulder. His skin shivered, made gooseflesh, his nipples erect. He pulled away from her touch and stood up. He lit a cigarette, shaking.

"You want me to go to a detox, don't you?" he said to Santana. "You want me to go get sober and clean myself up and then you want me to turn myself in."

Santana didn't answer and Cheyenne stood looking at him with wild eyes. "On the subway, you know," he said, "on the subway, leaving her, leaving that woman, through the window of the train on the opposite track I could read the graffiti — through the window I could read — it said: AND THERE ONCE WAS A KING NAMED BONY BONES. I thought of you, Santana. That's why I called you. It's why I got that seventeen-to-one shot, too, the horse's name was like that, Black Bones, King Bones, I don't know, Bony Bones, King Bony Bones — Death, you know, Santana, a black horse, maybe a white horse, isn't that what Death rides? There once was a king named Bony Bones. That was you, Santana. That's what came to my mind. Not God, Santana. Death. I killed that woman."

"Talk about her," Santana said.

"I saw the headlines at the racetrack on the *Post* and the *Daily News*. I didn't know she was dead. That was yesterday. Or maybe it wasn't. I don't remember. I need a drink."

"About her," Santana said.

Cheyenne shuddered and moved away from him, along the wall. "I won't," he said. "I won't listen to you. They'll find me here if I stay any longer. They'll match up those prints. How long does it take them to match up prints? My driver's license? That jail in Wyoming? They have computers for that. They'll know who I am. They'll telephone here. They could come knocking any minute. Isn't that true? Russell Jackson, next of kin? I shouldn't be here. They can find me here even while we hang around talking. My picture's everywhere. So what if nobody's recognized me? Even Jacks didn't recognize me. So what does that prove? It only means yet. What about somebody comes looking for me in the detox, maybe then they recognize me? Maybe they don't even match up fingerprints, they just start looking in the detox wards — they know this guy's a drunk, right? — this murderer they're looking for? Maybe they don't match my prints anywhere, why would they check Wyoming after all, maybe I have time to breathe for a while — maybe maybe maybe — "

Suddenly he sat down. "Okay," he said.

"You don't need him," Isabel said. "You have a passport. I have money."

"Stay out of it," he said.

"They don't know who you are," she said. "They don't know who they're looking for."

"The woman is dead," Santana said.

Isabel's face went hard. She stared at him in willful silence.

She would have been something like his mother, Russell thought in that moment. She would have had blue eyes, and sometimes a lost look. She would have loved Cheyenne. She would have looked at his beauty as Russell was looking at it: from a distance, through layers of glass. In sex she would have crossed over, passed through — only in sex. In sex Cheyenne would have killed her. Drunk, in love, in sex — a woman like their mother, like Isabel's mother, like Dominique—he would have killed her and almost himself. He was all scratched up. Traces of his skin must have been removed from under the dead woman's finger-nails, collected with samples of his hair, fibers of cloth, flakes of dried blood and semen scraped from the sheets, specimens neatly labeled, filed in plastic bags. For an instant Russell wanted to protect his brother, to save him. He remembered him para-lyzed: stopped in his rage, he had said, by a vision of snow. Isabel was like snow, but Isabel wouldn't save him. Maybe she wouldn't even stay with him long—how was anyone to know? Wasn't she her mother's daughter? Did she know what it meant that a woman was dead? Her mother knew. Her mother knew the dead. Santana knew. Even Russell knew—even he, no matter how much of his life he'd already lost in an effort to forget. But what about Isabel? He wanted to shake her, to break her—to stop her—but he was powerless. Santana also was powerless. He took comfort in that thought: he and Santana made equal in the face of the will of this girl.

"Tell me," he says to Santana now.

Santana looks at him without speaking. Finally, he says, "She babbled, sometimes in French, sometimes in Vietnamese."

He stops, as if to go on, to utter more than a sentence or two, would take too much out of him—Santana, who used to talk uninterrupted for hours—or maybe Russell only imagines he did. Behind him, the boiling water rattles the lid of the kettle, and Santana turns away to pour more water over the coffee.

"At the end," he says, "in the last contractions, when Isabel was leaving her body, she grabbed for my hand and said faintly, in French, for only me to hear—Of course there is a God. She denied it later, drinking, but that morning she said it again, she said that in that moment, as Isabel slid down out of her body, the pain resolved itself, physically, into ecstasy, and she was filled with an illumination of the certainty of God."

He looks at Russell. "That morning she told me she loved me, she had always loved me. They brought us Isabel, wrapped tight in hospital blankets, fat-cheeked, the rest of her scrawny, a black downy fuzz on her head and sleepy blackish blue eyes. Domi-

nique held her and said — You too, little one. I will love you too.
In loving this child, she said, maybe she would learn to love
herself.

"It's the only time I ever heard her speak of love."

At the table Cheyenne had begged him for reprieve. "I'm alive,
I don't want to think about her," he said. "She was crazy. She
went off sometimes. She talked about her father. She drank and
talked about her father. Half the time she thought I was somebody else. She thought I was him. I don't even know what
happened. How can I turn myself in?"

"Talk," Santana told him. "Remember her."

"She drank and smoked and aged and got harder," Santana
tells Russell now. "She did social work with refugees, Vietnamese. She tried to write about it, about them. That's what her
life was, and to be able to live it, she closed her heart to the good
she was doing. She was gentle with Isabel, whenever she could
be. It cost her a lot, even that effort of unguardedness with her
own child. All the hardness came from inside her. She never took
help, she didn't want help, she wouldn't let anyone touch her."

"For a while I loved her," Cheyenne said. "I wanted to love
her. She wouldn't let me." He stopped, helpless with fear. "She
was older. Beautiful once maybe. Beautiful with me sometimes.
She was a smart woman. Brainy. She thought. Read. Figured
things out. But thinking, I don't know, made her crazier — like
you, maybe, Jacks," he said quietly, "what do you say?"

Russell shook his head.

"When I woke up I wanted to hold her. I crawled across the
floor. I thought she'd be crying. I thought we'd been fighting,
maybe she had hurt me. My chest was cut up, my shoulder was
numb. I thought we'd passed out in our separate corners, each
with a bottle. I wanted to hold her — " He looked at Isabel. "I
don't know," he said. "Maybe it doesn't matter. Maybe I should
just as well go to jail. I didn't mean to hurt her. I can't — I
wouldn't — " Tears came to his eyes. He let Isabel take his hand.

"Leave him alone," she said to Santana.

"What will happen to me if they find me? Nothing good can
happen now. At least if I run there's a chance — it isn't too late,

maybe they don't know who I am yet, maybe they don't know who they're looking for, maybe they never will know—I have my passport—I'll get clean then, Santana, I will, I don't want to be crazy, I want a life too, we can have a life now if we leave now—she'll help me, she would—don't make me stop here—Santana?"

"When I came back this time I went to Washington," Santana said. "I went to the Vietnam wall. My name is on it. My real name. Do you hear what I'm telling you, Cheyenne? Cut into black marble with the honorably dead—my name."

"Would you rather have stayed there and died then?" Cheyenne asked, suddenly angry. "Do you want to go turn yourself in? What would he get?" he asked Russell. "For desertion, maybe treason? I mean, he's been working with the enemy hasn't he? Somebody's enemy. I'll bet La Migra wants his ass. Running refugees? Is that what you've been doing in L.A.? El Coyote Santana? Do you even think about turning yourself in? Have you gone to see your mother?" He laughed. He stood up. "Come on," he said to Isabel, pulling her to her feet. "We're wasting time here. I need a shower. Get packed."

"You watched over her," Russell says to Santana. "Even from Guatemala. And you never thought she might be yours?"

"I believed what Dominique told me. I still do."

"Isabel," he had said, trying to stop her: "I'm not your father."

"You think if Cheyenne's my uncle I won't go with him?" she had cried. "Maybe he is my uncle. So what? Nobody wants to be my father anyhow, so fine, I don't have a father, I never had a father—"

"Isabel—"

"No," she said. "I won't let you send him away. I can take care of him. I know how to take care of him. What do I know if I don't know how to take care of a drunk?"

"We live under threat of the disaster," Dominique had said one night on her roof. "Not just here," she said. "Everyone. Everywhere. It is the same for all. Thus it means nothing."

It means nothing.

"We shouldn't have called her," Russell says. "She won't help."

"Do you have another solution?"

Russell doesn't answer.

Santana watches him, unreadable. "She won't forgive you," he says at last, and Russell is suddenly more aware of fear than he has ever been.

"You suffer from a disaster of gentleness," Dominique had said when she walked away from him in the rain. "It is a madness," she said. "Your form of the disaster. The disaster lives in us all. In this child, too," she said, "already in this child, not even born, just beginning to grow, here in this vaguest, smallest, hint of a child-to-be. She is yours, he is yours. But never will be yours. Not mine either. No one's. Creature of the disaster. Like all of us, everywhere." She stood there in the rain, unprotected — her pale, pink-flowered dress clinging to her skin, revealing the new curving belly. "It means nothing," she said. "Not even this little life that is not yet."

Should he have stopped her from going then? Should he never have left her? As if there existed a single moment of the past that, lived differently, would change everything.

There is something he should do. There was something he should have done then, and there is something he should do now.

He knocks at Isabel's door.

"Go away," she says. "I'm still on the phone."

He wonders suddenly about the tequila, whether there is a drink or two more in it, a drink left for him. He could use a drink maybe. Maybe some of what is happening would reach him now if he had a drink in him. Maybe he wouldn't be so numb. Numb, he thinks. That was the word. All his life he has been numb. He would like to tell them: he didn't choose this.

But when Cheyenne comes out of the bathroom, clean-shaven, hair slicked back, asking for clothes, all Russell can say is "Take what you need."

"Beautiful photographs," Cheyenne says from the other side of the partition.

"What photographs?" Santana asks.

"Photographs of Isabel." Walls full of photographs of Isabel. They will be changed, Russell thinks. They will look like Dominique now. When he goes into his old files and pulls out negatives and prints them and hangs them side by side, mother and daughter, he will see what all this time has eluded him, what he is beginning to see already in his mind.

"Destroy them," Santana says.

Russell doesn't understand.

"If we can't stop her we have to help her," Santana says.

"Help her?" Russell repeats.

"Cooperate," Santana says. "With reality. Protect her. Help her."

"By destroying my photographs? My photographs of Isabel?"

"And anything else the police can use to find her."

"Why would the police come here?"

"They will come," Santana says.

Cheyenne reappears, wearing black, Russell's jeans and T-shirt hanging loose on his skinny body. Russell studies his face, the angular bones, the eyes, dark like Isabel's. A beautiful couple. A matched set. It's morning already. A beautiful morning. A fine day for flying. The rest is unreal. He is inert, as passive as in a dream: Cheyenne changing before him, shaken and docile, waiting for orders, Santana taking over, changing sides. The world is unstable. Nothing has ever been stable outside himself. Only his empty stillness remains. He will not be moved. He will wait it out, the way he would wait out a dream—the dream will make him stiller, the more frenzied the dream grows around him, or through him, the more immobile he really will be: it is the only safety he can recognize, the empty immobility of himself.

Around him the action continues: Santana strips the photographs from his walls and piles them under a window, and when he asks, "Negatives? Slides? Contact sheets?" Russell tells him, "In the darkroom. Take them all," his voice, like everything else in a dream, beyond his conscious control. At the table Cheyenne sits shaking, drinking coffee. Isabel, leaving the bedroom, holds out the phone: "She wants to talk to you."

They were the young people. There was supposed to be hope in the young. Instead there was only this destruction, self-destruction. Images come to him: smoke saturated with sunlight, insects sizzling in the Jamaican night. Guerrillas know how to slow down their heartbeats, Santana told him once. She is so young. He cannot remember ever having been so young himself.

"You can't do this," he says. "Isabel, don't do this."

"How are you going to stop me?"

"I can't," he says, and at the table Cheyenne laughs. "I want you to stay with me," Russell says, but he can't finish. He wants to warn her. There is no way to. He won't be heard. He takes the phone.

"Talk to me while she leaves, Jacks. Don't stop her."

"I can't stop anything."

Santana passes him by, carrying the big metal trash can from the darkroom to the windows. One by one he picks up a print, a strip of negatives, lights it, holds it carefully while it burns, then drops it smoking into the metal can. He opens the windows high. The smoke blows in, then out. Outside, birds sing. The buildings begin to glow — red, yellow, green. "I lay in bed and understood I had nothing to fear," Dominique says, continuing a story Russell only half hears. Isabel, wrapped in a towel, hair dripping, studies Cheyenne: "He needs sunglasses," she says. "Eat something," Santana says, still burning photographs. "Fix him something to eat," he says to Isabel. "Let her do what she wants to," Dominique says. "Desire is so fleeting, Jacks."

Santana goes out to buy Cheyenne a beer — "To stop that shaking," he says. At the table Isabel butters toast for Cheyenne. They are beautiful together. Out of a magazine. They eat eggs and toast and drink orange juice. The sun is coming up, the light keeps changing, it will be a clear bright day — a beautiful day for flying. He looks like my mother, Russell thinks. A child again. They are both children. Alone in a nightmare.

"While you were talking," he tells Dominique, "Santana burned every photograph of Isabel I've taken."

"You will miss her," she says. "You will miss her anyway."

"What have you done? Loaned her to me? Now you take her back again?"

"I didn't choose this, Jacks."

"Maybe," he says, and for a moment too terrible to speak aloud the whole thing is a game, nothing happened here, Cheyenne never killed a woman, Isabel isn't Dominique's daughter, everything is make-believe, dreamed up by Santana to punish him, again, finally, again and again. "Did you love Santana?" he asks. "Did you love Santana all along?"

"I loved you both," she says. "Equally," she says, and the word love becomes a zero.

"Isabel!" he cries. "Talk to your mother," and he walks away from the phone. The ashes in the garbage can are smoldering. A smell of chemical burning lingers in the air. There is more to be burned, he thinks. Everything. The dead flowers, the feathers, the playing cards, the scraps of leather and metal and plastic, the pushpins, the walls themselves, in bits and pieces — and the books, dear God, all his books, everything her hands have touched — is there nothing here her hands haven't touched? His files, his papers, his war photographs, his negatives — twenty years of negatives. "Burn it," he says out loud. "Burn it all."

In the street he sees Santana, wearing black shades.

Any minute now they will be gone.

"Russell," Isabel says. "Talk to her."

"I want to talk to you," he says. "Not to her. To you."

"I have to get dressed," she says. She hands him the phone.

Santana comes in, drops Isabel's keys on the table, passes Cheyenne the beer and sunglasses, and disappears behind the partition.

"They look so normal," Russell tells Dominique. "Like everyday life."

"They are everyday life," she says.

On his knees, Santana pulls gray socks up Cheyenne's ankles and slips his feet into black canvas shoes.

"Are they leaving now?" Dominique asks.

"Yes," Russell says. He lowers the phone.

Isabel comes out of her bedroom carrying the two small red nylon bags he bought her to take to Jamaica. She stands in front of him, wearing white now — as if for her wedding, he thinks.

"Well," she says. She looks at him with her crooked eyes. "Are you my father?"

"I don't know."

"Maybe it doesn't matter," she says.

"It does matter. I love you, Isabel."

"Do you?"

He doesn't know how to answer. "I love you," he says again. He doesn't know how he speaks. The words are in the air before he knows them.

"How do you?" she asks.

"Anyhow," he says. "However. You."

"Me," she says. "You know me?"

"I know you," he says.

She shrugs. "I don't know," she says. "I have to go now."

"But you'll come back."

"I don't know that."

"You will," he says.

"Don't believe it," she says. "You have no reason to believe it."

"I have no reason to let you go."

"Do you let me go? You love me that way?" she asks. "That proves it then. You're not my father." She smiles, a fleeting, scared little smile, a child. "Santana's not my father either," she says. "She says I misunderstood her." She shrugs. She rises on tiptoe to kiss Russell's cheek. Over her shoulder, he looks at his brother: almost himself, he thinks — a clown of himself, dressed in his clothes, his baggy jeans and linen jacket, flying away to Barcelona with his Isabel.

What is he to do? He almost asks Dominique.

"You're leaving too?" he asks Santana, who answers they still need him and takes Russell in his arms.

"And me?" Russell asks. "What about me?"

"We will talk a while longer," Dominique says. "I write pornography now," she says. "I moved. The cat ran away. I was a child in my parents' bedroom. I wonder sometimes what this means."

15

The trucks outside the Mae Son Waste Paper, Inc., fill the street, spewing diesel exhaust. The men are shouting. One of the drivers guns his engine, blackening the air. The noise is unbearable, the men are unbearable; the smell makes Russell sick. He closes the window. He lowers the shade. He turns his back on the street and looks at the empty room. It is bigger than he remembers. He has forgotten how big it is. It is full of their presence: the cigarette butts, the ashes, the used knives and forks, the crusts of toast on Cheyenne's plate, the open salsa jar, the clothes Cheyenne was wearing when he arrived — the army jacket, the cowboy boots, in the bathroom the dusty blue jeans, the blood-stained khaki shirt — in Isabel's bedroom the empty bottle. Everywhere her flowers, on the walls her cards and constructions and feathers and scraps. The end always comes too soon. Nothing now but secrets. Where he began, he thinks — in lassitude and secrecy. He will forget. Everything is over. Everything has taken place. What is left to happen? Ruin only. Destruction of the traces. He is reduced to silence. All his life he has been reduced to silence. But his mind goes on, unstoppable. Time goes on. Things run their course and still he stands here. They have hardly gone and already he begins to forget them. If there is no escape into the past or present, he will escape into the future, he will hide in the future tense. He will lie in her bed, in her sheets. He will look for her blood. He will burn her flowers — she'll disappear. He will put on Cheyenne's jacket, stolen from the closet of the dead woman. He will wear it as Cheyenne wore it, to make himself invisible. Cheyenne's jacket full of evidence. Santana told him to burn the evidence. It is time to start the burning. They are gone now, expelled. The ancient Greeks in times of calamity drove two scapegoats out of the city. They fed them cheese and figs and barley cakes, they beat them with leeks and wild plants, and in the end they burned them: two — one for the men, one for the women — chosen from a class of outcasts, in Athens maintained at public expense for just such times of crisis, social orphans kept like cattle to be sacrificed in this ritual of purification. Once the ashes were scattered on water and wind, the city closed back into itself, calamity appeased.

But what calamity? What is the disaster?

They will suffer, he thinks. If not for their suffering, he would be happy. Yes. And suddenly the suffering that will come to them fills him, his eyes, his throat, his frail human body. He will cry for them. He will feel himself cry for them. And then like the Greek city, he will close back in on himself, he will survive.

Himself, he thinks. I am the disaster.

He opens the window on the morning air. The trucks are gone now, the street almost quiet. The sky is bright, Mediterranean — what he thinks of as Mediterranean, he has not seen the Mediterranean sky, only has this idea of it, this clear, dry light, these supersaturated colors. He dreamed an air war in this sky. It is time for him to leave here.

Something should have been different. There was something he should have done. He doesn't know what. He doesn't know what to do now. It is too soon to burn the flowers. He wonders what they'll smell like, dried and dusty roses burning, carnations, daisies, a bird of paradise, flowers he's never known the names of, the purple sprays the flower vendors use in mixed bouquets, and iris, yes, and daffodils, and something white and wispy, virginal but dried to nothing now, forms so delicate they will disintegrate between his fingers.

"My mother made the orderly world," Isabel said once, "and then she made the break in the order. Again and again."

He might have recognized her even then.

Reality is what's forgotten.

Whatever he remembers didn't happen to him.

"I haven't slept," he says out loud. As if the sound of his voice will break through his torpor.

To be without sleep, he thinks. It alters reality as much as any drug can.

"It's all right to die," Santana said once. In Jamaica he said it. "Can you understand that, Jacks?" he said. "It's all right to die."

"Does that mean it's all right to kill then?" Russell had asked him.

And Santana had said, "No. Not anymore. I don't think so anymore."

To be without sleep makes the mind big. Too big inside the body. Maybe all his life he has been without sleep. All his life he has been an absence—he has covered his absence over, tried to cover it, but those closest to him, those who have left him, always knew. And maybe sleep was all he needed. Maybe now that they are gone he will be able to sleep, maybe there will be time now for sleeping, maybe in their absence he will find the time. It is they who will be absent now. He will prefer their absence to his own.

He would like to intervene. Here perhaps: at that moment in the future when something makes him happy and in that moment of happiness he remembers them as never having been.

He sits at the table. He plays with her fork against the plate. He reaches across the table and picks up Cheyenne's crusts. He chews on them. He is keeping watch, he thinks. As if they will come back to him. They will not come back.

At the zoo, with Isabel, he watched the peacocks' mating dance: the urgent fanning feathers, the erect blue throats. They shrieked before they made their display. "Like cats," Isabel said. They spread their fans and, turning slowly, waited for the hen to come within range, fan swaying, iridescent feathers all but vanishing at certain angles to the sun. "I thought they would be serene," she said. Their exotic frontal beauty couldn't hide their anguish, hind feathers ruffling, wild with agitation, small animal bodies in a frenzy of need. "Peacock feathers are bad luck," she said. "Now I know the reason."

She was a princess in a tower, Russell her keeper. To her Sleeping Beauty, the thorn hedge; to her Snow White, the seven dwarves. He would rather have been Beast to her Beauty. (If he cries, will she come back to him? If he falls down weeping in the garden of her dead flowers, will she feel his heart break and return?)

"Death to the fathers," Cheyenne said, leaving. "Death to the fathers, Jacks. What do you say?" He was the family symptom, he had said. "You grew up with her — you think you're so tightly wrapped?" At the door he said, "Sometimes I see her face. I see her face so vividly." And then he said, "I loved her. Did you love her, Jacks?"

But Russell couldn't answer.

"I'm sorry," Isabel said. "I'm sorry for you."

Angelino, she told him. "Why did she lie?" he asks out loud. Angelino. Was it her lie or Santana's? What was the reason? — as if in making things rational he could free himself from pain, as if it was the unreason that was unbearable, not the loss.

The loss.

He is cold now. Too cold for the summer weather. The world is cold, he thinks. In the heart of everything living. But Santana had told him that — the words were an old Guatemalan woman's.

"What's another story?" he had asked Isabel.

But this one was the truth.

He stretches his legs out onto another chair. If he had a cat, he thinks, it would come sit in his lap now. He takes a sip of cold coffee. The cup is heavy. He sets it on the table and closes his eyes. When he opens them again he is aware of having dreamed. A dream about insects. Cockroaches. He blushes. The memory of the dream fills him with repugnance and shame.

For its stupidity, he thinks.

He is with his father — he never sees his father in the dream, but his father is beside him, slightly behind, off to the right. They are standing at the table, Russell's eyes just peeking over its edge. They are setting a trap for cockroaches, meant to kill them with poisoned bait. But the roaches are already captured, held by strands of thread. The threads are long, like leashes. Russell is holding the threads. When the bait falls he is supposed to let them go, so the roaches can run for the food, to eat and die. (Something is wrong with this procedure. Even in the dream he knows it is illogical.) His father lowers the bait. Russell drops the threads. The cockroaches don't move. They are already dead. One of them (or more than one) has another insect body sticking out of its mouth. Suddenly it grows, or the dead insect body in its mouth grows, or both grow—two insects grow and are alive and crawl away, still growing. Not cockroaches any-more—they are inches long, with flat, segmented bodies. They've crawled away from the table, past Russell's father, to another piece of furniture—a piece of furniture from Russell's childhood, the wood waxed and deeply polished, with a fine, dark grain. One of the insects slithers into a seam in the wood, disappearing, and emerges at the bottom, close to Russell's feet. (He is a child—he has the legs and feet of a child.) When the insect disappears into the wood, he screams for Daddy to stop it, kill it, there it goes, it crawled into the wood, it's getting away—screaming in a panic to stop it, stop it. When it crawls out again onto the rug—a dark burgundy rug from his childhood—a barricade of furniture isolates the insect from him. Even so, he isn't safe. The second insect has reached the floor now, and both are multiplying: out of their mouths and heads new insects emerge; they multiply and eat one another and continue to grow. Four of them survive now, or five, in two tangled clumps, and Russell is screaming. *Daddy, stop them, make them stop,* he cries. *God help me.* A huge dark bird descends, an eagle but more enormous—Russell sees only its talons, bigger than his head, converging on the insects and snatching them up. Then there is nothing.

The dream makes him sick. It means nothing. It makes him angry.

"God help me," he says.

"God," he says.

("She will not forgive you," Santana said. What did he mean?) He wants to cry.

He gets to his feet. He listens without moving. Time to start the burning. "I want an explanation," he says out loud.

He tears a card down from the wall, another, playing cards and feathered earrings and constructions of paper and leather and metal and plastic. He gathers the bottles filled with dried flowers. He makes a pile of dried flowers under the window, next to the trash can where Santana burned his photographs.

"A bonfire of dead flowers then," he says. "Is that what you want?"

An eagle, he thinks. Eating the dream from inside. Everything eaten from inside out. Nothing left. He throws more flowers onto the pile. A sacrifice of flowers.

"I want the reasons," he says. "Tell me the reasons."

If he could understand he would not suffer.

He doesn't suffer now.

But suffering is waiting for him. He can feel it—just beyond him, waiting to snatch him up.

He is going to be afraid for a long time. He is going to expect them. He is going to know they are not here.

No one is watching.

He can tell himself the truth.

The truth.

She will never forgive him.

Silence is terrifying.

But there is no silence. The mind runs away from itself. If he listens he can hear the world: a car, a dripping faucet, a distant siren, another car, a mechanical whistling he can't identify, the building's creaking, an electric saw, a woman calling to someone on the street, hammering, more cars, something metal being dragged along the sidewalk, an airplane overhead, a honking horn, a bird, the squeaky wheels of the mailman's cart, a dog's bark. Sound after sound after sound. He is not alone. He will never be alone. His body lives in the world, surrounded. Not even sleep will stop it.

He goes to the darkroom for his negatives and contact sheets from Vietnam. He gets his notebooks and adds them to the pile of things to burn. Her bedroom too, he thinks. Her books, her clothes, her letters from Dominique. He could read the letters. He could save them long enough to read them. Maybe he would learn something. Unless she took them with her. He begins to shake. A cold sweat forms behind his knees. He goes to the table to look for a match, can't find the matches. He lights a candle at the stove and carries it back to the window. He burns a playing card. The ace of clubs. Then the king of clubs. Burgundy red feathered earrings. A flower—a rose, another. One by one he burns them, watching the flowers, dropping fire and ash into the trash can. If he were a movie, he thinks, the credits would begin to roll.

But he is not a movie. He is here—still here. And there is more.

He is waiting for magic words. Words to bring the eagle down.

He stops. He listens. He hears himself unraveling.

"Heroic stories are lies," Santana said once. "You tell heroic stories to get someone to go out and die for you."

"Tell me what you feel now," Dominique said on the phone.

"As if I'm living someone else's life," Russell told her.

"That is the human condition," she said.

"I don't think so," he said.

"You think Santana is different. Santana and his *compañeros.*"

"I do."

"Santana has surrendered to it. The *compañeros* surrender to it, perhaps from the day they are born—without choice. Your discomfort is your resistance. That is all."

"And you?" he asked. "Do you resist?"

"Oh, absolutely, Jacks," she said. She laughed. "You forget where we come from," she said. "All men kill."

What is he to do?

"Pray," he says out loud.

But—prayer, he thinks. What has he ever known about prayer? With his tears in the pillow and his already lost and ever absent love for Isabel? His daughter? Why not? Santana's? That too. It means nothing. He almost understands Dominique's indifference.

"Isabel," he says. But no one is with him.

"Cheyenne," he says. "Dominique. Santana."

But none of these words is the magic word.

He wants to find it anyway. If it doesn't exist, he will invent it. Isabel was magic. She came to him like magic. She changed him like magic. Her lies were magic. Magic didn't end. Not like this.

"It doesn't end like this," he says.

But it does end. He is powerless to change it. Everyone is powerless. He watches a plane cross the sky, disappearing, imagines it is their plane. ("Who is her father then?" he asked Dominique. "Who is not?" she answered, and he wanted to hit her.) The sky is blue, clear, Mediterranean. He will go to Barcelona too, he thinks. There is nothing to stop him. He will go to Barcelona. He will find Dominique and sit with her in a sidewalk café. He will hold her hand. This time he won't hide his tears from her. Cheyenne and Isabel will pass by and wave. In the early mornings when Dominique is sleeping off a hangover he will walk to the zoo to see the white gorilla. He will go every morning. And one morning he will find her there. She will be dressed all in white. Her hair will be long and wild, the way it was in Jamaica. He will take her photograph, with the gorilla. He will know whether she is his daughter. She will not be his daughter. She will be a woman. They will leave Barcelona. No one will follow them, no one will find them.

"Still in the nightmare," he says. None of this will happen. She will not forgive him.

He is fascinated by his fire. It burns in the trash can now. He is tired of the slow burning. He throws flowers in by the fistful, pages from his notebooks, leather scraps, plastic. The fire and smoke seem to laugh at him. He remembers his dream. It humiliates him. He doesn't know why. "Because it was so stupid," he says. The fire laughs. God laughs. He is laughing at himself. The smoke turns foul. He watches it billow out the window. He watches the sky.

At the center of all action is acceptance.

"The disaster is now," he says. He goes to the phone.

"The man you want," he says, "the man who killed that woman, is looking for a flight to Barcelona. He's wearing black shades, black levis, a black T-shirt, a gray linen jacket, gray socks, black canvas shoes. The clothes are too big for him. His name is William Jackson. He's traveling with a girl. She's wearing white. She's carrying red nylon bags."

He hangs up the phone.

In the pockets of the dead woman's jacket he finds Cheyenne's racetrack tickets, the woman's passport, her presence, her smell — a list of Alcoholics Anonymous meetings, from Boston, dated 1982, an old pack of Marlboros, a small black-bound sketchbook full of notes in a sloppy irregular hand. ("Illumination: the dread is not of doing it — it's of NOT doing it." And this: "Don't rely on the fear. Don't forget the fear. Feeling good is the greatest danger." And more: "I conspire against myself. I want to use him as a shield against all sexuality, idealize him, to hide behind, desexualize him to do it—— Forget all this, come down to earth, start on the ground." But: "Duplicity as I write this, nothing I write is real, not quite real, we know what the only reality is, it's never changed.")

"God blinds those who do not love," Santana had said to Cheyenne.

"What about your mother?" Cheyenne said. But Santana couldn't answer.

"I am not tough," the woman's notebook says. "This is not the way I want to live."

Another page: "So much sicker than I thought I was. Emotionally mangled. I do not want to know these things. I am lost, I lost, lost it. I'm lost — we're lost — she's lost — they're lost. Reality is lost. Gone forever now. Bye-bye."

Another: "Two. Four. Eight. Sixteen. Thirty-two. Sixty-four. One hundred twenty-eight. Two hundred fifty-six."

A drawing of a cat, in green ink.

A page of red stripes.

Some phone numbers and addresses — in Illinois, in Ohio, in Oregon, in California, Michigan, Iowa, Massachusetts, Florida, Vermont — in Ireland, England, Belgium, France — in Australia. Also names without numbers and numbers without names.

Isolated words (micro), phrases (the censorship of capitalism), beginnings of sentences (In the Museum of Science and Industry . . . On Liberty Street where so many rumors begin . . . The flashing red light on the corner of Limestone and High Streets . . .), quotations (Ecclesiastes 7:4 — "The heart of the wise is in the house of mourning, but the heart of fools is in the house of mirth"), book titles (*Conversation in the Cathedral, The Female Eunuch*), appointments (July 16, 9:30, home visit), unfinished lists (Karen — sweater / Jim & Di — trip / Smith and Mary ? / Hilmar — check / Maggie —).

And then whole pages — addressed, in a sense, directly to him: "Christmas Eve. A warm winter. New York. 1984. What am I doing here? I came here. When? Not recently. Why? I don't know. I am here. I came to escape. Now I am here. There is nothing to escape anymore. No way to escape. Not just by going. I am here now. Now what do I do? I don't know. I ramble. I go on. I go on and on and on. I will go on like this. I will write like this. You will keep reading. You will think this will go somewhere, and if you stay with me, believe me, it will. Your guess is as good as mine. I don't know where. Neither do you. But somewhere. Yes, we'll go together, you and I. We will start now, this minute, on Christmas Eve. Stop. I say it's Christmas Eve. As I write these words it is Christmas Eve, that is what it is. But not for you. For you it is some other day, some later day — if Christmas Eve, no longer 1984. You may not be in New York. You may not be in winter. You may be in some other winter, a colder winter, a final winter. Who knows? I don't. I don't know anything. I address you because I don't know anything. I am waiting to know something. So are you. Together we will find something out. But I am the leader. I don't want to be the leader. But here I am: I, the leader — completely at your mercy. You don't have to follow. You don't have to come along. You can turn away and leave me and I will talk to no one, no one will be here, no one reading, no one listening, only me, and still I will go on speaking as if you were here. I need you here. I need you with me. I need you beside the desk, in the other room, on the street, anywhere — in my head — I need to address you, as when I write a letter I know it

will be mailed and delivered and opened and read. In order to
continue here I need to know you will be here too. Stay with me.
When you leave me I'm lost. I watch television, eat, smoke, drink.
Unless I address you. I have to address you. I know I have to.
Now I have to discover what it is I have to say—what is necessary,
what it is that tells me to speak to you, that tells me I can't stop."

But then she does stop. On the next page in another ink she
writes: "I feel stupid and defeated. I don't know where to begin. I
don't know anything."

And then she begins again: "I want to kill my mother. I
am guilty toward my mother. My mother made of me a daughter who would not love her. It must have been what she wanted.
She was the grown-up, after all—I was only a child. I never believed I was a child. I believed I was a grown-up too. Now I am
a grown-up and for the first time I see the child I was. I am still
a child. I will be a child forever."

But not forever. Only a few months more.

She writes: "I know what my death will look like: Charming.
It will wear the face of a stranger. It will smile, like my father. I'll
invite it to come in. I will welcome it, like salvation. It will be
kind to me and let me live. Too kind. I will have to provoke it. I'll
insist. I'll rage. I'll demand: Let's get it over with. Take me. I'm
ready to die—ready."

Later she writes: "It was not my mother. It was before my
mother. Before my father. I came into life like this. Soul-sick.
Sick in my soul. What they did doesn't matter. They don't matter.
I'm alone here. I've always been alone."

Russell puts the notebook down.

"What if you were my father?" Isabel had asked him. "How
would you stop me then?"

He goes to the phone.

He hasn't told them enough. He hasn't been believed. How
many calls must they have had by now? How many false reports?

"The man is my brother," he says. "My half brother. He was
here all night. He told us everything. Everything he could
remember. The woman's jacket is here. Things he took from her.
Her passport, credit cards, everything—love letters," he says.

"I'm going through her pockets now. I'll tell you what's in her pockets. You have to stop them. Stop the girl."

She will not forgive him.

God blinds those who do not love, Santana said.

But who does love? Russell had wanted to ask him. Tell me, if you can, who does.

Wrong question, says the woman. The woman Cheyenne killed. The question is who does not, she says. Love is at fault, she says. To suffer from love is what we are born with. Like eyes to see and hands to grasp and little lungs to cry. We never don't suffer from love, she says.

Her jacket is in his hands. Her things are spread out before him. Her presence is in the room.

We will wait together then, he thinks. Her ghost will be his consolation.

He listens to himself. He is not afraid now.

The fear is over now, he thinks.

"The fear is over," he says.

"The disaster is now," he says.

Isabel will not speak to him again. But she will live.

16

In Barcelona Dominique sits in the Zurich Bar looking at the young people and tries to imagine her daughter.

"So how it begins," she says. "I can write pornography I told myself. I was taking a nap. It was Good Friday. I was not at my job. Not because of the holiday. I had been sick for two weeks. This was the first day I took off. I was tired, resting. Not really napping. I can write pornography, I thought. I needed a market. I had written so long, so many things, so many kinds of things, but had no market. So that afternoon lying there in bed alone with the sun coming in through the slats of the shades I thought I could write pornography."

But who is she talking to? Some German boy, skinny, blond and blue-eyed, barely older than Isabel. She has told this story already today. She told it to Jacks, but he wasn't listening. Or maybe she told it to Isabel.

She orders another glass of wine. "Not long after," she says, "I remembered the thought, but already I had dismissed it." She lights a cigarette. She looks at the German boy. She smiles at him suddenly. She can't remember who she told this story to. It doesn't matter. This seems to be the way things go now, she repeats herself and doesn't remember and repetition doesn't matter or memory either. Only the telling, again and again.

"The second thought I had," she says, "after the first, was that there wasn't much difference between pornography and art. Each was concerned with its own pleasures — not the world outside but the world within."

She speaks to him in English. The boy understands. He orders another drink for her and leans closer as the bar gets crowded and loud.

"When I got up," she says, "I wondered what to read. I had the continuing feeling of anticipation. Bach organ music came from the cassette player. I was boiling water to make tea. The cat chased a fly. I lived on the second floor, no balcony, no stairs. For the cat, no exit. The water boiled. Bach played on. The sun moved slowly in the room. Nothing happened."

But repetition was the wrong word. The word was revision: rewriting. I write pornography now, she had told Jacks, and maybe it was true. As a child she had slept in the same room with her mother and father. Maybe that was important. She listened to their gropings, their whisperings and tumblings, she heard the quiet of their sleep, and when she woke scared from dreams she crawled in bed between them. Her father, for all his stiffness, was gentle then, when she lay in bed beside him. Or maybe he was. When she drinks, and in nightmares, she is never sure. Other memories hover somewhere, just under her skin, behind her face, another reality, an altogether other life.

She sees her reflection in the glass.

"I remembered something else," she says. "And forgot it again. I told myself to wait, to get my tea, the forgotten thing would come back to me. But I didn't believe this. I began to argue with myself about disbelief and in the course of the argument came closer to the thing I had forgotten. Fear. It was fear. When I was lying in my bed, just before or just after thinking about pornography, I had experienced a sense of fear. No. The opposite. Fearlessness. It was fearlessness inside a fear. It was a feeling I knew. I had felt it the day before, in the early morning, still lying in bed. And I had felt it again that night, reading a letter from my daughter. But in neither instance had the experience become general — each time it lasted a moment only: came, had its effect, and disappeared into action. Now it was different: the feeling ended in knowledge. I lay there and knew. Fearlessness. Fear was an egg. Fearlessness was inside. Fear was the shell. All my life I had known only the shell. The fear. The toughness on the other side of fear. The shell was the toughness. What was the fear then? I didn't know.

"Start again."

While she talked, Russell had watched the others. While she talked, Isabel packed. In the bar now while she talks, the German boy leans closer and puts his hand lightly on the small of her back. She is still an attractive woman. She finds this hard to believe. She looks at herself in the mirror. She is old. She can see lines in her face. From such a distance, she thinks. But what did this boy see? Suddenly she laughs at herself: she had lived too long among Americans.

"I lay in bed and understood I had nothing to fear," she says. But the story is old. How many times now has she told it? To whom has she told it? She holds her glass up and switches to bourbon. The boy brushes her ear with his lips. He whispers. He smells of tapas, olives and garlic. "Isabel," she says, "what are you doing?" and Isabel, on a sidewalk in New York, lifts her head and looks at the sky. The day is bright, the air fresh, the heat just beginning to rise. "Santana?" Isabel says, and when he looks at her, she knows.

"I'm running away," she had told her mother. "Don't try to stop me."

But now she isn't sure. On the subway coming into Manhattan she had stood alone and watched them: Santana and Cheyenne. They talked and she stood apart from them and in the press of the rush-hour crowd, hearing only the thundering train and the voices close beside her, she watched Santana's face, Cheyenne's shaking hands. She had spent the night in his arms—she had opened her body to him. But who was he? What was he? When the train screeched to a stop at First Avenue, the sound was the sound of her fear.

Too early for the bank, they got off the train at Sixth Avenue and waited in a coffee shop, Cheyenne sipping beer.

"Change your clothes," Santana told her. "Go into the john and change."

She didn't ask why. Maybe she knew. In the little bathroom, she took off her dress and put on blue jeans and redid her hair, pulling it back from her forehead into a short, thick braid. She looked at herself in the mirror. She needed a hat, she thought. Straw, with a scarf. Sunglasses. Red lipstick. Dangling earrings. She did the lipstick and the earrings.

"How's this?" she asked Santana, and when he turned to look at her, she burst into tears.

"I'm sorry," she said. "I'm tired."

But now she isn't sure. She left them in the coffee shop to go to the bank for her money, and when the teller said, "This is a big withdrawal," and she asked was there a problem, she heard in her voice some part of herself that hoped there was. "I'm flying tonight," she said quickly. "I didn't think there would be a problem."

"Of course not," the teller said. "You just have to get it approved." He directed her to a man in a grayish blue suit who was occupied with another customer. Waiting, Isabel watched him. A white man, pink and puffy, a young man in a blue suit, a red tie, a little trim mustache. A married man, he wore a fat gold band on his wedding ring finger, displayed on his desk a brass-framed photo of a woman and children, his family. Maybe he kept a Bible in his desk, she thought. She imagined what she would say when she was sitting in that chair beside him: "Yes, $3600 is a large withdrawal. But I'm traveling suddenly to Spain, to visit my mother, you see, and I have to take my boyfriend with me — is boyfriend the right word, really? — for a man I've slept with once, when he was half drunk and dying? — for a man I'm rescuing you'd have to say from the law, a man who killed a woman only, I don't know, two days ago is it? Should I call him my boyfriend? Would you? Well, anyhow," she imagined — looking at her nails and thinking her outfit was incomplete without red polish, open sandals, painted toes — "you do understand my necessity, I believe, the hurry I'm in, the fact of these unforeseen circumstances that prevented my giving the bank notice of intent to withdraw. In fact there should be no problem, I can take traveler's checks for most of it, surely that won't upset the cash flow? Surely $3600 isn't really a problem? Not in such an emergency, would you say?" Then she would wink at him, of

course, and feel up his thigh, offer him what she assumed he
wanted, they all wanted, these respectable men in their fat little
suits, with their wives and families and heroes and lies. She
blushed suddenly as he glanced over at her and flashed her a
smile, cool and professional, a smile that said be patient, only a
moment more now, and she was ashamed and her imagined plea
changed tone: "I'm scared. I'm at your mercy. This man is a
stranger to me and I slept with him and I begged him to let me
help, I wanted to help him, I loved him so long. But who was he?
Who is he? Who did I love? This drunk? This killer? Did you
always love your wife? Do you still? If she was a drunk and she
scared you would you love her then? Would your children? If she
killed someone would you? What does it mean, kill someone? I
don't know. Do you? They say he stabbed her seventeen times. In
the night with me he thought there was blood. Maybe I don't
love him. Maybe I never loved him. Maybe love —" But the man
interrupted her thoughts then to call her to his desk, she smiled,
and when he asked was anything wrong as he OK'd her withdrawal, she realized he'd seen tears in her eyes and she answered
no, well yes, she was just in a hurry, her mother was sick, in
France, she was traveling suddenly, she would take most of the
money in checks, and she was on the street again in no time, light
as a balloon on air, another cord binding her to earth severed.
Humming "New York, New York," she made it a farewell song,
and stopped to buy sunglasses, a straw hat, and nail polish, fire-
engine red. The plane wouldn't leave until evening. She would
have time to buy sandals too, maybe a Walkman, music to listen
to, a present for her mother. Her mother. She was going to see
her mother. "Mama," she said out loud, and took the sunglasses
off and wiped away the tears that suddenly came to her eyes. Up
ahead she saw Cheyenne and Santana waiting outside the coffee
shop. "What now?" she asked when she reached them and
Santana told her the bags, change her bags, buy one, not red,
small enough for carry-on, they'd meet her in Washington
Square — Cheyenne standing apart from them, indifferent, eyes
raking the street: pedestrians, trucks, buses, bicycles, cars — birds

in the sky. She looked at the sky and turned back around. "Santana?" she asked, and when he looked at her, she knew.

"Don't try to stop me," she had said to her mother.

"Talk to me," Dominique said.

"Talk," Isabel had said. "That's all anyone wants to do now. I've had enough of talking."

"Enough of talking," Dominique says to the German boy. "We don't have to talk," she had said to Jacks. "I'll wait here with you. Tell me when they say good-bye."

"I lay in bed," she tells the German boy — so lean, so angular — so attentive — so young, "and felt a knowledge of myself that was outside all — what? — authority? — rules? — law? There was this core of myself I had never met before — no, this was not the fearlessness of youthful folly or drunken bravado or hysterical passion — not that — this was essentially calm — serene — still. Yes, still. The still, deep center of myself. But not myself. Just in there. Fearless.

"Then I thought about writing pornography.

"Was that the answer? It seemed to be an alien thought, unrelated to the fearlessness, a distraction. But what was the fearlessness looking for then? I didn't know. I spent the afternoon in anticipation. I felt the presence of someone with me. Someone forgotten. I didn't know who. I tried to imagine. I couldn't. I felt the presence leave. I felt I had disappointed it. But I could summon myself to fearlessness at will. Or at the opposite of will. As if laying my will down. I waited. Nothing happened."

On the phone she had said, "Perhaps it was you, Jacks.

"Perhaps you were having a dream that morning. A dream I was in. We watched the world end together, Jacks. We stood at my window and watched the world end. Anything else is repetition."

(Repetition: He dreamed of his father. An eagle ate the dream from inside.)

"Let her do what she wants to," she said. "Desire is so fleeting. Let her have it while she can. It is the only illusion left for them. They are born after disaster, heading into disaster. They have nothing else. They have less than we did, Jacks. Even less than we.

"You forget where we come from," she said. "All men kill."

"All men kill," she said to Isabel. "Get used to it."

On the bench beside Santana, painting her toenails red, out the corner of her eye Isabel watches Cheyenne sit brooding, staring into space. In paper bags at her feet are the new black carry-on, a green floral scarf, a floppy-brimmed straw hat, and the flats she'd shed in the shoe store for undyed leather sandals. Two mustached policemen pass them by, Cheyenne following their progress across the square, then losing interest and staring at his feet. Students cross the square, and office workers and women and men with strollers and children, people with dogs, laughing teenagers traveling in packs, someone in a clown suit selling balloons, homeless men begging with paper cups, others drinking out of bottles, a hot-dog vendor setting up his cart, musicians opening guitar cases, a student film crew with camera and tripod, tape recorder, mike, and boom. Three black musicians setting up congas and steel drums attract Cheyenne's attention as Isabel wiggles her toes dry and slips her feet into her shoes.

"Chey?" she says when he stands up, but he doesn't hear her, drawn away to the saxophone and drums. Half rising, she's about to follow, when Santana stops her, and together they watch Cheyenne nod and talk and offer cigarettes around and reach out tentatively to touch the skin of the congas.

"Pack," Santana tells her. "What doesn't fit I'll send you."

"I can't run anymore," she says suddenly, and at the congas Cheyenne begins to drum.

"Come to Barcelona," her mother had said. "Bring him with you if you have to, but come to Barcelona," and in Barcelona now Dominique says, "I'm tired," and the German boy smiles and with naive bravado promises to wake her up. She touches his shoulder. She pities him. So much life still ahead of him. So many years still to go. To go, she thinks. To go on. On and on. "The cat ran away," she says. "I moved." She orders another whiskey. The light begins to fade. She wonders if Isabel really will come. She imagines Santana.

"Santana," she says. She talks to the mirror. The boy is gone. Or maybe he isn't. He lights her cigarette. He hides behind smoke. Jacks was in the north and Santana stood beside her at the window next to the fan. The war stopped. Just for a moment. For a moment she saw a different life: a life. An ordinary life. A man, a woman, a child. Sunshine and rain. Plants growing out of the earth. Animals. A life of animals, and friends. Her mother. Her father. But the war began again. Animals died. Friends disappeared. Her father betrayed her. Touched her. Used her. Her father lied. And Santana was already gone somewhere, far away in his heart and mind—standing at the window beside her. He touched her but the war had come back. His touch brought it back. The world came with him. Time. "Santana," she said.

"Santana," Isabel says in New York, and he sees her, so like her mother: changeable as water, fierce, determined—so suddenly sane.

"It's all right," he says. "I've got the lawyer. I've got the detox. I've got a place for him reserved."

"All I have to do is let him go?"

He nods.

"What if I can't?"

"Don't think. Just do."

"How?"

"Pack," he says. "What you need in the black bag, what you don't in the red."

She lifts one red bag to the bench, unzips it, and stops at the sight of the clothes and shoes and papers it holds. "I don't know what I need," she says. "I don't need anything."

"Begin," Santana says. "Here. Where's the new one? Pass me things. Open your shopping bags. What'd you buy?"

She takes out the hat, ties the scarf around its brim, and plants it on her head.

"Beautiful," he says, packing. "Sunglasses?"

"Here somewhere," she says, and searching through the things that surround her, tissue, nail polish, shopping bags, notebooks, letters, clothes half packed and unpacked, stops and lifts her face to him, eyes filling with tears: "What should I do?"

"Keep packing," he says. "Listen to the music. Look at him now."

At the congas Cheyenne plays in a frenzy, the steel drums and saxophone picking up his beat, communicating with him and with each other, working off him, following and leading him on, the conga player dancing with gourds and bells, and at the center of the music, the intruder, the shaking white boy, crazy Cheyenne — deep in some trance of forgetfulness and memory, confessing in the drumming, drumming his confession, sweating memory and forgetfulness, guilt and loss, down his face, out his hands.

"And then?" Isabel whispers.

"Find a travel agent on West Fourth Street. Buy one ticket, one-way. Take the train to the plane. Go to your mother."

"Just walk away?"

"Yes," Santana says. "Sit with me and listen a while and then just walk away."

She is silent, watching Cheyenne.

"You knew I would do this."

"I hoped," he admits.

"Are you my father?" she asks him.

"Do you want a father?"

"Only the truth," she says, and he restrains a smile at the paradox, a riddle he recalls only in the sound of it: a paradox of liars, like a pride of lions, a wilderness of spiders — only the sound, and the silence at that point where lies and truth-telling converge.

"Believe your mother," he says gravely.

But Isabel says, "No." She turns to look at him. "If I push her for an answer, she says I'm forcing her to lie. But what if she lied to you? What if you are my father?" — so young and earnest beneath her sun hat, behind her bright lipstick. Would he tell her the truth if he knew?

"If I am?" he asks.

"I don't know. I — I want you to tell me."

"What could I tell you that I can't tell you now?"

"Could I live with you? Could I come live with you in L.A.?"

"You don't have to be my daughter to come to L.A."

"You are my father," she says. "Tell me you're not"—insisting, he thinks, on some bodily knowledge that had nothing to do with history or facts.

He wants to say it's impossible. But impossible isn't quite true. "Words kill," he says.

But she shakes her head. "No," she says, and turns away from him, standing suddenly, collecting her trash. When she uncovers her sunglasses, she pushes them onto her face. She takes the black bag out of his hands, hastily fills it, zips it shut, says, "Throw out the rest, leave it for the homeless, don't send me a thing," and swings the bag up over her shoulder and walks away.

"Death to the fathers," Cheyenne had said when they left Russell, and as night begins to fall in Barcelona, Santana follows Isabel across the square, in and out of patches of sunlight, finally stopping her, holding her, kissing her good-bye. "Don't be angry, now," he says. "Not with me. Do you think I could love you any more than I do?"

"Again," Dominique says, seeking oblivion in the arms of the boy from the Zurich Bar, and in the detox Santana's brought him to on Lafayette Street, Cheyenne pulls blankets tight around himself and shivers and rocks. "Again, again," Dominique says, waking in the night, and in the room feels the presence of the dead woman. Perhaps she is coming for me, she thinks. She will come for me now. I am alone again in Barcelona. Barcelona is a foreign city. I live here because it is foreign, because I am foreign, because I am a stranger anywhere I go. "I feel the dead woman in this room," she says, and the boy, thinking she's dreaming, holds her and caresses her hair. "At my side in the night," she says. "I invite her to lie down. I ask her can she help me sleep. I ask her to stay, not to leave me. We are sisters in the skin. She knows everything about me. In the darkness I see her eyes. We are daughters of the same father—who meant us no harm. Not now," she says to the boy, and on Lafayette Street Cheyenne says, "I'm cold," and when from some terrible distance Santana tells him it will get better now, everything will get better, in a cell somewhere in his body, in a space in his mind or his heart, in a sliver of time, less than a second, a zero between one moment and another, bright and quick as the knife blade, a door opens and light penetrates, the cold vanishes and returns, when he breathes the breath goes all the way down in his body, and through the rest of the night he will watch himself as if from up on the ceiling and listen and hear himself cry.

"Again, again," Dominique says as light reaches her in the morning, filtered through dusty rose-golden shades. The boy is beside her. What boy? "Again," she says, and Isabel, waking as her plane lands in Madrid, pushes her face against the window and decides that before doing anything else she will see the white gorilla. "No more," Dominique says, not sure quite where she is. "I have to go," she says, "I have to sleep," and drifts again into icy dreaming, while Isabel, after entering the country quickly on her French passport, changing money, and taking the short flight to Barcelona, stands watching the gorilla, disappointed now, thinking how ugly he is, gorillas weren't meant to be white, how arrogant, how rude to his fellows, feeling betrayed by the attraction and sympathy she has felt for him, a creature who should have lived free, who like other caged gorillas she has seen should still have had his dignity, his nobility intact. Instead she sees this—what can she call him?—manlike, egotistical king of the mountain, who treats the other apes like slaves and smears shit on the glass of their common cage. She would like to regard this act as some noble protest, some gesture of rebellion against the hordes of people who come every day to peer at him—and it is at him, not at the others, that the crowds come to peer, she knows that, and he knows it too, she can see it in him, he thinks he's god, god of the gorillas. But what is he? Dirty. In the wild maybe he would have washed, maybe kept himself clean. In the wild he would have been noble, taken care of his fellows, they him, in the wild he would have been good to his family, his wife, his babies. But here? It isn't his fault, of course, she knows it's not, he's a captive creature, like everyone, she thinks, all of us, but does he have to be so mean? She turns away from him, to hide her tears. She puts her dark glasses on and leaves the gorillas. A little boy runs across the grass, chasing peacocks and pigeons. *"Palomas,"* he cries, running with arms outstretched, the awkward, stately peacock, slower than the child, somehow evading his chunky little legs as he lunges more insistently at the skittering pigeons, who fly up almost into his face while he claps his hands and laughs and laughs.

Leaving the zoo, Isabel telephones her mother, Dominique finally waking in the bed of the young stranger, waking enough to wake herself, finally to move, to make her way to the bath, to call for coffee, which the boy brings her, devoted, sitting at her feet in the thick hotel carpeting while she brushes out her hair. So he is a rich boy, she thinks, and laughs in her heart for him. A rich young German boy who loves his mother, and she shakes her head and touches his cheek and tells him he is dear but she must go now, and old as she is and tired, she feels her heart flutter at the words and knows it is not for him she flutters but for Isabel — making her way now from the zoo to the center of the city, and later, crossing the Plaza de Cataluña, realizing as she walks under the warm wide sky that it never was the gorilla she wanted to see in Barcelona. And understanding, as Dominique finally leaves the boy's hotel, that she is someone separate from the events that have surrounded her, that she is neither her mother nor her father, any father, nor made up of their parts, not her love for Cheyenne, not love for anyone, or anyone's love for her, or their idea of her either, but free, all her own, and altogether other, Isabel stands in the doorway lingering in the lingering light of day before stepping into the shadows to find her mother among the smoking, drinking patrons of the Zurich Bar.

Catherine Gammon

My life as a writer began when I was a child, with the story of my mother and father. There was glamour in their story, and I am still sometimes in thrall to that spellbinding childhood myth, its figures cut from some heyday-of-Hollywood scrapbook: my father the dashing newspaperman, with his mustache and rolled-up shirtsleeves and dark handsome eyes; my reserved, intelligent, independent-minded mother — and her profound and mysterious patience with every excess of my father's.

My father and mother taught me to write, in ways they intended and ways they didn't. Defending myself against the power of their presence, in writing I found my privacy and my own voice (I, who so much wanted to be heard) — the only world within my world that they couldn't invade, although on occasion they tried. Editors at heart, reviewing my writing for school, they taught me in more conventional ways. But fiction remained mine alone.

The pull of childhood is great. With the parental myth comes another: myself as isolated intelligence, witness, secret child hidden in a secret cave.

The two myths can work together to crowd out the living world. Asked to describe herself, the child becomes reticent, says: "The writer exists to protect the person. Read the fiction. Forget the life." But behind the reticent child stands another—willing to answer, learning to tell.